PEOPLE AND STORIES THAT SHOULD NOT BE FORGOTTEN
ADVENTURES

ADVENTURES

PEOPLE AND STORIES THAT SHOULD NOT BE FORGOTTEN

Fall 2023

COPYRIGHT ©2023, OFFBEAT PUBLISHING, LLC

All rights reserved. No part of this publication may be reproduced, distributed, or transmitted in any form or by any means, including photocopying, recording, or other electronic or mechanical methods, without the prior written permission of the publisher, except in the case of brief quotations embodied in critical reviews and certain other noncommercial uses permitted by copyright law.

This publication includes works of fiction. Any resemblance to actual events or persons, living or dead, is entirely coincidental.

ISBN: (PAPERBACK) 978-1-950464-54-8
ISBN: (EBOOK) 978-1-950464-55-5

WWW.OFFBEATREADS.COM

ADVENTURES

PEOPLE AND STORIES THAT SHOULD NOT BE FORGOTTEN

FALL, 2023

ISSUE #9

WHAT

WHERE

Editor's Note

Who better to grace the cover of our Fall Issue (#9) than the in-sanely gorgeous Yvonne De Carlo? Because the Canadian-born actress contributed to television and film far beyond her role as Lily Munster, we include an alternate picture of her here.

Her beauty in the cover photo goes beyond aesthetics. The apprehension you feel within includes fright, just under the skin, and not ready for what may exist beyond your sight. Her eyes suggest she is unafraid and slightly amused, and she dares you to step over the line. What do you see?

Before 2023 is done, we'll bring you the Winter Issue of **Adventures** and, our special two-year Anniversary Issue. I also want to make you are aware of another change. Because other projects require that I tend to them, Michael Brian will be taking the helm as editor. He is a father, author, novel editor, book reviewer, and more. His vast insight into books of all genres can only be a benefit to each issue, and to you.

At the end of this book I have included a poem. This poem is one I wrote when my mom was slipping away in the hospital a few years ago. I still shake my head, wondering how she gathered the strength to come back from being so weak. Surrounding the poem are images of my very first serious try at writing when I was around eight years old. Thanks you mom for letting me be a kid.

Let's meet where sad jazz plays. Drinks are on me.

Robert Kimbrell

Letters to the editor:

Comments/Questions are accepted. Put *Letter to Editor* in Subject and send to: OffBeatReads@pm.me
*Email content could be published in future *Adventures To Go*.

CARMILLA
BY JOSEPH SHERIDAN LE FANU

PROLOGUE

Upon a paper attached to the Narrative which follows, Doctor Hesselius has written a rather elaborate note, which he accompanies with a reference to his Essay on the strange subject which the MS. illuminates.

This mysterious subject he treats, in that Essay, with his usual learning and acumen, and with remarkable directness and condensation. It will form but one volume of the series of that extraordinary man's collected papers.

As I publish the case, in this volume, simply to interest the "laity," I shall forestall the intelligent lady, who relates it, in nothing; and after due consideration, I have determined, therefore, to abstain from presenting any précis of the learned Doctor's reasoning, or extract from his statement on a subject which he describes as "involving, not improbably, some of the profoundest arcana of our dual existence, and its intermediates."

I was anxious on discovering this paper, to reopen the correspondence commenced by Doctor Hesselius, so many years before, with a person so clever and careful as his informant seems to have been. Much to my regret, however, I found that she had died in the interval.

She, probably, could have added little to the Narrative which she communicates in the following pages, with, so far as I can pronounce, such conscientious particularity.

I

AN EARLY FRIGHT

In Styria, we, though by no means magnificent people, inhabit a castle, or schloss. A small income, in that part of the world, goes a great way. Eight or nine hundred a year does wonders. Scantily enough ours would have answered among wealthy people at home. My father is English, and I bear an English name, although I never saw England. But here, in this lonely and primitive place, where everything is so marvelously cheap, I really don't see how ever so much more money would at all materially add to our comforts, or even luxuries.

My father was in the Austrian service, and retired upon a pension and his patrimony, and purchased this feudal residence, and the small estate on which it stands, a bargain.

Nothing can be more picturesque or solitary. It stands on a slight eminence in a forest. The road, very old and narrow, passes in front of its drawbridge, never raised in my time, and its moat, stocked with perch, and sailed over by many swans, and floating on its surface white fleets of water lilies.

Over all this the schloss shows its many-windowed front; its towers, and its Gothic chapel.

The forest opens in an irregular and very picturesque glade before its gate, and at the right a steep Gothic bridge carries the road over a stream that winds in deep shadow through the wood. I have said that this is a very lonely place. Judge whether I say truth. Looking from the hall door towards the road, the forest in which our castle stands extends fifteen miles to the right, and twelve to the left. The nearest inhabited village is about seven of your English miles to the left. The nearest inhabited schloss of any historic associations, is that of old General Spielsdorf, nearly twenty miles away to the right.

I have said "the nearest *inhabited* village," because there is, only three miles westward, that is to say in the direction of General Spielsdorf's schloss, a ruined village, with its quaint little church, now roofless, in the aisle of which are the moldering tombs of the proud family of Karnstein, now extinct, who once owned the equally desolate chateau which, in the thick of the forest, overlooks the silent ruins of the town.

Respecting the cause of the desertion of this striking and melancholy spot, there is a legend which I shall relate to you another time.

I must tell you now, how very small is the party who constitute the inhabitants of our castle. I don't include servants, or those dependents who occupy rooms in the buildings attached to the schloss. Listen, and wonder! My father, who is the kindest man on earth, but growing old; and I, at the date of my story, only nineteen. Eight years have passed since then.

I and my father constituted the family at the schloss. My mother, a Styrian lady, died in my infancy, but I had a good-natured governess, who had been with me from, I might almost say, my infancy. I could not remember the time when her fat, benignant face was not a familiar picture in my memory.

This was Madame Perrodon, a native of Berne, whose care and good nature now in part supplied to me the loss of my mother, whom I do not even remember, so early I lost her. She made a third at our little dinner party. There was a fourth, Mademoiselle De Lafontaine, a lady such as you term, I believe, a "finishing governess." She spoke French and German, Madame Perrodon French and broken English, to which my father and I added English, which, partly to prevent its becoming a lost language among us, and partly from patriotic motives, we spoke every day. The consequence was a Babel, at which strangers used to laugh, and which I shall make no attempt to reproduce in this narrative. And there were two or three young lady friends besides, pretty nearly of my own age, who were occasional visitors, for longer or shorter terms; and these visits I sometimes returned.

These were our regular social resources; but of course there were chance visits from "neighbors" of only five or six leagues distance. My life was, notwithstanding, rather a solitary one, I can assure you.

My gouvernantes had just so much control over me as you might conjecture such sage persons would have in the case of a rather spoiled girl, whose only parent allowed her pretty nearly her own way in everything.

The first occurrence in my existence, which produced a terrible impression upon my mind, which, in fact, never has been effaced, was one of the very earliest incidents of my life which I can recollect. Some people will think it so trifling that it should not be recorded here. You will see, however, by-and-by, why I mention it. The nursery, as it was called, though I had it all to myself, was a large room in the upper story of the castle, with a steep oak roof. I can't have been more than six years old, when one night I awoke, and looking round the room from my bed, failed to see the nursery maid. Neither was my nurse there; and I thought myself alone. I was not frightened, for I was one of those happy children who are studiously kept in ignorance of ghost stories, of fairy tales, and of all such lore as makes us cover up our heads when the door cracks suddenly, or the flicker of an expiring candle makes the shadow of a bedpost dance upon the wall, nearer to our faces. I was vexed and insulted at finding myself, as I conceived, neglected, and I began to whimper, preparatory to a hearty bout of roaring; when to my surprise, I saw a solemn, but very pretty face looking at me from the side of the bed. It was that of a young lady who was kneeling, with her hands under the coverlet. I looked at her with a kind of pleased wonder, and ceased whimpering. She caressed me with her hands, and lay down beside me on the bed, and drew me towards her, smiling; I felt immediately delightfully soothed, and fell asleep again. I was wakened by a sensation as if two needles ran into my breast very deep at the same moment, and I cried loudly. The lady started back, with her eyes fixed on me, and then slipped down upon the floor, and, as I thought, hid herself under the bed.

I was now for the first time frightened, and I yelled with all my might and main. Nurse, nursery maid, housekeeper, all came running in, and hearing my story, they made light of it, soothing me all they could meanwhile. But, child as I was, I could perceive that their faces were pale with an unwonted look of anxiety, and I saw them look under the bed, and about the room, and peep under tables and pluck open cupboards; and the housekeeper whispered to the nurse: "Lay your hand along that hollow in the bed; someone *did* lie there, so sure as you did not; the place is still warm."

I remember the nursery maid petting me, and all three examining my chest, where I told them I felt the puncture, and pronouncing that there was no sign visible that any such thing had happened to me.

The housekeeper and the two other servants who were in charge of the nursery, remained sitting up all night; and from that time a servant always sat up in the nursery until I was about fourteen.

I was very nervous for a long time after this. A doctor was called in, he was pallid and elderly. How well I remember his long saturnine face, slightly pitted with smallpox, and his chestnut wig. For a good while, every second day, he came and gave me medicine, which of course I hated.

The morning after I saw this apparition I was in a state of terror, and could not bear to be left alone, daylight though it was, for a moment.

I remember my father coming up and standing at the bedside, and talking cheerfully, and asking the nurse a number of questions, and laughing very heartily at one of the answers; and patting me on the shoulder, and kissing me, and telling me not to be frightened, that it was nothing but a dream and could not hurt me.

But I was not comforted, for I knew the visit of the strange woman was *not* a dream; and I was *awfully* frightened.

I was a little consoled by the nursery maid's assuring me that it was she who had come and looked at me, and lain down beside me in the bed, and that I must have been half-dreaming not to have known her face. But this, though supported by the nurse, did not quite satisfy me.

I remembered, in the course of that day, a venerable old man, in a black cassock, coming into the room with the nurse and housekeeper, and talking a little to them, and very kindly to me; his face was very sweet and gentle, and he told me they were going to pray, and joined my hands together, and desired me to say, softly, while they were praying, "Lord hear all good prayers for us, for Jesus' sake." I think these were the very words, for I often repeated them to myself, and my nurse used for years to make me say them in my prayers.

I remembered so well the thoughtful sweet face of that white-haired old man, in his black cassock, as he stood in that rude, lofty, brown room, with the clumsy furniture of a fashion three hundred years old about him, and the scanty light entering its shadowy atmosphere through the small lattice. He kneeled, and the three women with him, and he prayed aloud with an earnest quavering voice for, what appeared to me, a long time. I forget all my life preceding that event, and for some time after it is all obscure also, but the scenes I have just described stand out vivid as the isolated pictures of the phantasmagoria surrounded by darkness.

II
A GUEST

I am now going to tell you something so strange that it will require all your faith in my veracity to believe my story. It is not only true, nevertheless, but truth of which I have been an eyewitness.

It was a sweet summer evening, and my father asked me, as he sometimes did, to take a little ramble with him along that beautiful forest vista which I have mentioned as lying in front of the schloss.

"General Spielsdorf cannot come to us so soon as I had hoped," said my father, as we pursued our walk.

He was to have paid us a visit of some weeks, and we had expected his arrival next day. He was to have brought with him a young lady, his niece and ward, Mademoiselle Rheinfeldt, whom I had never seen, but whom I had heard described as a very charming girl, and in whose society I had promised myself many happy days. I was more disappointed than a young lady living in a town, or a bustling neighborhood can possibly imagine. This visit, and the new acquaintance it promised, had furnished my day dream for many weeks.

"And how soon does he come?" I asked.

"Not till autumn. Not for two months, I dare say," he answered. "And I am very glad now, dear, that you never knew Mademoiselle Rheinfeldt."

"And why?" I asked, both mortified and curious.

"Because the poor young lady is dead," he replied. "I quite forgot I had not told you, but you were not in the room when I received the General's letter this evening."

I was very much shocked. General Spielsdorf had mentioned in his first letter, six or seven weeks before, that she was not so well as he would wish her, but there was nothing to suggest the remotest suspicion of danger.

"Here is the General's letter," he said, handing it to me. "I am afraid he is in great affliction; the letter appears to me to have been written very nearly in distraction."

We sat down on a rude bench, under a group of magnificent lime trees. The sun was setting with all its melancholy splendor behind the sylvan horizon, and the stream that flows beside our home, and passes under the steep old bridge I have mentioned, wound through many a group of noble trees, almost at our feet, reflecting in its current the fading crimson of the sky. General Spielsdorf's letter was so extraordinary, so vehement, and in some places so self-contradictory, that I read it twice over—the second time aloud to my father—and was still unable to account for it, except by supposing that grief had unsettled his mind.

It said "I have lost my darling daughter, for as such I loved her. During the last days of dear Bertha's illness I was not able to write to you.

Before then I had no idea of her danger. I have lost her, and now learn *all*, too late. She died in the peace of innocence, and in the glorious hope of a blessed futurity. The fiend who betrayed our infatuated hospitality has done it all. I thought I was receiving into my house innocence, gaiety, a charming companion for my lost Bertha. Heavens! what a fool have I been!

I thank God my child died without a suspicion of the cause of her sufferings. She is gone without so much as conjecturing the nature of her illness, and the accursed passion of the agent of all this misery. I devote my remaining days to tracking and extinguishing a monster. I am told I may hope to accomplish my righteous and merciful purpose. At present there is scarcely a gleam of light to guide me. I curse my conceited incredulity, my despicable affectation of superiority, my blindness, my obstinacy—all— too late. I cannot write or talk collectedly now. I am distracted. So soon as I shall have a little recovered, I mean to devote myself for a time to enquiry, which may possibly lead me as far as Vienna. Some time in the autumn, two months hence, or earlier if I live, I will see you—that is, if you permit me; I will then tell you all that I scarce dare put upon paper now. Farewell. Pray for me, dear friend."

In these terms ended this strange letter. Though I had never seen Bertha Rheinfeldt my eyes filled with tears at the sudden intelligence; I was startled, as well as profoundly disappointed.

The sun had now set, and it was twilight by the time I had returned the General's letter to my father.

It was a soft clear evening, and we loitered, speculating upon the possible meanings of the violent and incoherent sentences which I had just been reading. We had nearly a mile to walk before reaching the road that passes the schloss in front, and by that time the moon was shining brilliantly. At the drawbridge we met Madame Perrodon and Mademoiselle De Lafontaine, who had come out, without their bonnets, to enjoy the exquisite moonlight.

We heard their voices gabbling in animated dialogue as we approached. We joined them at the drawbridge, and turned about to admire with them the beautiful scene.

The glade through which we had just walked lay before us. At our left the narrow road wound away under clumps of lordly trees, and was lost to sight amid the thickening forest. At the right the same road crosses the steep and picturesque bridge, near which stands a ruined tower which once guarded that pass; and beyond the bridge an abrupt eminence rises, covered with trees, and showing in the shadows some grey ivy-clustered rocks.

Over the sward and low grounds a thin film of mist was stealing like smoke, marking the distances with a transparent veil; and here and there we could see the river faintly flashing in the moonlight.

No softer, sweeter scene could be imagined. The news I had just heard made it melancholy; but nothing could disturb its character of profound serenity, and the enchanted glory and vagueness of the prospect.

My father, who enjoyed the picturesque, and I, stood looking in silence over the expanse beneath us. The two good governesses, standing a little way behind us, discoursed upon the scene, and were eloquent upon the moon.

Madame Perrodon was fat, middle-aged, and romantic, and talked and sighed poetically. Mademoiselle De Lafontaine—in right of her father who was a German, assumed to be psychological, metaphysical, and something of a mystic—now declared that when the moon shone with a light so intense it was well known that it indicated a special spiritual activity. The effect of the full moon in such a state of brilliancy was manifold. It acted on dreams, it acted on lunacy, it acted on nervous people, it had marvelous physical influences connected with life. Mademoiselle related that her cousin, who was mate of a merchant ship, having taken a nap on deck on such a night, lying on his back, with his face full in the light on the moon, had wakened, after a dream of an old woman clawing him by the cheek, with his features horribly drawn to one side; and his countenance had never quite recovered its equilibrium.

"The moon, this night," she said, "is full of idyllic and magnetic influence—and see, when you look behind you at the front of the schloss how all its windows flash and twinkle with that silvery splendor, as if unseen hands had lighted up the rooms to receive fairy guests."

There are indolent styles of the spirits in which, indisposed to talk ourselves, the talk of others is pleasant to our listless ears; and I gazed on, pleased with the tinkle of the ladies' conversation.

"I have got into one of my moping moods tonight," said my father, after a silence, and quoting Shakespeare, whom, by way of keeping up our English, he used to read aloud, he said:

In truth I know not why I am so sad.

It wearies me: you say it wearies you;

But how I got it—came by it.'

"I forget the rest. But I feel as if some great misfortune were hanging over us. I suppose the poor General's afflicted letter has had something to do with it."

At this moment the unwonted sound of carriage wheels and many hoofs upon the road, arrested our attention.

They seemed to be approaching from the high ground overlooking the bridge, and very soon the equipage emerged from that point. Two horsemen first crossed the bridge, then came a carriage drawn by four horses, and two men rode behind.

It seemed to be the traveling carriage of a person of rank; and we were all immediately absorbed in watching that very unusual spectacle. It became, in a few moments, greatly more interesting, for just as the carriage had passed the summit of the steep bridge, one of the leaders, taking fright, communicated his panic to the rest, and after a plunge or two, the whole team broke into a wild gallop together, and dashing between the horsemen who rode in front, came thundering along the road towards us with the speed of a hurricane.

The excitement of the scene was made more painful by the clear, long-drawn screams of a female voice from the carriage window.

We all advanced in curiosity and horror; me rather in silence, the rest with various ejaculations of terror.

Our suspense did not last long. Just before you reach the castle drawbridge, on the route they were coming, there stands by the roadside a magnificent lime tree, on the other stands an ancient stone cross, at sight of which the horses, now going at a pace that was perfectly frightful, swerved so as to bring the wheel over the projecting roots of the tree.

I knew what was coming. I covered my eyes, unable to see it out, and turned my head away; at the same moment I heard a cry from my lady friends, who had gone on a little.

Curiosity opened my eyes, and I saw a scene of utter confusion. Two of the horses were on the ground, the carriage lay upon its side with two wheels in the air; the men were busy removing the traces, and a lady with a commanding air and figure had got out, and stood with clasped hands, raising the handkerchief that was in them every now and then to her eyes.

Through the carriage door was now lifted a young lady, who appeared to be lifeless. My dear old father was already beside the elder lady, with his hat in his hand, evidently tendering his aid and the resources of his schloss. The lady did not appear to hear him, or to have eyes for anything but the slender girl who was being placed against the slope of the bank.

I approached; the young lady was apparently stunned, but she was certainly not dead. My father, who piqued himself on being something of a physician, had just had his fingers on her wrist and assured the lady, who declared herself her mother, that her pulse, though faint and irregular, was undoubtedly still distinguishable. The lady clasped her hands and looked upward, as if in a momentary transport of gratitude; but immediately she broke out again in that theatrical way which is, I believe, natural to some people.

She was what is called a fine looking woman for her time of life, and must have been handsome; she was tall, but not thin, and dressed in black velvet, and looked rather pale, but with a proud and commanding countenance, though now agitated strangely.

"Who was ever being so born to calamity?" I heard her say, with clasped hands, as I came up. "Here am I, on a journey of life and death, in prosecuting which to lose an hour is possibly to lose all. My child will not have recovered sufficiently to resume her route for who can say how long. I must leave her: I cannot, dare not, delay. How far on, sir, can you tell, is the nearest village? I must leave her there; and shall not see my darling, or even hear of her till my return, three months hence."

I plucked my father by the coat, and whispered earnestly in his ear: "Oh! papa, pray ask her to let her stay with us—it would be so delightful. Do, pray."

"If Madame will entrust her child to the care of my daughter, and of her good gouvernante, Madame Perrodon, and permit her to remain as our guest, under my charge, until her return, it will confer a distinction and an obligation upon us, and we shall treat her with all the care and devotion which so sacred a trust deserves."

"I cannot do that, sir, it would be to task your kindness and chivalry too cruelly," said the lady, distractedly.

"It would, on the contrary, be to confer on us a very great kindness at the moment when we most need it. My daughter has just been disappointed by a cruel misfortune, in a visit from which she had long anticipated a great deal of happiness. If you confide this young lady to our care it will be her best consolation. The nearest village on your route is distant, and affords no such inn as you could think of placing your daughter at; you cannot allow her to continue her journey for any considerable distance without danger. If, as you say, you cannot suspend your journey, you must part with her tonight, and nowhere could you do so with more honest assurances of care and tenderness than here."

There was something in this lady's air and appearance so distinguished and even imposing, and in her manner so engaging, as to impress one, quite apart from the dignity of her equipage, with a conviction that she was a person of consequence.

By this time the carriage was replaced in its upright position, and the horses, quite tractable, in the traces again.

The lady threw on her daughter a glance which I fancied was not quite so affectionate as one might have anticipated from the beginning of the scene; then she beckoned slightly to my father, and withdrew two or three steps with him out of hearing; and talked to him with a fixed and stern countenance, not at all like that with which she had hitherto spoken.

I was filled with wonder that my father did not seem to perceive the change, and also unspeakably curious to learn what it could be that she was speaking, almost in his ear, with so much earnestness and rapidity.

Two or three minutes at most I think she remained thus employed, then she turned, and a few steps brought her to where her daughter lay, supported by Madame Perrodon. She kneeled beside her for a moment and whispered, as Madame supposed, a little benediction in her ear; then hastily kissing her she stepped into her carriage, the door was closed, the footmen in stately liveries jumped up behind, the outriders spurred on, the postilions cracked their whips, the horses plunged and broke suddenly into a furious canter that threatened soon again to become a gallop, and the carriage whirled away, followed at the same rapid pace by the two horsemen in the rear.

III

WE COMPARE NOTES

We followed the *cortege* with our eyes until it was swiftly lost to sight in the misty wood; and the very sound of the hoofs and the wheels died away in the silent night air.

Nothing remained to assure us that the adventure had not been an illusion of a moment but the young lady, who just at that moment opened her eyes. I could not see, for her face was turned from me, but she raised her head, evidently looking about her, and I heard a very sweet voice ask complainingly, "Where is mamma?"

Our good Madame Perrodon answered tenderly, and added some comfortable assurances.

I then heard her ask:

"Where am I? What is this place?" and after that she said, "I don't see the carriage; and Matska, where is she?"

Madame answered all her questions in so far as she understood them; and gradually the young lady remembered how the misadventure came about, and was glad to hear that no one in, or in attendance on, the carriage was hurt; and on learning that her mamma had left her here, till her return in about three months, she wept.

I was going to add my consolations to those of Madame Perrodon when Mademoiselle De Lafontaine placed her hand upon my arm, saying:

"Don't approach, one at a time is as much as she can at present converse with; a very little excitement would possibly overpower her now."

As soon as she is comfortably in bed, I thought, I will run up to her room and see her.

My father in the meantime had sent a servant on horseback for the physician, who lived about two leagues away; and a bedroom was being prepared for the young lady's reception.

The stranger now rose, and leaning on Madame's arm, walked slowly over the drawbridge and into the castle gate.

In the hall, servants waited to receive her, and she was conducted forthwith to her room. The room we usually sat in as our drawing room is long, having four windows, that looked over the moat and drawbridge, upon the forest scene I have just described.

It is furnished in old carved oak, with large carved cabinets, and the chairs are cushioned with crimson Utrecht velvet. The walls are covered with tapestry, and surrounded with great gold frames, the figures being as large as life, in ancient and very curious costume, and the subjects represented are hunting, hawking, and generally festive. It is not too stately to be extremely comfortable; and here we had our tea, for with his usual patriotic leanings he insisted that the national beverage should make its appearance regularly with our coffee and chocolate.

We sat here this night, and with candles lighted, were talking over the adventure of the evening.

Madame Perrodon and Mademoiselle De Lafontaine were both of our party. The young stranger had hardly lain down in her bed when she sank into a deep sleep; and those ladies had left her in the care of a servant.

"How do you like our guest?" I asked, as soon as Madame entered. "Tell me all about her?"

"I like her extremely," answered Madame, "she is, I almost think, the prettiest creature I ever saw; about your age, and so gentle and nice."

"She is absolutely beautiful," threw in Mademoiselle, who had peeped for a moment into the stranger's room.

"And such a sweet voice!" added Madame Perrodon.

"Did you remark a woman in the carriage, after it was set up again, who did not get out," inquired Mademoiselle, "but only looked from the window?"

"No, we had not seen her."

Then she described a hideous black woman, with a sort of colored turban on her head, and who was gazing all the time from the carriage window, nodding and grinning derisively towards the ladies, with gleaming eyes and large white eyeballs, and her teeth set as if in fury.

"Did you remark what an ill-looking pack of men the servants were?" asked Madame.

"Yes," said my father, who had just come in, "ugly, hang-dog looking fellows as ever I beheld in my life. I hope they mayn't rob the poor lady in the forest. They are clever rogues, however; they got everything to rights in a minute."

"I dare say they are worn out with too long traveling," said Madame.

"Besides looking wicked, their faces were so strangely lean, and dark, and sullen. I am very curious, I own; but I dare say the young lady will tell you all about it tomorrow, if she is sufficiently recovered."

"I don't think she will," said my father, with a mysterious smile, and a little nod of his head, as if he knew more about it than he cared to tell us.

This made us all the more inquisitive as to what had passed between him and the lady in the black velvet, in the brief but earnest interview that had immediately preceded her departure.

We were scarcely alone, when I entreated him to tell me. He did not need much pressing.

"There is no particular reason why I should not tell you. She expressed a reluctance to trouble us with the care of her daughter, saying she was in delicate health, and nervous, but not subject to any kind of seizure—she volunteered that—nor to any illusion; being, in fact, perfectly sane."

"How very odd to say all that!" I interpolated. "It was so unnecessary."

"At all events it *was* said," he laughed, "and as you wish to know all that passed, which was indeed very little, I tell you. She then said, 'I am making a long journey of *vital* importance—she emphasized the word—rapid and secret; I shall return for my child in three months; in the meantime, she will be silent as to who we are, whence we come, and whither we are traveling.' That is all she said. She spoke very pure French. When she said the word 'secret,' she paused for a few seconds, looking sternly, her eyes fixed on mine. I fancy she makes a great point of that. You saw how quickly she was gone. I hope I have not done a very foolish thing, in taking charge of the young lady."

For my part, I was delighted. I was longing to see and talk to her; and only waiting till the doctor should give me leave. You, who live in towns, can have no idea how great an event the introduction of a new friend is, in such a solitude as surrounded us.

The doctor did not arrive till nearly one o'clock; but I could no more have gone to my bed and slept, than I could have overtaken, on foot, the carriage in which the princess in black velvet had driven away.

When the physician came down to the drawing room, it was to report very favorably upon his patient. She was now sitting up, her pulse quite regular, apparently perfectly well. She had sustained no injury, and the little shock to her nerves had passed away quite harmlessly. There could be no harm certainly in my seeing her, if we both wished it; and, with this permission I sent, forthwith, to know whether she would allow me to visit her for a few minutes in her room.

The servant returned immediately to say that she desired nothing more.

You may be sure I was not long in availing myself of this permission.

Our visitor lay in one of the handsomest rooms in the schloss. It was, perhaps, a little stately. There was a somber piece of tapestry opposite the foot of the bed, representing Cleopatra with the asps to her bosom; and other solemn classic scenes were displayed, a little faded, upon the other walls. But there was gold carving, and rich and varied color enough in the other decorations of the room, to more than redeem the gloom of the old tapestry.

There were candles at the bedside. She was sitting up; her slender pretty figure enveloped in the soft silk dressing gown, embroidered with flowers, and lined with thick quilted silk, which her mother had thrown over her feet as she lay upon the ground.

What was it that, as I reached the bedside and had just begun my little greeting, struck me dumb in a moment, and made me recoil a step or two from before her? I will tell you.

I saw the very face which had visited me in my childhood at night, which remained so fixed in my memory, and on which I had for so many years so often ruminated with horror, when no one suspected of what I was thinking.

It was pretty, even beautiful; and when I first beheld it, wore the same melancholy expression.

But this almost instantly lighted into a strange fixed smile of recognition.

There was a silence of fully a minute, and then at length she spoke; I could not.

"How wonderful!" she exclaimed. "Twelve years ago, I saw your face in a dream, and it has haunted me ever since."

"Wonderful indeed!" I repeated, overcoming with an effort the horror that had for a time suspended my utterances. "Twelve years ago, in vision or reality, I certainly saw you. I could not forget your face. It has remained before my eyes ever since."

Her smile had softened. Whatever I had fancied strange in it, was gone, and it and her dimpling cheeks were now delightfully pretty and intelligent.

I felt reassured, and continued more in the vein which hospitality indicated, to bid her welcome, and to tell her how much pleasure her accidental arrival had given us all, and especially what a happiness it was to me.

I took her hand as I spoke. I was a little shy, as lonely people are, but the situation made me eloquent, and even bold. She pressed my hand, she laid hers upon it, and her eyes glowed, as, looking hastily into mine, she smiled again, and blushed.

She answered my welcome very prettily. I sat down beside her, still wondering; and she said:

"I must tell you my vision about you; it is so very strange that you and I should have had, each of the other so vivid a dream, that each should have seen, I you and you me, looking as we do now, when of course we both were mere children. I was a child, about six years old, and I awoke from a confused and troubled dream, and found myself in a room, unlike my nursery, wainscoted clumsily in some dark wood, and with cupboards and bedsteads, and chairs, and benches placed about it. The beds were, I thought, all empty, and the room itself without anyone but myself in it; and I, after looking about me for some time, and admiring especially an iron candlestick with two branches, which I should certainly know again, crept under one of the beds to reach the window; but as I got from under the bed, I heard someone crying; and looking up, while I was still upon my knees, I saw you—most assuredly you—as I see you now; a beautiful young lady, with golden hair and large blue eyes, and lips—your lips—you as you are here.

"Your looks won me; I climbed on the bed and put my arms about you, and I think we both fell asleep. I was aroused by a scream; you were sitting up screaming. I was frightened, and slipped down upon the ground, and, it seemed to me, lost consciousness for a moment; and when I came to myself, I was again in my nursery at home. Your face I have never forgotten since. I could not be misled by mere resemblance. *You are* the lady whom I saw then."

It was now my turn to relate my corresponding vision, which I did, to the undisguised wonder of my new acquaintance.

"I don't know which should be most afraid of the other," she said, again smiling—"If you were less pretty I think I should be very much afraid of you, but being as you are, and you and I both so young, I feel only that I have made your acquaintance twelve years ago, and have already a right to your intimacy; at all events it does seem as if we were destined, from our earliest childhood, to be friends. I wonder whether you feel as strangely drawn towards me as I do to you; I have never had a friend—shall I find one now?" She sighed, and her fine dark eyes gazed passionately on me.

Now the truth is, I felt rather unaccountably towards the beautiful stranger. I did feel, as she said, "drawn towards her," but there was also something of repulsion. In this ambiguous feeling, however, the sense of attraction immensely prevailed. She interested and won me; she was so beautiful and so indescribably engaging.

I perceived now something of languor and exhaustion stealing over her, and hastened to bid her good night.

"The doctor thinks," I added, "that you ought to have a maid to sit up with you tonight; one of ours is waiting, and you will find her a very useful and quiet creature."

"How kind of you, but I could not sleep, I never could with an attendant in the room. I shan't require any assistance—and, shall I confess my weakness, I am haunted with a terror of robbers. Our house was robbed once, and two servants murdered, so I always lock my door. It has become a habit—and you look so kind I know you will forgive me. I see there is a key in the lock."

She held me close in her pretty arms for a moment and whispered in my ear, "Good night, darling, it is very hard to part with you, but good night; tomorrow, but not early, I shall see you again."

She sank back on the pillow with a sigh, and her fine eyes followed me with a fond and melancholy gaze, and she murmured again "Good night, dear friend."

Young people like, and even love, on impulse. I was flattered by the evident, though as yet undeserved, fondness she showed me. I liked the confidence with which she at once received me. She was determined that we should be very near friends.

Next day came and we met again. I was delighted with my companion; that is to say, in many respects.

Her looks lost nothing in daylight—she was certainly the most beautiful creature I had ever seen, and the unpleasant remembrance of the face presented in my early dream, had lost the effect of the first unexpected recognition.

She confessed that she had experienced a similar shock on seeing me, and precisely the same faint antipathy that had mingled with my admiration of her. We now laughed together over our momentary horrors.

IV

HER HABITS—A SAUNTER

I told you that I was charmed with her in most particulars.

There were some that did not please me so well.

She was above the middle height of women. I shall begin by describing her.

She was slender, and wonderfully graceful. Except that her movements were languid—very languid—indeed, there was nothing in her appearance to indicate an invalid. Her complexion was rich and brilliant; her features were small and beautifully formed; her eyes large, dark, and lustrous; her hair was quite wonderful, I never saw hair so magnificently thick and long when it was down about her shoulders; I have often placed my hands under it, and laughed with wonder at its weight. It was exquisitely fine and soft, and in color a rich very dark brown, with something of gold. I loved to let it down, tumbling with its own weight, as, in her room, she lay back in her chair talking in her sweet low voice, I used to fold and braid it, and spread it out and play with it. Heavens! If I had but known all!

I said there were particulars which did not please me. I have told you that her confidence won me the first night I saw her; but I found that she exercised with respect to herself, her mother, her history, everything in fact connected with her life, plans, and people, an ever wakeful reserve. I dare say I was unreasonable, perhaps I was wrong; I dare say I ought to have respected the solemn injunction laid upon my father by the stately lady in black velvet. But curiosity is a restless and unscrupulous passion, and no one girl can endure, with patience, that hers should be baffled by another. What harm could it do anyone to tell me what I so ardently desired to know? Had she no trust in my good sense or honor? Why would she not believe me when I assured her, so solemnly, that I would not divulge one syllable of what she told me to any mortal breathing.

There was a coldness, it seemed to me, beyond her years, in her smiling melancholy persistent refusal to afford me the least ray of light.

I cannot say we quarreled upon this point, for she would not quarrel upon any. It was, of course, very unfair of me to press her, very ill-bred, but I really could not help it; and I might just as well have let it alone.

What she did tell me amounted, in my unconscionable estimation—to nothing.

It was all summed up in three very vague disclosures:

First—Her name was Carmilla.

Second—Her family was very ancient and noble.

Third—Her home lay in the direction of the west.

She would not tell me the name of her family, nor their armorial bearings, nor the name of their estate, nor even that of the country they lived in.

You are not to suppose that I worried her incessantly on these subjects. I watched opportunity, and rather insinuated than urged my inquiries. Once or twice, indeed, I did attack her more directly. But no matter what my tactics, utter failure was invariably the result. Reproaches and caresses were all lost upon her. But I must add this, that her evasion was conducted with so pretty a melancholy and deprecation, with so many, and even passionate declarations of her liking for me, and trust in my honor, and with so many promises that I should at last know all, that I could not find it in my heart long to be offended with her.

She used to place her pretty arms about my neck, draw me to her, and laying her cheek to mine, murmur with her lips near my ear, "Dearest, your little heart is wounded; think me not cruel because I obey the irresistible law of my strength and weakness; if your dear heart is wounded, my wild heart bleeds with yours. In the rapture of my enormous humiliation I live in your warm life, and you shall die—die, sweetly die—into mine. I cannot help it; as I draw near to you, you, in your turn, will draw near to others, and learn the rapture of that cruelty, which yet is love; so, for a while, seek to know no more of me and mine, but trust me with all your loving spirit."

And when she had spoken such a rhapsody, she would press me more closely in her trembling embrace, and her lips in soft kisses gently glow upon my cheek.

Her agitations and her language were unintelligible to me.

From these foolish embraces, which were not of very frequent occurrence, I must allow, I used to wish to extricate myself; but my energies seemed to fail me. Her murmured words sounded like a lullaby in my ear, and soothed my resistance into a trance, from which I only seemed to recover myself when she withdrew her arms.

In these mysterious moods I did not like her. I experienced a strange tumultuous excitement that was pleasurable, ever and anon, mingled with a vague sense of fear and disgust. I had no distinct thoughts about her while such scenes lasted, but I was conscious of a love growing into adoration, and also of abhorrence. This I know is paradox, but I can make no other attempt to explain the feeling.

I now write, after an interval of more than ten years, with a trembling hand, with a confused and horrible recollection of certain occurrences and situations, in the ordeal through which I was unconsciously passing; though with a vivid and very sharp remembrance of the main current of my story.

But, I suspect, in all lives there are certain emotional scenes, those in which our passions have been most wildly and terribly roused, that are of all others the most vaguely and dimly remembered.

Sometimes after an hour of apathy, my strange and beautiful companion would take my hand and hold it with a fond pressure, renewed again and again; blushing softly, gazing in my face with languid and burning eyes, and breathing so fast that her dress rose and fell with the tumultuous respiration. It was like the ardor of a lover; it embarrassed me; it was hateful and yet over-powering; and with gloating eyes she drew me to her, and her hot lips traveled along my cheek in kisses; and she would whisper, almost in sobs, "You are mine, you *shall* be mine, you and I are one for ever." Then she had thrown herself back in her chair, with her small hands over her eyes, leaving me trembling.

"Are we related," I used to ask; "what can you mean by all this? I remind you perhaps of someone whom you love; but you must not, I hate it; I don't know you—I don't know myself when you look so and talk so."

She used to sigh at my vehemence, then turn away and drop my hand.

Respecting these very extraordinary manifestations I strove in vain to form any satisfactory theory—I could not refer them to affectation or trick. It was unmistakably the momentary breaking out of suppressed instinct and emotion. Was she, notwithstanding her mother's volunteered denial, subject to brief visitations of insanity; or was there here a disguise and a romance? I had read in old storybooks of such things. What if a boyish lover had found his way into the house, and sought to prosecute his suit in masquerade, with the assistance of a clever old adventuress. But there were many things against this hypothesis, highly interesting as it was to my vanity.

I could boast of no little attentions such as masculine gallantry delights to offer. Between these passionate moments there were long intervals of commonplace, of gaiety, of brooding melancholy, during which, except that I detected her eyes so full of melancholy fire, following me, at times I might have been as nothing to her. Except in these brief periods of mysterious excitement her ways were girlish; and there was always a languor about her, quite incompatible with a masculine system in a state of health.

In some respects her habits were odd. Perhaps not so singular in the opinion of a town lady like you, as they appeared to us rustic people. She used to come down very late, generally not till one o'clock, she would then take a cup of chocolate, but eat nothing; we then went out for a walk, which was a mere saunter, and she seemed, almost immediately, exhausted, and either returned to the schloss or sat on one of the benches that were placed, here and there, among the trees. This was a bodily languor in which her mind did not sympathize. She was always an animated talker, and very intelligent.

She sometimes alluded for a moment to her own home, or mentioned an adventure or situation, or an early recollection, which indicated a people of strange manners, and described customs of which we knew nothing. I gathered from these chance hints that her native country was much more remote than I had at first fancied.

As we sat thus one afternoon under the trees a funeral passed us by. It was that of a pretty young girl, whom I had often seen, the daughter of one of the rangers of the forest. The poor man was walking behind the coffin of his darling; she was his only child, and he looked quite heartbroken.

Peasants walking two-and-two came behind, they were singing a funeral hymn.

I rose to mark my respect as they passed, and joined in the hymn they were very sweetly singing.

My companion shook me a little roughly, and I turned surprised.

She said brusquely, "Don't you perceive how discordant that is?"

"I think it very sweet, on the contrary," I answered, vexed at the interruption, and very uncomfortable, lest the people who composed the little procession should observe and resent what was passing.

I resumed, therefore, instantly, and was again interrupted. "You pierce my ears," said Carmilla, almost angrily, and stopping her ears with her tiny fingers. "Besides, how can you tell that your religion and mine are the same; your forms wound me, and I hate funerals. What a fuss! Why you must die—*everyone* must die; and all are happier when they do. Come home."

"My father has gone on with the clergyman to the churchyard. I thought you knew she was to be buried today."

"She? I don't trouble my head about peasants. I don't know who she is," answered Carmilla, with a flash from her fine eyes.

"She is the poor girl who fancied she saw a ghost a fortnight ago, and has been dying ever since, till yesterday, when she expired."

"Tell me nothing about ghosts. I shan't sleep tonight if you do."

"I hope there is no plague or fever coming; all this looks very like it," I continued. "The swineherd's young wife died only a week ago, and she thought something seized her by the throat as she lay in her bed, and nearly strangled her. Papa says such horrible fancies do accompany some forms of fever. She was quite well the day before. She sank afterwards, and died before a week."

"Well, *her* funeral is over, I hope, and *her* hymn sung; and our ears shan't be tortured with that discord and jargon. It has made me nervous. Sit down here, beside me; sit close; hold my hand; press it hard-hard-harder."

We had moved a little back, and had come to another seat.

She sat down. Her face underwent a change that alarmed and even terrified me for a moment. It darkened, and became horribly livid; her teeth and hands were clenched, and she frowned and compressed her lips, while she stared down upon the ground at her feet, and trembled all over with a continued shudder as irrepressible as ague. All her energies seemed strained to suppress a fit, with which she was then breathlessly tugging; and at length a low convulsive cry of suffering broke from her, and gradually the hysteria subsided. "There! That comes of strangling people with hymns!" she said at last. "Hold me, hold me still. It is passing away."

And so gradually it did; and perhaps to dissipate the somber impression which the spectacle had left upon me, she became unusually animated and chatty; and so we got home.

This was the first time I had seen her exhibit any definable symptoms of that delicacy of health which her mother had spoken of. It was the first time, also, I had seen her exhibit anything like temper.

Both passed away like a summer cloud; and never but once afterwards did I witness on her part a momentary sign of anger. I will tell you how it happened.

She and I were looking out of one of the long drawing room windows, when there entered the courtyard, over the drawbridge, a figure of a wanderer whom I knew very well. He used to visit the schloss generally twice a year.

It was the figure of a hunchback, with the sharp lean features that generally accompany deformity. He wore a pointed black beard, and he was smiling from ear to ear, showing his white fangs. He was dressed in buff, black, and scarlet, and crossed with more straps and belts than I could count, from which hung all manner of things. Behind, he carried a magic lantern, and two boxes, which I well knew, in one of which was a salamander, and in the other a mandrake. These monsters used to make my father laugh. They were compounded of parts of monkeys, parrots, squirrels, fish, and hedgehogs, dried and stitched together with great neatness and startling effect. He had a fiddle, a box of conjuring apparatus, a pair of foils and masks attached to his belt, several other mysterious cases dangling about him, and a black staff with copper ferrules in his hand. His companion was a rough spare dog, that followed at his heels, but stopped short, suspiciously at the drawbridge, and in a little while began to howl dismally.

In the meantime, the mountebank, standing in the midst of the courtyard, raised his grotesque hat, and made us a very ceremonious bow, paying his compliments very volubly in execrable French, and German not much better.

Then, disengaging his fiddle, he began to scrape a lively air to which he sang with a merry discord, dancing with ludicrous airs and activity, that made me laugh, in spite of the dog's howling.

Then he advanced to the window with many smiles and salutations, and his hat in his left hand, his fiddle under his arm, and with a fluency that never took breath, he gabbled a long advertisement of all his accomplishments, and the resources of the various arts which he placed at our service, and the curiosities and entertainments which it was in his power, at our bidding, to display.

"Will your ladyships be pleased to buy an amulet against the oupire, which is going like the wolf, I hear, through these woods," he said dropping his hat on the pavement. "They are dying of it right and left and here is a charm that never fails; only pinned to the pillow, and you may laugh in his face."

These charms consisted of oblong slips of vellum, with cabalistic ciphers and diagrams upon them.

Carmilla instantly purchased one, and so did I.

He was looking up, and we were smiling down upon him, amused; at least, I can answer for myself. His piercing black eye, as he looked up in our faces, seemed to detect something that fixed for a moment his curiosity,

In an instant he unrolled a leather case, full of all manner of odd little steel instruments.

"See here, my lady," he said, displaying it, and addressing me, "I profess, among other things less useful, the art of dentistry. Plague take the dog!" he interpolated. "Silence, beast! He howls so that your ladyships can scarcely hear a word. Your noble friend, the young lady at your right, has the sharpest tooth,—long, thin, pointed, like an awl, like a needle; ha, ha! With my sharp and long sight, as I look up, I have seen it distinctly; now if it happens to hurt the young lady, and I think it must, here am I, here are my file, my punch, my nippers; I will make it round and blunt, if her ladyship pleases; no longer the tooth of a fish, but of a beautiful young lady as she is. Hey? Is the young lady displeased? Have I been too bold? Have I offended her?"

The young lady, indeed, looked very angry as she drew back from the window.

"How dares that mountebank insult us so? Where is your father? I shall demand redress from him. My father would have had the wretch tied up to the pump, and flogged with a cart whip, and burnt to the bones with the cattle brand!"

She retired from the window a step or two, and sat down, and had hardly lost sight of the offender, when her wrath subsided as suddenly as it had risen, and she gradually recovered her usual tone, and seemed to forget the little hunchback and his follies.

My father was out of spirits that evening. On coming in he told us that there had been another case very similar to the two fatal ones which had lately occurred. The sister of a young peasant on his estate, only a mile away, was very ill, had been, as she described it, attacked very nearly in the same way, and was now slowly but steadily sinking.

"All this," said my father, "is strictly referable to natural causes. These poor people infect one another with their superstitions, and so repeat in imagination the images of terror that have infested their neighbors."

"But that very circumstance frightens one horribly," said Carmilla.

"How so?" inquired my father.

"I am so afraid of fancying I see such things; I think it would be as bad as reality."

"We are in God's hands: nothing can happen without his permission, and all will end well for those who love him. He is our faithful creator; He has made us all, and will take care of us."

"Creator! *Nature!*" said the young lady in answer to my gentle father. "And this disease that invades the country is natural. Nature. All things proceed from Nature—don't they? All things in the heaven, in the earth, and under the earth, act and live as Nature ordains? I think so."

"The doctor said he would come here today," said my father, after a silence. "I want to know what he thinks about it, and what he thinks we had better do."

"Doctors never did me any good," said Carmilla.

"Then you have been ill?" I asked.

"More ill than ever you were," she answered.

"Long ago?"

"Yes, a long time. I suffered from this very illness; but I forget all but my pain and weakness, and they were not so bad as are suffered in other diseases."

"You were very young then?"

"I dare say, let us talk no more of it. You would not wound a friend?"

She looked languidly in my eyes, and passed her arm round my waist lovingly, and led me out of the room. My father was busy over some papers near the window.

"Why does your papa like to frighten us?" said the pretty girl with a sigh and a little shudder.

"He doesn't, dear Carmilla, it is the very furthest thing from his mind."

"Are you afraid, dearest?"

"I should be very much if I fancied there was any real danger of my being attacked as those poor people were."

"You are afraid to die?"

"Yes, every one is."

"But to die as lovers may—to die together, so that they may live together.

Girls are caterpillars while they live in the world, to be finally butterflies when the summer comes; but in the meantime there are grubs and larvae, don't you see—each with their peculiar propensities, necessities and structure. So says Monsieur Buffon, in his big book, in the next room."

Later in the day the doctor came, and was closeted with papa for some time.

He was a skilful man, of sixty and upwards, he wore powder, and shaved his pale face as smooth as a pumpkin. He and papa emerged from the room together, and I heard papa laugh, and say as they came out:

"Well, I do wonder at a wise man like you. What do you say to hippogriffs and dragons?"

The doctor was smiling, and made answer, shaking his head—

"Nevertheless life and death are mysterious states, and we know little of the resources of either."

And so they walked on, and I heard no more. I did not then know what the doctor had been broaching, but I think I guess it now.

V

A WONDERFUL LIKENESS

This evening there arrived from Gratz the grave, dark-faced son of the picture cleaner, with a horse and cart laden with two large packing cases, having many pictures in each. It was a journey of ten leagues, and whenever a messenger arrived at the schloss from our little capital of Gratz, we used to crowd about him in the hall, to hear the news.

This arrival created in our secluded quarters quite a sensation. The cases remained in the hall, and the messenger was taken charge of by the servants till he had eaten his supper. Then with assistants, and armed with hammer, ripping chisel, and turnscrew, he met us in the hall, where we had assembled to witness the unpacking of the cases.

Carmilla sat looking listlessly on, while one after the other the old pictures, nearly all portraits, which had undergone the process of renovation, were brought to light. My mother was of an old Hungarian family, and most of these pictures, which were about to be restored to their places, had come to us through her.

My father had a list in his hand, from which he read, as the artist rummaged out the corresponding numbers. I don't know that the pictures were very good, but they were, undoubtedly, very old, and some of them very curious also. They had, for the most part, the merit of being now seen by me, I may say, for the first time; for the smoke and dust of time had all but obliterated them.

"There is a picture that I have not seen yet," said my father. "In one corner, at the top of it, is the name, as well as I could read, 'Marcia Karnstein,' and the date '1698'; and I am curious to see how it has turned out."

I remembered it; it was a small picture, about a foot and a half high, and nearly square, without a frame; but it was so blackened by age that I could not make it out.

The artist now produced it, with evident pride. It was quite beautiful; it was startling; it seemed to live. It was the effigy of Carmilla!

"Carmilla, dear, here is an absolute miracle. Here you are, living, smiling, ready to speak, in this picture. Isn't it beautiful, Papa? And see, even the little mole on her throat."

My father laughed, and said "Certainly it is a wonderful likeness," but he looked away, and to my surprise seemed but little struck by it, and went on talking to the picture cleaner, who was also something of an artist, and discoursed with intelligence about the portraits or other works, which his art had just brought into light and color, while I was more and more lost in wonder the more I looked at the picture.

"Will you let me hang this picture in my room, papa?" I asked.

"Certainly, dear," said he, smiling, "I'm very glad you think it so like.

It must be prettier even than I thought it, if it is."

The young lady did not acknowledge this pretty speech, did not seem to hear it. She was leaning back in her seat, her fine eyes under their long lashes gazing on me in contemplation, and she smiled in a kind of rapture.

"And now you can read quite plainly the name that is written in the corner.

It is not Marcia; it looks as if it was done in gold. The name is Mircalla, Countess Karnstein, and this is a little coronet over and underneath A.D.

1698. I am descended from the Karnsteins; that is, mamma was."

"Ah!" said the lady, languidly, "so am I, I think, a very long descent, very ancient. Are there any Karnsteins living now?"

"None who bear the name, I believe. The family were ruined, I believe, in some civil wars, long ago, but the ruins of the castle are only about three miles away."

"How interesting!" she said, languidly. "But see what beautiful moonlight!" She glanced through the hall door, which stood a little open. "Suppose you take a little ramble round the court, and look down at the road and river."

"It is so like the night you came to us," I said.

She sighed; smiling.

She rose, and each with her arm about the other's waist, we walked out upon the pavement.

In silence, slowly we walked down to the drawbridge, where the beautiful landscape opened before us.

"And so you were thinking of the night I came here?" she almost whispered.

"Are you glad I came?"

"Delighted, dear Carmilla," I answered.

"And you asked for the picture you think like me, to hang in your room," she murmured with a sigh, as she drew her arm closer about my waist, and let her pretty head sink upon my shoulder. "How romantic you are, Carmilla," I said. "Whenever you tell me your story, it will be made up chiefly of some one great romance."

She kissed me silently.

"I am sure, Carmilla, you have been in love; that there is, at this moment, an affair of the heart going on."

"I have been in love with no one, and never shall," she whispered, "unless it should be with you."

How beautiful she looked in the moonlight!

Shy and strange was the look with which she quickly hid her face in my neck and hair, with tumultuous sighs, that seemed almost to sob, and pressed in mine a hand that trembled.

Her soft cheek was glowing against mine. "Darling, darling," she murmured, "I live in you; and you would die for me, I love you so."

I started from her.

She was gazing on me with eyes from which all fire, all meaning had flown, and a face colorless and apathetic.

"Is there a chill in the air, dear?" she said drowsily. "I almost shiver; have I been dreaming? Let us come in. Come; come; come in."

"You look ill, Carmilla; a little faint. You certainly must take some wine," I said.

"Yes. I will. I'm better now. I shall be quite well in a few minutes. Yes, do give me a little wine," answered Carmilla, as we approached the door.

"Let us look again for a moment; it is the last time, perhaps, I shall see the moonlight with you."

"How do you feel now, dear Carmilla? Are you really better?" I asked.

I was beginning to take alarm, lest she should have been stricken with the strange epidemic that they said had invaded the country about us.

"Papa would be grieved beyond measure," I added, "if he thought you were ever so little ill, without immediately letting us know. We have a very skilful doctor near us, the physician who was with papa today."

"I'm sure he is. I know how kind you all are; but, dear child, I am quite well again. There is nothing ever wrong with me, but a little weakness.

People say I am languid; I am incapable of exertion; I can scarcely walk as far as a child of three years old: and every now and then the little strength I have falters, and I become as you have just seen me. But after all I am very easily set up again; in a moment I am perfectly myself. See how I have recovered."

So, indeed, she had; and she and I talked a great deal, and very animated she was; and the remainder of that evening passed without any recurrence of what I called her infatuations. I mean her crazy talk and looks, which embarrassed, and even frightened me.

But there occurred that night an event which gave my thoughts quite a new turn, and seemed to startle even Carmilla's languid nature into momentary energy.

VI

A VERY STRANGE AGONY

When we got into the drawing room, and had sat down to our coffee and chocolate, although Carmilla did not take any, she seemed quite herself again, and Madame, and Mademoiselle De Lafontaine, joined us, and made a little card party, in the course of which papa came in for what he called his "dish of tea."

When the game was over he sat down beside Carmilla on the sofa, and asked her, a little anxiously, whether she had heard from her mother since her arrival.

She answered "No."

He then asked whether she knew where a letter would reach her at present.

"I cannot tell," she answered ambiguously, "but I have been thinking of leaving you; you have been already too hospitable and too kind to me. I have given you an infinity of trouble, and I should wish to take a carriage tomorrow, and post in pursuit of her; I know where I shall ultimately find her, although I dare not yet tell you."

"But you must not dream of any such thing," exclaimed my father, to my great relief. "We can't afford to lose you so, and I won't consent to your leaving us, except under the care of your mother, who was so good as to consent to your remaining with us till she should herself return. I should be quite happy if I knew that you heard from her: but this evening the accounts of the progress of the mysterious disease that has invaded our neighborhood, grow even more alarming; and my beautiful guest, I do feel the responsibility, unaided by advice from your mother, very much. But I shall do my best; and one thing is certain, that you must not think of leaving us without her distinct direction to that effect. We should suffer too much in parting from you to consent to it easily."

"Thank you, sir, a thousand times for your hospitality," she answered, smiling bashfully. "You have all been too kind to me; I have seldom been so happy in all my life before, as in your beautiful chateau, under your care, and in the society of your dear daughter."

So he gallantly, in his old-fashioned way, kissed her hand, smiling and pleased at her little speech.

I accompanied Carmilla as usual to her room, and sat and chatted with her while she was preparing for bed.

"Do you think," I said at length, "that you will ever confide fully in me?"

She turned round smiling, but made no answer, only continued to smile on me.

"You won't answer that?" I said. "You can't answer pleasantly; I ought not to have asked you."

"You were quite right to ask me that, or anything. You do not know how dear you are to me, or you could not think any confidence too great to look for.

But I am under vows, no nun half so awfully, and I dare not tell my story yet, even to you. The time is very near when you shall know everything. You will think me cruel, very selfish, but love is always selfish; the more ardent the more selfish. How jealous I am you cannot know. You must come with me, loving me, to death; or else hate me and still come with me. and *hating* me through death and after. There is no such word as indifference in my apathetic nature."

"Now, Carmilla, you are going to talk your wild nonsense again," I said hastily.

"Not I, silly little fool as I am, and full of whims and fancies; for your sake I'll talk like a sage. Were you ever at a ball?"

"No; how you do run on. What is it like? How charming it must be."

"I almost forget, it is years ago."

I laughed.

"You are not so old. Your first ball can hardly be forgotten yet."

"I remember everything about it—with an effort. I see it all, as divers see what is going on above them, through a medium, dense, rippling, but transparent. There occurred that night what has confused the picture, and made its colours faint. I was all but assassinated in my bed, wounded here," she touched her breast, "and never was the same since."

"Were you near dying?"

"Yes, very—a cruel love—strange love, that would have taken my life. Love will have its sacrifices. No sacrifice without blood. Let us go to sleep now; I feel so lazy. How can I get up just now and lock my door?"

She was lying with her tiny hands buried in her rich wavy hair, under her cheek, her little head upon the pillow, and her glittering eyes followed me wherever I moved, with a kind of shy smile that I could not decipher.

I bid her good night, and crept from the room with an uncomfortable sensation.

I often wondered whether our pretty guest ever said her prayers. I certainly had never seen her upon her knees. In the morning she never came down until long after our family prayers were over, and at night she never left the drawing room to attend our brief evening prayers in the hall.

If it had not been that it had casually come out in one of our careless talks that she had been baptised, I should have doubted her being a Christian. Religion was a subject on which I had never heard her speak a word. If I had known the world better, this particular neglect or antipathy would not have so much surprised me.

The precautions of nervous people are infectious, and persons of a like temperament are pretty sure, after a time, to imitate them. I had adopted Carmilla's habit of locking her bedroom door, having taken into my head all her whimsical alarms about midnight invaders and prowling assassins. I had also adopted her precaution of making a brief search through her room, to satisfy herself that no lurking assassin or robber was "ensconced."

These wise measures taken, I got into my bed and fell asleep. A light was burning in my room. This was an old habit, of very early date, and which nothing could have tempted me to dispense with.

Thus fortifed I might take my rest in peace. But dreams come through stone walls, light up dark rooms, or darken light ones, and their persons make their exits and their entrances as they please, and laugh at locksmiths.

I had a dream that night that was the beginning of a very strange agony.

I cannot call it a nightmare, for I was quite conscious of being asleep.

But I was equally conscious of being in my room, and lying in bed, precisely as I actually was. I saw, or fancied I saw, the room and its furniture just as I had seen it last, except that it was very dark, and I saw something moving round the foot of the bed, which at first I could not accurately distinguish. But I soon saw that it was a sooty-black animal that resembled a monstrous cat. It appeared to me about four or five feet long for it measured fully the length of the hearthrug as it passed over it; and it continued to-ing and fro-ing with the lithe, sinister restlessness of a beast in a cage. I could not cry out, although as you may suppose, I was terrified. Its pace was growing faster, and the room rapidly darker and darker, and at length so dark that I could no longer see anything of it but its eyes. I felt it spring lightly on the bed. The two broad eyes approached my face, and suddenly I felt a stinging pain as if two large needles darted, an inch or two apart, deep into my breast. I waked with a scream. The room was lighted by the candle that burnt there all through the night, and I saw a female figure standing at the foot of the bed, a little at the right side. It was in a dark loose dress, and its hair was down and covered its shoulders. A block of stone could not have been more still. There was not the slightest stir of respiration. As I stared at it, the figure appeared to have changed its place, and was now nearer the door; then, close to it, the door opened, and it passed out.

I was now relieved, and able to breathe and move. My first thought was that Carmilla had been playing me a trick, and that I had forgotten to secure my door. I hastened to it, and found it locked as usual on the inside. I was afraid to open it—I was horrified. I sprang into my bed and covered my head up in the bedclothes, and lay there more dead than alive till morning.

VII
DESCENDING

It would be vain my attempting to tell you the horror with which, even now, I recall the occurrence of that night. It was no such transitory terror as a dream leaves behind it. It seemed to deepen by time, and communicated itself to the room and the very furniture that had encompassed the apparition.

I could not bear next day to be alone for a moment. I should have told papa, but for two opposite reasons. At one time I thought he would laugh at my story, and I could not bear its being treated as a jest; and at another I thought he might fancy that I had been attacked by the mysterious complaint which had invaded our neighborhood. I had myself no misgiving of the kind, and as he had been rather an invalid for some time, I was afraid of alarming him.

I was comfortable enough with my good-natured companions, Madame Perrodon, and the vivacious Mademoiselle Lafontaine. They both perceived that I was out of spirits and nervous, and at length I told them what lay so heavy at my heart.

Mademoiselle laughed, but I fancied that Madame Perrodon looked anxious.

"By-the-by," said Mademoiselle, laughing, "the long lime tree walk, behind Carmilla's bedroom window, is haunted!"

"Nonsense!" exclaimed Madame, who probably thought the theme rather inopportune, "and who tells that story, my dear?"

"Martin says that he came up twice, when the old yard gate was being repaired, before sunrise, and twice saw the same female figure walking down the lime tree avenue."

"So he well might, as long as there are cows to milk in the river fields," said Madame.

"I daresay; but Martin chooses to be frightened, and never did I see fool more frightened."

"You must not say a word about it to Carmilla, because she can see down that walk from her room window," I interposed, "and she is, if possible, a greater coward than I."

Carmilla came down rather later than usual that day.

"I was so frightened last night," she said, so soon as were together, "and I am sure I should have seen something dreadful if it had not been for that charm I bought from the poor little hunchback whom I called such hard names. I had a dream of something black coming round my bed, and I awoke in a perfect horror, and I really thought, for some seconds, I saw a dark figure near the chimneypiece, but I felt under my pillow for my charm, and the moment my fingers touched it, the figure disappeared, and I felt quite certain, only that I had it by me, that something frightful would have made its appearance, and, perhaps, throttled me, as it did those poor people we heard of.

"Well, listen to me," I began, and recounted my adventure, at the recital of which she appeared horrified.

"And had you the charm near you?" she asked, earnestly.

"No, I had dropped it into a china vase in the drawing room, but I shall certainly take it with me tonight, as you have so much faith in it."

At this distance of time I cannot tell you, or even understand, how I overcame my horror so effectually as to lie alone in my room that night. I remember distinctly that I pinned the charm to my pillow. I fell asleep almost immediately, and slept even more soundly than usual all night.

Next night I passed as well. My sleep was delightfully deep and dreamless.

But I wakened with a sense of lassitude and melancholy, which, however, did not exceed a degree that was almost luxurious.

"Well, I told you so," said Carmilla, when I described my quiet sleep, "I had such delightful sleep myself last night; I pinned the charm to the breast of my nightdress. It was too far away the night before. I am quite sure it was all fancy, except the dreams. I used to think that evil spirits made dreams, but our doctor told me it is no such thing. Only a fever passing by, or some other malady, as they often do, he said, knocks at the door, and not being able to get in, passes on, with that alarm."

"And what do you think the charm is?" said I.

"It has been fumigated or immersed in some drug, and is an antidote against the malaria," she answered.

"Then it acts only on the body?"

"Certainly; you don't suppose that evil spirits are frightened by bits of ribbon, or the perfumes of a druggist's shop? No, these complaints, wandering in the air, begin by trying the nerves, and so infect the brain, but before they can seize upon you, the antidote repels them. That I am sure is what the charm has done for us. It is nothing magical, it is simply natural.

I should have been happier if I could have quite agreed with Carmilla, but I did my best, and the impression was a little losing its force.

For some nights I slept profoundly; but still every morning I felt the same lassitude, and a languor weighed upon me all day. I felt myself a changed girl. A strange melancholy was stealing over me, a melancholy that I would not have interrupted. Dim thoughts of death began to open, and an idea that I was slowly sinking took gentle, and, somehow, not unwelcome, possession of me. If it was sad, the tone of mind which this induced was also sweet.

Whatever it might be, my soul acquiesced in it.

I would not admit that I was ill, I would not consent to tell my papa, or to have the doctor sent for.

Carmilla became more devoted to me than ever, and her strange paroxysms of languid adoration more frequent. She used to gloat on me with increasing ardor the more my strength and spirits waned. This always shocked me like a momentary glare of insanity.

Without knowing it, I was now in a pretty advanced stage of the strangest illness under which mortal ever suffered. There was an unaccountable fascination in its earlier symptoms that more than reconciled me to the incapacitating effect of that stage of the malady. This fascination increased for a time, until it reached a certain point, when gradually a sense of the horrible mingled itself with it, deepening, as you shall hear, until it discolored and perverted the whole state of my life.

The first change I experienced was rather agreeable. It was very near the turning point from which began the descent of Avernus.

Certain vague and strange sensations visited me in my sleep. The prevailing one was of that pleasant, peculiar cold thrill which we feel in bathing, when we move against the current of a river. This was soon accompanied by dreams that seemed interminable, and were so vague that I could never recollect their scenery and persons, or any one connected portion of their action. But they left an awful impression, and a sense of exhaustion, as if I had passed through a long period of great mental exertion and danger.

After all these dreams there remained on waking a remembrance of having been in a place very nearly dark, and of having spoken to people whom I could not see; and especially of one clear voice, of a female's, very deep, that spoke as if at a distance, slowly, and producing always the same sensation of indescribable solemnity and fear. Sometimes there came a sensation as if a hand was drawn softly along my cheek and neck. Sometimes it was as if warm lips kissed me, and longer and longer and more lovingly as they reached my throat, but there the caress fixed itself. My heart beat faster, my breathing rose and fell rapidly and full drawn; a sobbing, that rose into a sense of strangulation, supervened, and turned into a dreadful convulsion, in which my senses left me and I became unconscious.

It was now three weeks since the commencement of this unaccountable state.

My sufferings had, during the last week, told upon my appearance. I had grown pale, my eyes were dilated and darkened underneath, and the languor which I had long felt began to display itself in my countenance.

My father asked me often whether I was ill; but, with an obstinacy which now seems to me unaccountable, I persisted in assuring him that I was quite well.

In a sense this was true. I had no pain, I could complain of no bodily derangement. My complaint seemed to be one of the imagination, or the nerves, and, horrible as my sufferings were, I kept them, with a morbid reserve, very nearly to myself.

It could not be that terrible complaint which the peasants called the oupire, for I had now been suffering for three weeks, and they were seldom ill for much more than three days, when death put an end to their miseries.

Carmilla complained of dreams and feverish sensations, but by no means of so alarming a kind as mine. I say that mine were extremely alarming. Had I been capable of comprehending my condition, I would have invoked aid and advice on my knees. The narcotic of an unsuspected influence was acting upon me, and my perceptions were benumbed.

I am going to tell you now of a dream that led immediately to an odd discovery.

One night, instead of the voice I was accustomed to hear in the dark, I heard one, sweet and tender, and at the same time terrible, which said,

"Your mother warns you to beware of the assassin." At the same time a light unexpectedly sprang up, and I saw Carmilla, standing, near the foot of my bed, in her white nightdress, bathed, from her chin to her feet, in one great stain of blood.

I wakened with a shriek, possessed with the one idea that Carmilla was being murdered. I remember springing from my bed, and my next recollection is that of standing on the lobby, crying for help.

Madame and Mademoiselle came scurrying out of their rooms in alarm; a lamp burned always on the lobby, and seeing me, they soon learned the cause of my terror.

I insisted on our knocking at Carmilla's door. Our knocking was unanswered.

It soon became a pounding and an uproar. We shrieked her name, but all was vain.

We all grew frightened, for the door was locked. We hurried back, in panic, to my room. There we rang the bell long and furiously. If my father's room had been at that side of the house, we would have called him up at once to our aid. But, alas! he was quite out of hearing, and to reach him involved an excursion for which we none of us had courage.

Servants, however, soon came running up the stairs; I had got on my dressing gown and slippers meanwhile, and my companions were already similarly furnished. Recognizing the voices of the servants on the lobby, we sallied out together; and having renewed, as fruitlessly, our summons at Carmilla's door, I ordered the men to force the lock. They did so, and we stood, holding our lights aloft, in the doorway, and so stared into the room.

We called her by name; but there was still no reply. We looked round the room. Everything was undisturbed. It was exactly in the state in which I had left it on bidding her good night. But Carmilla was gone.

VIII
SEARCH

At sight of the room, perfectly undisturbed except for our violent entrance, we began to cool a little, and soon recovered our senses sufficiently to dismiss the men. It had struck Mademoiselle that possibly Carmilla had been wakened by the uproar at her door, and in her first panic had jumped from her bed, and hid herself in a press, or behind a curtain, from which she could not, of course, emerge until the majordomo and his myrmidons had withdrawn. We now recommenced our search, and began to call her name again.

It was all to no purpose. Our perplexity and agitation increased. We examined the windows, but they were secured. I implored of Carmilla, if she had concealed herself, to play this cruel trick no longer—to come out and to end our anxieties. It was all useless. I was by this time convinced that she was not in the room, nor in the dressing room, the door of which was still locked on this side. She could not have passed it. I was utterly puzzled. Had Carmilla discovered one of those secret passages which the old housekeeper said were known to exist in the schloss, although the tradition of their exact situation had been lost? A little time would, no doubt, explain all—utterly perplexed as, for the present, we were.

It was past four o'clock, and I preferred passing the remaining hours of darkness in Madame's room. Daylight brought no solution of the difficulty.

The whole household, with my father at its head, was in a state of agitation next morning. Every part of the chateau was searched. The grounds were explored. No trace of the missing lady could be discovered. The stream was about to be dragged; my father was in distraction; what a tale to have to tell the poor girl's mother on her return. I, too, was almost beside myself, though my grief was quite of a different kind.

The morning was passed in alarm and excitement. It was now one o'clock, and still no tidings. I ran up to Carmilla's room, and found her standing at her dressing table. I was astounded. I could not believe my eyes. She beckoned me to her with her pretty finger, in silence. Her face expressed extreme fear.

I ran to her in an ecstasy of joy; I kissed and embraced her again and again. I ran to the bell and rang it vehemently, to bring others to the spot who might at once relieve my father's anxiety.

"Dear Carmilla, what has become of you all this time? We have been in agonies of anxiety about you," I exclaimed. "Where have you been? How did you come back?"

"Last night has been a night of wonders," she said.

"For mercy's sake, explain all you can."

"It was past two last night," she said, "when I went to sleep as usual in my bed, with my doors locked, that of the dressing room, and that opening upon the gallery. My sleep was uninterrupted, and, so far as I know, dreamless; but I woke just now on the sofa in the dressing room there, and I found the door between the rooms open, and the other door forced. How could all this have happened without my being wakened? It must have been accompanied with a great deal of noise, and I am particularly easily wakened; and how could I have been carried out of my bed without my sleep having been interrupted, I whom the slightest stir startles?"

By this time, Madame, Mademoiselle, my father, and a number of the servants were in the room. Carmilla was, of course, overwhelmed with inquiries, congratulations, and welcomes. She had but one story to tell, and seemed the least able of all the party to suggest any way of accounting for what had happened.

My father took a turn up and down the room, thinking. I saw Carmilla's eye follow him for a moment with a sly, dark glance.

When my father had sent the servants away, Mademoiselle having gone in search of a little bottle of valerian and salvolatile, and there being no one now in the room with Carmilla, except my father, Madame, and myself, he came to her thoughtfully, took her hand very kindly, led her to the sofa, and sat down beside her.

"Will you forgive me, my dear, if I risk a conjecture, and ask a question?"

"Who can have a better right?" she said. "Ask what you please, and I will tell you everything. But my story is simply one of bewilderment and darkness. I know absolutely nothing. Put any question you please, but you know, of course, the limitations mamma has placed me under."

"Perfectly, my dear child. I need not approach the topics on which she desires our silence. Now, the marvel of last night consists in your having been removed from your bed and your room, without being wakened, and this removal having occurred apparently while the windows were still secured, and the two doors locked upon the inside. I will tell you my theory and ask you a question."

Carmilla was leaning on her hand dejectedly; Madame and I were listening breathlessly.

"Now, my question is this. Have you ever been suspected of walking in your sleep?"

"Never, since I was very young indeed."

"But you did walk in your sleep when you were young?"

"Yes; I know I did. I have been told so often by my old nurse."

My father smiled and nodded.

"Well, what has happened is this. You got up in your sleep, unlocked the door, not leaving the key, as usual, in the lock, but taking it out and locking it on the outside; you again took the key out, and carried it away with you to some one of the five-and-twenty rooms on this floor, or perhaps upstairs or downstairs. There are so many rooms and closets, so much heavy furniture, and such accumulations of lumber, that it would require a week to search this old house thoroughly. Do you see, now, what I mean?"

"I do, but not all," she answered.

"And how, papa, do you account for her finding herself on the sofa in the dressing room, which we had searched so carefully?"

"She came there after you had searched it, still in her sleep, and at last awoke spontaneously, and was as much surprised to find herself where she was as any one else. I wish all mysteries were as easily and innocently explained as yours, Carmilla," he said, laughing. "And so we may congratulate ourselves on the certainty that the most natural explanation of the occurrence is one that involves no drugging, no tampering with locks, no burglars, or poisoners, or witches—nothing that need alarm Carmilla, or anyone else, for our safety."

Carmilla was looking charmingly. Nothing could be more beautiful than her tints. Her beauty was, I think, enhanced by that graceful languor that was peculiar to her. I think my father was silently contrasting her looks with mine, for he said:

"I wish my poor Laura was looking more like herself"; and he sighed.

So our alarms were happily ended, and Carmilla restored to her friends.

IX
THE DOCTOR

As Carmilla would not hear of an attendant sleeping in her room, my father arranged that a servant should sleep outside her door, so that she would not attempt to make another such excursion without being arrested at her own door.

That night passed quietly; and next morning early, the doctor, whom my father had sent for without telling me a word about it, arrived to see me.

Madame accompanied me to the library; and there the grave little doctor, with white hair and spectacles, whom I mentioned before, was waiting to receive me.

I told him my story, and as I proceeded he grew graver and graver.

We were standing, he and I, in the recess of one of the windows, facing one another. When my statement was over, he leaned with his shoulders against the wall, and with his eyes fixed on me earnestly, with an interest in which was a dash of horror.

After a minute's reflection, he asked Madame if he could see my father.

He was sent for accordingly, and as he entered, smiling, he said:

"I dare say, doctor, you are going to tell me that I am an old fool for having brought you here; I hope I am."

But his smile faded into shadow as the doctor, with a very grave face, beckoned him to him.

He and the doctor talked for some time in the same recess where I had just conferred with the physician. It seemed an earnest and argumentative conversation. The room is very large, and I and Madame stood together, burning with curiosity, at the farther end. Not a word could we hear, however, for they spoke in a very low tone, and the deep recess of the window quite concealed the doctor from view, and very nearly my father, whose foot, arm, and shoulder only could we see; and the voices were, I suppose, all the less audible for the sort of closet which the thick wall and window formed.

After a time my father's face looked into the room; it was pale, thoughtful, and, I fancied, agitated.

"Laura, dear, come here for a moment. Madame, we shan't trouble you, the doctor says, at present."

Accordingly I approached, for the first time a little alarmed; for, although I felt very weak, I did not feel ill; and strength, one always fancies, is a thing that may be picked up when we please.

My father held out his hand to me, as I drew near, but he was looking at the doctor, and he said:

"It certainly is very odd; I don't understand it quite. Laura, come here, dear; now attend to Doctor Spielsberg, and recollect yourself."

"You mentioned a sensation like that of two needles piercing the skin, somewhere about your neck, on the night when you experienced your first horrible dream. Is there still any soreness?"

"None at all," I answered.

"Can you indicate with your finger about the point at which you think this occurred?"

"Very little below my throat—here," I answered.

I wore a morning dress, which covered the place I pointed to.

"Now you can satisfy yourself," said the doctor. "You won't mind your papa's lowering your dress a very little. It is necessary, to detect a symptom of the complaint under which you have been suffering."

I acquiesced. It was only an inch or two below the edge of my collar.

"God bless me!—so it is," exclaimed my father, growing pale.

"You see it now with your own eyes," said the doctor, with a gloomy triumph.

"What is it?" I exclaimed, beginning to be frightened.

"Nothing, my dear young lady, but a small blue spot, about the size of the tip of your little finger; and now," he continued, turning to papa, "the question is what is best to be done?"

Is there any danger?"I urged, in great trepidation.

"I trust not, my dear," answered the doctor. "I don't see why you should not recover. I don't see why you should not begin immediately to get better. That is the point at which the sense of strangulation begins?"

"Yes," I answered.

"And—recollect as well as you can—the same point was a kind of center of that thrill which you described just now, like the current of a cold stream running against you?"

"It may have been; I think it was."

"Ay, you see?" he added, turning to my father. "Shall I say a word to Madame?"

"Certainly," said my father.

He called Madame to him, and said:

"I find my young friend here far from well. It won't be of any great consequence, I hope; but it will be necessary that some steps be taken, which I will explain by-and-by; but in the meantime, Madame, you will be so good as not to let Miss Laura be alone for one moment. That is the only direction I need give for the present. It is indispensable."

"We may rely upon your kindness, Madame, I know," added my father.

Madame satisfied him eagerly.

"And you, dear Laura, I know you will observe the doctor's direction."

"I shall have to ask your opinion upon another patient, whose symptoms slightly resemble those of my daughter, that have just been detailed to you—very much milder in degree, but I believe quite of the same sort. She is a young lady—our guest; but as you say you will be passing this way again this evening, you can't do better than take your supper here, and you can then see her. She does not come down till the afternoon."

"I thank you," said the doctor. "I shall be with you, then, at about seven this evening."

And then they repeated their directions to me and to Madame, and with this parting charge my father left us, and walked out with the doctor; and I saw them pacing together up and down between the road and the moat, on the grassy platform in front of the castle, evidently absorbed in earnest conversation.

The doctor did not return. I saw him mount his horse there, take his leave, and ride away eastward through the forest.

Nearly at the same time I saw the man arrive from Dranfield with the letters, and dismount and hand the bag to my father.

In the meantime, Madame and I were both busy, lost in conjecture as to the reasons of the singular and earnest direction which the doctor and my father had concurred in imposing. Madame, as she afterwards told me, was afraid the doctor apprehended a sudden seizure, and that, without prompt assistance, I might either lose my life in a fit, or at least be seriously hurt.

The interpretation did not strike me; and I fancied, perhaps luckily for my nerves, that the arrangement was prescribed simply to secure a companion, who would prevent my taking too much exercise, or eating unripe fruit, or doing any of the fifty foolish things to which young people are supposed to be prone.

About half an hour after my father came in—he had a letter in his hand—and said:

"This letter had been delayed; it is from General Spielsdorf. He might have been here yesterday, he may not come till tomorrow or he may be here today."

He put the open letter into my hand; but he did not look pleased, as he used when a guest, especially one so much loved as the General, was coming.

On the contrary, he looked as if he wished him at the bottom of the Red Sea. There was plainly something on his mind which he did not choose to divulge.

"Papa, darling, will you tell me this?" said I, suddenly laying my hand on his arm, and looking, I am sure, imploringly in his face.

"Perhaps," he answered, smoothing my hair caressingly over my eyes.

"Does the doctor think me very ill?"

"No, dear; he thinks, if right steps are taken, you will be quite well again, at least, on the high road to a complete recovery, in a day or two," he answered, a little dryly. "I wish our good friend, the General, had chosen any other time; that is, I wish you had been perfectly well to receive him."

"But do tell me, papa," I insisted, "what does he think is the matter with me?"

"Nothing; you must not plague me with questions," he answered, with more irritation than I ever remember him to have displayed before; and seeing that I looked wounded, I suppose, he kissed me, and added, "You shall know all about it in a day or two; that is, all that I know. In the meantime you are not to trouble your head about it."

He turned and left the room, but came back before I had done wondering and puzzling over the oddity of all this; it was merely to say that he was going to Karnstein, and had ordered the carriage to be ready at twelve, and that I and Madame should accompany him; he was going to see the priest who lived near those picturesque grounds, upon business, and as Carmilla had never seen them, she could follow, when she came down, with Mademoiselle, who would bring materials for what you call a picnic, which might be laid for us in the ruined castle.

At twelve o'clock, accordingly, I was ready, and not long after, my father, Madame and I set out upon our projected drive.

Passing the drawbridge we turn to the right, and follow the road over the steep Gothic bridge, westward, to reach the deserted village and ruined castle of Karnstein.

No sylvan drive can be fancied prettier. The ground breaks into gentle hills and hollows, all clothed with beautiful wood, totally destitute of the comparative formality which artificial planting and early culture and pruning impart.

The irregularities of the ground often lead the road out of its course, and cause it to wind beautifully round the sides of broken hollows and the steeper sides of the hills, among varieties of ground almost inexhaustible.

Turning one of these points, we suddenly encountered our old friend, the General, riding towards us, attended by a mounted servant. His portmanteaus were following in a hired wagon, such as we term a cart.

The General dismounted as we pulled up, and, after the usual greetings, was easily persuaded to accept the vacant seat in the carriage and send his horse on with his servant to the schloss.

X

BEREAVED

It was about ten months since we had last seen him: but that time had sufficed to make an alteration of years in his appearance. He had grown thinner; something of gloom and anxiety had taken the place of that cordial serenity which used to characterize his features. His dark blue eyes, always penetrating, now gleamed with a sterner light from under his shaggy grey eyebrows. It was not such a change as grief alone usually induces, and angrier passions seemed to have had their share in bringing it about.

We had not long resumed our drive, when the General began to talk, with his usual soldierly directness, of the bereavement, as he termed it, which he had sustained in the death of his beloved niece and ward; and he then broke out in a tone of intense bitterness and fury, inveighing against the "hellish arts" to which she had fallen a victim, and expressing, with more exasperation than piety, his wonder that Heaven should tolerate so monstrous an indulgence of the lusts and malignity of hell.

My father, who saw at once that something very extraordinary had befallen, asked him, if not too painful to him, to detail the circumstances which he thought justified the strong terms in which he expressed himself.

"I should tell you all with pleasure," said the General, "but you would not believe me."

"Why should I not?" he asked.

"Because," he answered testily, "you believe in nothing but what consists with your own prejudices and illusions. I remember when I was like you, but I have learned better."

"Try me," said my father; "I am not such a dogmatist as you suppose. Besides which, I very well know that you generally require proof for what you believe, and am, therefore, very strongly predisposed to respect your conclusions."

"You are right in supposing that I have not been led lightly into a belief in the marvelous—for what I have experienced is marvelous—and I have been forced by extraordinary evidence to credit that which ran counter, diametrically, to all my theories. I have been made the dupe of a preternatural conspiracy."

Notwithstanding his professions of confidence in the General's penetration, I saw my father, at this point, glance at the General, with, as I thought, a marked suspicion of his sanity.

The General did not see it, luckily. He was looking gloomily and curiously into the glades and vistas of the woods that were opening before us.

"You are going to the Ruins of Karnstein?" he said. "Yes, it is a lucky coincidence; do you know I was going to ask you to bring me there to inspect them. I have a special object in exploring. There is a ruined chapel, ain't there, with a great many tombs of that extinct family?"

"So there are—highly interesting," said my father. "I hope you are thinking of claiming the title and estates?"

My father said this gaily, but the General did not recollect the laugh, or even the smile, which courtesy exacts for a friend's joke; on the contrary, he looked grave and even fierce, ruminating on a matter that stirred his anger and horror.

"Something very different," he said, gruffly. "I mean to unearth some of those fine people. I hope, by God's blessing, to accomplish a pious sacrilege here, which will relieve our earth of certain monsters, and enable honest people to sleep in their beds without being assailed by murderers. I have strange things to tell you, my dear friend, such as I myself would have scouted as incredible a few months since."

My father looked at him again, but this time not with a glance of suspicion—with an eye, rather, of keen intelligence and alarm.

"The house of Karnstein," he said, "has been long extinct: a hundred years at least. My dear wife was maternally descended from the Karnsteins. But the name and title have long ceased to exist. The castle is a ruin; the very village is deserted; it is fifty years since the smoke of a chimney was seen there; not a roof left."

"Quite true. I have heard a great deal about that since I last saw you; a great deal that will astonish you. But I had better relate everything in the order in which it occurred," said the General. "You saw my dear ward— my child, I may call her. No creature could have been more beautiful, and only three months ago none more blooming."

"Yes, poor thing! when I saw her last she certainly was quite lovely," said my father. "I was grieved and shocked more than I can tell you, my dear friend; I knew what a blow it was to you."

He took the General's hand, and they exchanged a kind pressure. Tears gathered in the old soldier's eyes. He did not seek to conceal them. He said:

"We have been very old friends; I knew you would feel for me, childless as I am. She had become an object of very near interest to me, and repaid my care by an affection that cheered my home and made my life happy. That is all gone. The years that remain to me on earth may not be very long; but by God's mercy I hope to accomplish a service to mankind before I die, and to subserve the vengeance of Heaven upon the fiends who have murdered my poor child in the spring of her hopes and beauty!"

"You said, just now, that you intended relating everything as it occurred," said my father. "Pray do; I assure you that it is not mere curiosity that prompts me."

By this time we had reached the point at which the Drunstall road, by which the General had come, diverges from the road which we were traveling to Karnstein.

"How far is it to the ruins?" inquired the General, looking anxiously forward.

"About half a league," answered my father. "Pray let us hear the story you were so good as to promise."

XI

THE STORY

With all my heart," said the General, with an effort; and after a short pause in which to arrange his subject, he commenced one of the strangest narratives I ever heard.

"My dear child was looking forward with great pleasure to the visit you had been so good as to arrange for her to your charming daughter." Here he made me a gallant but melancholy bow. "In the meantime we had an invitation to my old friend the Count Carlsfeld, whose schloss is about six leagues to the other side of Karnstein. It was to attend the series of fetes which, you remember, were given by him in honor of his illustrious visitor, the Grand Duke Charles."

"Yes; and very splendid, I believe, they were," said my father.

"Princely! But then his hospitalities are quite regal. He has Aladdin's lamp. The night from which my sorrow dates was devoted to a magnificent masquerade. The grounds were thrown open, the trees hung with colored lamps. There was such a display of fireworks as Paris itself had never witnessed. And such music—music, you know, is my weakness—such ravishing music! The finest instrumental band, perhaps, in the world, and the finest singers who could be collected from all the great operas in Europe. As you wandered through these fantastically illuminated grounds, the moon-lighted chateau throwing a rosy light from its long rows of

60

windows, you would suddenly hear these ravishing voices stealing from the silence of some grove, or rising from boats upon the lake. I felt myself, as I looked and listened, carried back into the romance and poetry of my early youth.

"When the fireworks were ended, and the ball beginning, we returned to the noble suite of rooms that were thrown open to the dancers. A masked ball, you know, is a beautiful sight; but so brilliant a spectacle of the kind I never saw before.

"It was a very aristocratic assembly. I was myself almost the only 'nobody' present.

"My dear child was looking quite beautiful. She wore no mask. Her excitement and delight added an unspeakable charm to her features, always lovely. I remarked a young lady, dressed magnificently, but wearing a mask, who appeared to me to be observing my ward with extraordinary interest. I had seen her, earlier in the evening, in the great hall, and again, for a few minutes, walking near us, on the terrace under the castle windows, similarly employed. A lady, also masked, richly and gravely dressed, and with a stately air, like a person of rank, accompanied her as a chaperon.

Had the young lady not worn a mask, I could, of course, have been much more certain upon the question whether she was really watching my poor darling.

I am now well assured that she was.

"We were now in one of the salons. My poor dear child had been dancing, and was resting a little in one of the chairs near the door; I was standing near. The two ladies I have mentioned had approached and the younger took the chair next my ward; while her companion stood beside me, and for a little time addressed herself, in a low tone, to her charge.

"Availing herself of the privilege of her mask, she turned to me, and in the tone of an old friend, and calling me by my name, opened a conversation with me, which piqued my curiosity a good deal. She referred to many scenes where she had met me—at Court, and at distinguished houses. She alluded to little incidents which I had long ceased to think of, but which, I found, had only lain in abeyance in my memory, for they instantly started into life at her touch.

"I became more and more curious to ascertain who she was, every moment. She parried my attempts to discover very adroitly and pleasantly.

The knowledge she showed of many passages in my life seemed to me all but unaccountable; and she appeared to take a not unnatural pleasure in foiling my curiosity, and in seeing me flounder in my eager perplexity, from one conjecture to another.

"In the meantime the young lady, whom her mother called by the odd name of Millarca, when she once or twice addressed her, had, with the same ease and grace, got into conversation with my ward.

"She introduced herself by saying that her mother was a very old acquaintance of mine. She spoke of the agreeable audacity which a mask rendered practicable; she talked like a friend; she admired her dress, and insinuated very prettily her admiration of her beauty. She amused her with laughing criticisms upon the people who crowded the ballroom, and laughed at my poor child's fun. She was very witty and lively when she pleased, and after a time they had grown very good friends, and the young stranger lowered her mask, displaying a remarkably beautiful face. I had never seen it before, neither had my dear child. But though it was new to us, the features were so engaging, as well as lovely, that it was impossible not to feel the attraction powerfully. My poor girl did so. I never saw anyone more taken with another at first sight, unless, indeed, it was the stranger herself, who seemed quite to have lost her heart to her.

"In the meantime, availing myself of the license of a masquerade, I put not a few questions to the elder lady.

"'You have puzzled me utterly,' I said, laughing. 'Is that not enough?

Won't you, now, consent to stand on equal terms, and do me the kindness to remove your mask?'

"'Can any request be more unreasonable?' she replied. 'Ask a lady to yield an advantage! Beside, how do you know you should recognize me? Years make changes.'

"'As you see,' I said, with a bow, and, I suppose, a rather melancholy little laugh.

"'As philosophers tell us,' she said; 'and how do you know that a sight of my face would help you?'

"'I should take chance for that,' I answered. 'It is vain trying to make yourself out an old woman; your figure betrays you.'

"'Years, nevertheless, have passed since I saw you, rather since you saw me, for that is what I am considering. Millarca, there, is my daughter;

I cannot then be young, even in the opinion of people whom time has taught to be indulgent, and I may not like to be compared with what you remember me.

You have no mask to remove. You can offer me nothing in exchange.'

"My petition is to your pity, to remove it.'

"And mine to yours, to let it stay where it is,' she replied.

"Well, then, at least you will tell me whether you are French or German; you speak both languages so perfectly.'

"I don't think I shall tell you that, General; you intend a surprise, and are meditating the particular point of attack.'

"At all events, you won't deny this,' I said, 'that being honored by your permission to converse, I ought to know how to address you. Shall I say Madame la Comtesse?'

"She laughed, and she would, no doubt, have met me with another evasion—if, indeed, I can treat any occurrence in an interview every circumstance of which was prearranged, as I now believe, with the profoundest cunning, as liable to be modified by accident.

"As to that,' she began; but she was interrupted, almost as she opened her lips, by a gentleman, dressed in black, who looked particularly elegant and distinguished, with this drawback, that his face was the most deadly pale I ever saw, except in death. He was in no masquerade—in the plain evening dress of a gentleman; and he said, without a smile, but with a courtly and unusually low bow:—

"Will Madame la Comtesse permit me to say a very few words which may interest her?'

"The lady turned quickly to him, and touched her lip in token of silence; she then said to me, 'Keep my place for me, General; I shall return when I have said a few words.'

"And with this injunction, playfully given, she walked a little aside with the gentleman in black, and talked for some minutes, apparently very earnestly. They then walked away slowly together in the crowd, and I lost them for some minutes.

"I spent the interval in cudgeling my brains for a conjecture as to the identity of the lady who seemed to remember me so kindly, and I was thinking of turning about and joining in the conversation between my pretty ward and the Countess's daughter, and trying whether, by the time she returned, I might not have a surprise in store for her, by having her name, title, chateau, and estates at my fingers' ends. But at this moment she returned, accompanied by the pale man in black, who said:

"I shall return and inform Madame la Comtesse when her carriage is at the door.'

"He withdrew with a bow."

XII

A PETITION

"Then we are to lose Madame la Comtesse, but I hope only for a few hours,' I said, with a low bow.

"It may be that only, or it may be a few weeks. It was very unlucky his speaking to me just now as he did. Do you now know me?'

"I assured her I did not.

"You shall know me,' she said, 'but not at present. We are older and better friends than, perhaps, you suspect. I cannot yet declare myself. I shall in three weeks pass your beautiful schloss, about which I have been making enquiries. I shall then look in upon you for an hour or two, and renew a friendship which I never think of without a thousand pleasant recollections. This moment a piece of news has reached me like a thunderbolt. I must set out now, and travel by a devious route, nearly a hundred miles, with all the dispatch I can possibly make. My perplexities multiply. I am only deterred by the compulsory reserve I practice as to my name from making a very singular request of you. My poor child has not quite recovered her strength. Her horse fell with her, at a hunt which she had ridden out to witness, her nerves have not yet recovered the shock, and our physician says that she must on no account exert herself for some time to come. We came here, in consequence, by very easy stages—hardly six leagues a day. I must now travel day and night, on a mission of life and death—a mission the critical and momentous nature of which I shall be able to explain to you when we meet, as I hope we shall, in a few weeks, without the necessity of any concealment.'

"She went on to make her petition, and it was in the tone of a person from whom such a request amounted to conferring, rather than seeking a favor.

This was only in manner, and, as it seemed, quite unconsciously. Than the terms in which it was expressed, nothing could be more deprecatory. It was simply that I would consent to take charge of her daughter during her absence.

"This was, all things considered, a strange, not to say, an audacious request. She in some sort disarmed me, by stating and admitting everything that could be urged against it, and throwing herself entirely upon my chivalry. At the same moment, by a fatality that seems to have predetermined all that happened, my poor child came to my side, and, in an undertone, besought me to invite her new friend, Millarca, to pay us a visit. She had just been sounding her, and thought, if her mamma would allow her, she would like it extremely.

"At another time I should have told her to wait a little, until, at least, we knew who they were. But I had not a moment to think in. The two ladies assailed me together, and I must confess the refined and beautiful face of the young lady, about which there was something extremely engaging, as well as the elegance and fire of high birth, determined me; and, quite overpowered, I submitted, and undertook, too easily, the care of the young lady, whom her mother called Millarca.

"The Countess beckoned to her daughter, who listened with grave attention while she told her, in general terms, how suddenly and peremptorily she had been summoned, and also of the arrangement she had made for her under my care, adding that I was one of her earliest and most valued friends.

"I made, of course, such speeches as the case seemed to call for, and found myself, on reflection, in a position which I did not half like.

"The gentleman in black returned, and very ceremoniously conducted the lady from the room.

"The demeanor of this gentleman was such as to impress me with the conviction that the Countess was a lady of very much more importance than her modest title alone might have led me to assume.

"Her last charge to me was that no attempt was to be made to learn more about her than I might have already guessed, until her return. Our distinguished host, whose guest she was, knew her reasons.

"But here,' she said, 'neither I nor my daughter could safely remain for more than a day. I removed my mask imprudently for a moment, about an hour ago, and, too late, I fancied you saw me. So I resolved to seek an opportunity of talking a little to you. Had I found that you had seen me, I would have thrown myself on your high sense of honor to keep my secret some weeks. As it is, I am satisfied that you did not see me; but if you now suspect, or, on reflection, should suspect, who I am, I commit myself, in like manner, entirely to your honor. My daughter will observe the same secrecy, and I well know that you will, from time to time, remind her, lest she should thoughtlessly disclose it.'

"She whispered a few words to her daughter, kissed her hurriedly twice, and went away, accompanied by the pale gentleman in black, and disappeared in the crowd.

"In the next room,' said Millarca, 'there is a window that looks upon the hall door. I should like to see the last of mamma, and to kiss my hand to her.'

"We assented, of course, and accompanied her to the window. We looked out, and saw a handsome old-fashioned carriage, with a troop of couriers and footmen. We saw the slim figure of the pale gentleman in black, as he held a thick velvet cloak, and placed it about her shoulders and threw the hood over her head. She nodded to him, and just touched his hand with hers. He bowed low repeatedly as the door closed, and the carriage began to move.

"She is gone,' said Millarca, with a sigh.

"She is gone,' I repeated to myself, for the first time—in the hurried moments that had elapsed since my consent—reflecting upon the folly of my act.

"She did not look up,' said the young lady, plaintively.

"The Countess had taken off her mask, perhaps, and did not care to show her face,' I said; 'and she could not know that you were in the window.'

"She sighed, and looked in my face. She was so beautiful that I relented. I was sorry I had for a moment repented of my hospitality, and I determined to make her amends for the unavowed churlishness of my reception.

"The young lady, replacing her mask, joined my ward in persuading me to return to the grounds, where the concert was soon to be renewed. We did so, and walked up and down the terrace that lies under the castle windows.

Millarca became very intimate with us, and amused us with lively descriptions and stories of most of the great people whom we saw upon the terrace. I liked her more and more every minute. Her gossip without being ill-natured, was extremely diverting to me, who had been so long out of the great world. I thought what life she would give to our sometimes lonely evenings at home.

"This ball was not over until the morning sun had almost reached the horizon. It pleased the Grand Duke to dance till then, so loyal people could not go away, or think of bed.

"We had just got through a crowded saloon, when my ward asked me what had become of Millarca. I thought she had been by her side, and she fancied she was by mine. The fact was, we had lost her.

"All my efforts to find her were vain. I feared that she had mistaken, in the confusion of a momentary separation from us, other people for her new friends, and had, possibly, pursued and lost them in the extensive grounds which were thrown open to us.

"Now, in its full force, I recognized a new folly in my having undertaken the charge of a young lady without so much as knowing her name; and fettered as I was by promises, of the reasons for imposing which I knew nothing, I could not even point my inquiries by saying that the missing young lady was the daughter of the Countess who had taken her departure a few hours before.

"Morning broke. It was clear daylight before I gave up my search. It was not till near two o'clock next day that we heard anything of my missing charge.

"At about that time a servant knocked at my niece's door, to say that he had been earnestly requested by a young lady, who appeared to be in great distress, to make out where she could find the General Baron Spielsdorf and the young lady his daughter, in whose charge she had been left by her mother.

"There could be no doubt, notwithstanding the slight inaccuracy, that our young friend had turned up; and so she had. Would to heaven we had lost her!

"She told my poor child a story to account for her having failed to recover us for so long. Very late, she said, she had got to the housekeeper's bedroom in despair of finding us, and had then fallen into a deep sleep which, long as it was, had hardly sufficed to recruit her strength after the fatigues of the ball.

"That day Millarca came home with us. I was only too happy, after all, to have secured so charming a companion for my dear girl."

XIII

THE WOODMAN

"There soon, however, appeared some drawbacks. In the first place, Millarca complained of extreme languor—the weakness that remained after her late illness—and she never emerged from her room till the afternoon was pretty far advanced. In the next place, it was accidentally discovered, although she always locked her door on the inside, and never disturbed the key from its place till she admitted the maid to assist at her toilet, that she was undoubtedly sometimes absent from her room in the very early morning, and at various times later in the day, before she wished it to be understood that she was stirring. She was repeatedly seen from the windows of the schloss, in the first faint grey of the morning, walking through the trees, in an easterly direction, and looking like a person in a trance. This convinced me that she walked in her sleep. But this hypothesis did not solve the puzzle. How did she pass out from her room, leaving the door locked on the inside? How did she escape from the house without unbarring door or window?

"In the midst of my perplexities, an anxiety of a far more urgent kind presented itself.

"My dear child began to lose her looks and health, and that in a manner so mysterious, and even horrible, that I became thoroughly frightened.

"She was at first visited by appalling dreams; then, as she fancied, by a specter, sometimes resembling Millarca, sometimes in the shape of a beast, indistinctly seen, walking round the foot of her bed, from side to side.

Lastly came sensations. One, not unpleasant, but very peculiar, she said, resembled the flow of an icy stream against her breast. At a later time, she felt something like a pair of large needles pierce her, a little below the throat, with a very sharp pain. A few nights after, followed a gradual and convulsive sense of strangulation; then came unconsciousness."

I could hear distinctly every word the kind old General was saying, because by this time we were driving upon the short grass that spreads on either side of the road as you approach the roofless village which had not shown the smoke of a chimney for more than half a century.

You may guess how strangely I felt as I heard my own symptoms so exactly described in those which had been experienced by the poor girl who, but for the catastrophe which followed, would have been at that moment a visitor at my father's chateau. You may suppose, also, how I felt as I heard him detail habits and mysterious peculiarities which were, in fact, those of our beautiful guest, Carmilla!

A vista opened in the forest; we were on a sudden under the chimneys and gables of the ruined village, and the towers and battlements of the dismantled castle, round which gigantic trees are grouped, overhung us from a slight eminence.

In a frightened dream I got down from the carriage, and in silence, for we had each abundant matter for thinking; we soon mounted the ascent, and were among the spacious chambers, winding stairs, and dark corridors of the castle.

"And this was once the palatial residence of the Karnsteins!" said the old General at length, as from a great window he looked out across the village, and saw the wide, undulating expanse of forest. "It was a bad family, and here its bloodstained annals were written," he continued. "It is hard that they should, after death, continue to plague the human race with their atrocious lusts. That is the chapel of the Karnsteins, down there."

He pointed down to the grey walls of the Gothic building partly visible through the foliage, a little way down the steep. "And I hear the axe of a woodman," he added, "busy among the trees that surround it; he possibly may give us the information of which I am in search, and point out the grave of Mircalla, Countess of Karnstein. These rustics preserve the local traditions of great families, whose stories die out among the rich and titled so soon as the families themselves become extinct."

"We have a portrait, at home, of Mircalla, the Countess Karnstein; should you like to see it?" asked my father.

"Time enough, dear friend," replied the General. "I believe that I have seen the original; and one motive which has led me to you earlier than I at first intended, was to explore the chapel which we are now approaching."

"What! see the Countess Mircalla," exclaimed my father; "why, she has been dead more than a century!"

"Not so dead as you fancy, I am told," answered the General.

"I confess, General, you puzzle me utterly," replied my father, looking at him, I fancied, for a moment with a return of the suspicion I detected before. But although there was anger and detestation, at times, in the old General's manner, there was nothing flighty.

"There remains to me," he said, as we passed under the heavy arch of the Gothic church—for its dimensions would have justified its being so styled—"but one object which can interest me during the few years that remain to me on earth, and that is to wreak on her the vengeance which, I thank God, may still be accomplished by a mortal arm."

"What vengeance can you mean?" asked my father, in increasing amazement.

"I mean, to decapitate the monster," he answered, with a fierce flush, and a stamp that echoed mournfully through the hollow ruin, and his clenched hand was at the same moment raised, as if it grasped the handle of an axe, while he shook it ferociously in the air.

"What?" exclaimed my father, more than ever bewildered.

"To strike her head off."

"Cut her head off!"

"Aye, with a hatchet, with a spade, or with anything that can cleave through her murderous throat. You shall hear," he answered, trembling with rage. And hurrying forward he said:

"That beam will answer for a seat; your dear child is fatigued; let her be seated, and I will, in a few sentences, close my dreadful story."

The squared block of wood, which lay on the grass-grown pavement of the chapel, formed a bench on which I was very glad to seat myself, and in the meantime the General called to the woodman, who had been removing some boughs which leaned upon the old walls; and, axe in hand, the hardy old fellow stood before us.

He could not tell us anything of these monuments; but there was an old man, he said, a ranger of this forest, at present sojourning in the house of the priest, about two miles away, who could point out every monument of the old Karnstein family; and, for a trifle, he undertook to bring him back with him, if we would lend him one of our horses, in little more than half an hour.

"Have you been long employed about this forest?" asked my father of the old man.

"I have been a woodman here," he answered in his patois, "under the forester, all my days; so has my father before me, and so on, as many generations as I can count up. I could show you the very house in the village here, in which my ancestors lived."

"How came the village to be deserted?" asked the General.

"It was troubled by revenants, sir; several were tracked to their graves, there detected by the usual tests, and extinguished in the usual way, by decapitation, by the stake, and by burning; but not until many of the villagers were killed.

"But after all these proceedings according to law," he continued—"so many graves opened, and so many vampires deprived of their horrible animation—the village was not relieved. But a Moravian nobleman, who happened to be traveling this way, heard how matters were, and being skilled—as many people are in his country—in such affairs, he offered to deliver the village from its tormentor. He did so thus: There being a bright moon that night, he ascended, shortly after sunset, the towers of the chapel here, from whence he could distinctly see the churchyard beneath him; you can see it from that window. From this point he watched until he saw the vampire come out of his grave, and place near it the linen clothes in which he had been folded, and then glide away towards the village to plague its inhabitants.

"The stranger, having seen all this, came down from the steeple, took the linen wrappings of the vampire, and carried them up to the top of the tower, which he again mounted. When the vampire returned from his prowlings and missed his clothes, he cried furiously to the Moravian, whom he saw at the summit of the tower, and who, in reply, beckoned him to ascend and take them. Whereupon the vampire, accepting his invitation, began to climb the steeple, and so soon as he had reached the battlements, the Moravian, with a stroke of his sword, clove his skull in twain, hurling him down to the churchyard, whither, descending by the winding stairs, the stranger followed and cut his head off, and next day delivered it and the body to the villagers, who duly impaled and burnt them.

"This Moravian nobleman had authority from the then head of the family to remove the tomb of Mircalla, Countess Karnstein, which he did effectually, so that in a little while its site was quite forgotten."

"Can you point out where it stood?" asked the General, eagerly.

The forester shook his head, and smiled.

"Not a soul living could tell you that now," he said; "besides, they say her body was removed; but no one is sure of that either."

Having thus spoken, as time pressed, he dropped his axe and departed, leaving us to hear the remainder of the General's strange story.

XIV
THE MEETING

"My beloved child," he resumed, "was now growing rapidly worse. The physician who attended her had failed to produce the slightest impression on her disease, for such I then supposed it to be. He saw my alarm, and suggested a consultation. I called in an abler physician, from Gratz.

Several days elapsed before he arrived. He was a good and pious, as well as a learned man. Having seen my poor ward together, they withdrew to my library to confer and discuss. I, from the adjoining room, where I awaited their summons, heard these two gentlemen's voices raised in something sharper than a strictly philosophical discussion. I knocked at the door and entered. I found the old physician from Gratz maintaining his theory. His rival was combating it with undisguised ridicule, accompanied with bursts of laughter. This unseemly manifestation subsided and the altercation ended on my entrance.

"Sir,' said my first physician,'my learned brother seems to think that you want a conjuror, and not a doctor.'

"Pardon me,' said the old physician from Gratz, looking displeased, 'I shall state my own view of the case in my own way another time. I grieve, Monsieur le General, that by my skill and science I can be of no use.

Before I go I shall do myself the honor to suggest something to you.'

"He seemed thoughtful, and sat down at a table and began to write.

Profoundly disappointed, I made my bow, and as I turned to go, the other doctor pointed over his shoulder to his companion who was writing, and then, with a shrug, significantly touched his forehead.

"This consultation, then, left me precisely where I was. I walked out into the grounds, all but distracted. The doctor from Gratz, in ten or fifteen minutes, overtook me. He apologized for having followed me, but said that he could not conscientiously take his leave without a few words more. He told me that he could not be mistaken; no natural disease exhibited the same symptoms; and that death was already very near. There remained, however, a day, or possibly two, of life. If the fatal seizure were at once arrested, with great care and skill her strength might possibly return. But all hung now upon the confines of the irrevocable. One more assault might extinguish the last spark of vitality which is, every moment, ready to die.

"And what is the nature of the seizure you speak of?' I entreated.

"I have stated all fully in this note, which I place in your hands upon the distinct condition that you send for the nearest clergyman, and open my letter in his presence, and on no account read it till he is with you; you would despise it else, and it is a matter of life and death. Should the priest fail you, then, indeed, you may read it.'

"He asked me, before taking his leave finally, whether I would wish to see a man curiously learned upon the very subject, which, after I had read his letter, would probably interest me above all others, and he urged me earnestly to invite him to visit him there; and so took his leave.

"The ecclesiastic was absent, and I read the letter by myself. At another time, or in another case, it might have excited my ridicule. But into what quackeries will not people rush for a last chance, where all accustomed means have failed, and the life of a beloved object is at stake?

"Nothing, you will say, could be more absurd than the learned man's letter.

It was monstrous enough to have consigned him to a madhouse. He said that the patient was suffering from the visits of a vampire! The punctures which she described as having occurred near the throat, were, he insisted, the insertion of those two long, thin, and sharp teeth which, it is well known, are peculiar to vampires; and there could be no doubt, he added, as to the well-defined presence of the small livid mark which all concurred in describing as that induced by the demon's lips, and every symptom described by the sufferer was in exact conformity with those recorded in every case of a similar visitation.

"Being myself wholly skeptical as to the existence of any such portent as the vampire, the supernatural theory of the good doctor furnished, in my opinion, but another instance of learning and intelligence oddly associated with some one hallucination. I was so miserable, however, that, rather than try nothing, I acted upon the instructions of the letter.

"I concealed myself in the dark dressing room, that opened upon the poor patient's room, in which a candle was burning, and watched there till she was fast asleep. I stood at the door, peeping through the small crevice, my sword laid on the table beside me, as my directions prescribed, until, a little after one, I saw a large black object, very ill-defined, crawl, as it seemed to me, over the foot of the bed, and swiftly spread itself up to the poor girl's throat, where it swelled, in a moment, into a great, palpitating mass.

"For a few moments I had stood petrified. I now sprang forward, with my sword in my hand. The black creature suddenly contracted towards the foot of the bed, glided over it, and, standing on the floor about a yard below the foot of the bed, with a glare of skulking ferocity and horror fixed on me, I saw Millarca. Speculating I know not what, I struck at her instantly with my sword; but I saw her standing near the door, unscathed. Horrified, I pursued, and struck again. She was gone; and my sword flew to shivers against the door.

"I can't describe to you all that passed on that horrible night. The whole house was up and stirring. The specter Millarca was gone. But her victim was sinking fast, and before the morning dawned, she died."

The old General was agitated. We did not speak to him. My father walked to some little distance, and began reading the inscriptions on the tombstones; and thus occupied, he strolled into the door of a side chapel to prosecute his researches. The General leaned against the wall, dried his eyes, and sighed heavily. I was relieved on hearing the voices of Carmilla and Madame, who were at that moment approaching. The voices died away.

In this solitude, having just listened to so strange a story, connected, as it was, with the great and titled dead, whose monuments were moldering among the dust and ivy round us, and every incident of which bore so awfully upon my own mysterious case—in this haunted spot, darkened by the towering foliage that rose on every side, dense and high above its noiseless walls—a horror began to steal over me, and my heart sank as I thought that my friends were, after all, not about to enter and disturb this triste and ominous scene.

The old General's eyes were fixed on the ground, as he leaned with his hand upon the basement of a shattered monument.

Under a narrow, arched doorway, surmounted by one of those demoniacal grotesques in which the cynical and ghastly fancy of old Gothic carving delights, I saw very gladly the beautiful face and figure of Carmilla enter the shadowy chapel.

I was just about to rise and speak, and nodded smiling, in answer to her peculiarly engaging smile; when with a cry, the old man by my side caught up the woodman's hatchet, and started forward. On seeing him a brutalized change came over her features. It was an instantaneous and horrible transformation, as she made a crouching step backwards. Before I could utter a scream, he struck at her with all his force, but she dived under his blow, and unscathed, caught him in her tiny grasp by the wrist. He struggled for a moment to release his arm, but his hand opened, the axe fell to the ground, and the girl was gone.

He staggered against the wall. His grey hair stood upon his head, and a moisture shone over his face, as if he were at the point of death.

The frightful scene had passed in a moment. The first thing I recollect after, is Madame standing before me, and impatiently repeating again and again, the question, "Where is Mademoiselle Carmilla?"

I answered at length, "I don't know—I can't tell—she went there," and I pointed to the door through which Madame had just entered; "only a minute or two since."

"But I have been standing there, in the passage, ever since Mademoiselle Carmilla entered; and she did not return."

She then began to call "Carmilla," through every door and passage and from the windows, but no answer came.

"She called herself Carmilla?" asked the General, still agitated.

"Carmilla, yes," I answered.

"Aye," he said; "that is Millarca. That is the same person who long ago was called Mircalla, Countess Karnstein. Depart from this accursed ground, my poor child, as quickly as you can. Drive to the clergyman's house, and stay there till we come. Begone! May you never behold Carmilla more; you will not find her here."

XV
ORDEAL AND EXECUTION

As he spoke one of the strangest looking men I ever beheld entered the chapel at the door through which Carmilla had made her entrance and her exit. He was tall, narrow-chested, stooping, with high shoulders, and dressed in black. His face was brown and dried in with deep furrows; he wore an oddly-shaped hat with a broad leaf. His hair, long and grizzled, hung on his shoulders. He wore a pair of gold spectacles, and walked slowly, with an odd shambling gait, with his face sometimes turned up to the sky, and sometimes bowed down towards the ground, seemed to wear a perpetual smile; his long thin arms were swinging, and his lank hands, in old black gloves ever so much too wide for them, waving and gesticulating in utter abstraction.

"The very man!" exclaimed the General, advancing with manifest delight. "My dear Baron, how happy I am to see you, I had no hope of meeting you so soon." He signed to my father, who had by this time returned, and leading the fantastic old gentleman, whom he called the Baron to meet him. He introduced him formally, and they at once entered into earnest conversation. The stranger took a roll of paper from his pocket, and spread it on the worn surface of a tomb that stood by. He had a pencil case in his fingers, with which he traced imaginary lines from point to point on the paper, which from their often glancing from it, together, at certain points of the building, I concluded to be a plan of the chapel. He accompanied, what I may term, his lecture, with occasional readings from a dirty little book, whose yellow leaves were closely written over.

They sauntered together down the side aisle, opposite to the spot where I was standing, conversing as they went; then they began measuring distances by paces, and finally they all stood together, facing a piece of the sidewall, which they began to examine with great minuteness; pulling off the ivy that clung over it, and rapping the plaster with the ends of their sticks, scraping here, and knocking there. At length they ascertained the existence of a broad marble tablet, with letters carved in relief upon it.

With the assistance of the woodman, who soon returned, a monumental inscription, and carved escutcheon, were disclosed. They proved to be those of the long lost monument of Mircalla, Countess Karnstein.

The old General, though not I fear given to the praying mood, raised his hands and eyes to heaven, in mute thanksgiving for some moments.

"Tomorrow," I heard him say; "the commissioner will be here, and the Inquisition will be held according to law."

Then turning to the old man with the gold spectacles, whom I have described, he shook him warmly by both hands and said:

"Baron, how can I thank you? How can we all thank you? You will have delivered this region from a plague that has scourged its inhabitants for more than a century. The horrible enemy, thank God, is at last tracked."

My father led the stranger aside, and the General followed. I know that he had led them out of hearing, that he might relate my case, and I saw them glance often quickly at me, as the discussion proceeded.

My father came to me, kissed me again and again, and leading me from the chapel, said:

"It is time to return, but before we go home, we must add to our party the good priest, who lives but a little way from this; and persuade him to accompany us to the schloss."

In this quest we were successful: and I was glad, being unspeakably fatigued when we reached home. But my satisfaction was changed to dismay, on discovering that there were no tidings of Carmilla. Of the scene that had occurred in the ruined chapel, no explanation was offered to me, and it was clear that it was a secret which my father for the present determined to keep from me.

The sinister absence of Carmilla made the remembrance of the scene more horrible to me. The arrangements for the night were singular. Two servants, and Madame were to sit up in my room that night; and the ecclesiastic with my father kept watch in the adjoining dressing room.

The priest had performed certain solemn rites that night, the purport of which I did not understand any more than I comprehended the reason of this extraordinary precaution taken for my safety during sleep.

I saw all clearly a few days later.

The disappearance of Carmilla was followed by the discontinuance of my nightly sufferings.

You have heard, no doubt, of the appalling superstition that prevails in Upper and Lower Styria, in Moravia, Silesia, in Turkish Serbia, in Poland, even in Russia; the superstition, so we must call it, of the Vampire.

If human testimony, taken with every care and solemnity, judicially, before commissions innumerable, each consisting of many members, all chosen for integrity and intelligence, and constituting reports more voluminous perhaps than exist upon any one other class of cases, is worth anything, it is difficult to deny, or even to doubt the existence of such a phenomenon as the Vampire.

For my part I have heard no theory by which to explain what I myself have witnessed and experienced, other than that supplied by the ancient and well-attested belief of the country.

The next day the formal proceedings took place in the Chapel of Karnstein.

The grave of the Countess Mircalla was opened; and the General and my father recognized each his perfidious and beautiful guest, in the face now disclosed to view. The features, though a hundred and fifty years had passed since her funeral, were tinted with the warmth of life. Her eyes were open; no cadaverous smell exhaled from the coffin. The two medical men, one officially present, the other on the part of the promoter of the inquiry, attested the marvelous fact that there was a faint but appreciable respiration, and a corresponding action of the heart. The limbs were perfectly flexible, the flesh elastic; and the leaden coffin floated with blood, in which to a depth of seven inches, the body lay immersed.

Here then, were all the admitted signs and proofs of vampirism. The body, therefore, in accordance with the ancient practice, was raised, and a sharp stake driven through the heart of the vampire, who uttered a piercing shriek at the moment, in all respects such as might escape from a living person in the last agony. Then the head was struck off, and a torrent of blood flowed from the severed neck. The body and head was next placed on a pile of wood, and reduced to ashes, which were thrown upon the river and borne away, and that territory has never since been plagued by the visits of a vampire.

My father has a copy of the report of the Imperial Commission, with the signatures of all who were present at these proceedings, attached in verification of the statement. It is from this official paper that I have summarized my account of this last shocking scene.

XVI
CONCLUSION

I write all this you suppose with composure. But far from it; I cannot think of it without agitation. Nothing but your earnest desire so repeatedly expressed, could have induced me to sit down to a task that has unstrung my nerves for months to come, and reinduced a shadow of the unspeakable horror which years after my deliverance continued to make my days and nights dreadful, and solitude insupportably terrific.

Let me add a word or two about that quaint Baron Vordenburg, to whose curious lore we were indebted for the discovery of the Countess Mircalla's grave.

He had taken up his abode in Gratz, where, living upon a mere pittance, which was all that remained to him of the once princely estates of his family, in Upper Styria, he devoted himself to the minute and laborious investigation of the marvelously authenticated tradition of Vampirism. He had at his fingers' ends all the great and little works upon the subject.

"Magia Posthuma," "Phlegon de Mirabilibus," "Augustinus de cura pro Mortuis," "Philosophicae et Christianae Cogitationes de Vampiris," by John Christofer Herenberg; and a thousand others, among which I remember only a few of those which he lent to my father. He had a voluminous digest of all the judicial cases, from which he had extracted a system of principles that appear to govern—some always, and others occasionally only—the condition of the vampire. I may mention, in passing, that the deadly pallor attributed to that sort of revenants, is a mere melodramatic fiction. They present, in the grave, and when they show themselves in human society, the appearance of healthy life. When disclosed to light in their coffins, they exhibit all the symptoms that are enumerated as those which proved the vampire-life of the long-dead Countess Karnstein.

How they escape from their graves and return to them for certain hours every day, without displacing the clay or leaving any trace of disturbance in the state of the coffin or the cerements, has always been admitted to be utterly inexplicable. The amphibious existence of the vampire is sustained by daily renewed slumber in the grave. Its horrible lust for living blood supplies the vigor of its waking existence. The vampire is prone to be fascinated with an engrossing vehemence, resembling the passion of love, by particular persons. In pursuit of these it will exercise inexhaustible patience and stratagem, for access to a particular object may be obstructed in a hundred ways. It will never desist until it has satiated its passion, and drained the very life of its coveted victim. But it will, in these cases, husband and protract its murderous enjoyment with the refinement of an epicure, and heighten it by the gradual approaches of an artful courtship. In these cases it seems to yearn for something like sympathy and consent. In ordinary ones it goes direct to its object, overpowers with violence, and strangles and exhausts often at a single feast.

The vampire is, apparently, subject, in certain situations, to special conditions. In the particular instance of which I have given you a relation, Mircalla seemed to be limited to a name which, if not her real one, should at least reproduce, without the omission or addition of a single letter, those, as we say, anagrammatically, which compose it.

Carmilla did this; so did Millarca.

My father related to the Baron Vordenburg, who remained with us for two or three weeks after the expulsion of Carmilla, the story about the Moravian nobleman and the vampire at Karnstein churchyard, and then he asked the Baron how he had discovered the exact position of the long-concealed tomb of the Countess Mircalla? The Baron's grotesque features puckered up into a mysterious smile; he looked down, still smiling on his worn spectacle case and fumbled with it. Then looking up, he said:

"I have many journals, and other papers, written by that remarkable man; the most curious among them is one treating of the visit of which you speak, to Karnstein. The tradition, of course, discolors and distorts a little. He might have been termed a Moravian nobleman, for he had changed his abode to that territory, and was, beside, a noble. But he was, in truth, a native of Upper Styria. It is enough to say that in very early youth he had been a passionate and favored lover of the beautiful Mircalla, Countess Karnstein. Her early death plunged him into inconsolable grief. It is the nature of vampires to increase and multiply, but according to an ascertained and ghostly law.

"Assume, at starting, a territory perfectly free from that pest. How does it begin, and how does it multiply itself? I will tell you. A person, more or less wicked, puts an end to himself. A suicide, under certain circumstances, becomes a vampire. That specter visits living people in their slumbers; they die, and almost invariably, in the grave, develop into vampires. This happened in the case of the beautiful Mircalla, who was haunted by one of those demons. My ancestor, Vordenburg, whose title I still bear, soon discovered this, and in the course of the studies to which he devoted himself, learned a great deal more.

"Among other things, he concluded that suspicion of vampirism would probably fall, sooner or later, upon the dead Countess, who in life had been his idol. He conceived a horror, be she what she might, of her remains being profaned by the outrage of a posthumous execution. He has left a curious paper to prove that the vampire, on its expulsion from its amphibious existence, is projected into a far more horrible life; and he resolved to save his once beloved Mircalla from this.

"He adopted the stratagem of a journey here, a pretended removal of her remains, and a real obliteration of her monument. When age had stolen upon him, and from the vale of years, he looked back on the scenes he was leaving, he considered, in a different spirit, what he had done, and a horror took possession of him. He made the tracings and notes which have guided me to the very spot, and drew up a confession of the deception that he had practiced. If he had intended any further action in this matter, death prevented him; and the hand of a remote descendant has, too late for many, directed the pursuit to the lair of the beast."

We talked a little more, and among other things he said was this:

"One sign of the vampire is the power of the hand. The slender hand of Mircalla closed like a vice of steel on the General's wrist when he raised the hatchet to strike. But its power is not confined to its grasp; it leaves a numbness in the limb it seizes, which is slowly, if ever, recovered from."

The following Spring my father took me a tour through Italy. We remained away for more than a year. It was long before the terror of recent events subsided; and to this hour the image of Carmilla returns to memory with ambiguous alternations—sometimes the playful, languid, beautiful girl; sometimes the writhing fiend I saw in the ruined church; and often from a reverie I have started, fancying I heard the light step of Carmilla at the drawing room door.

The End

ACTRESS KAY FRANCIS

Dark
Corners
Elmedina Hota

The Craft of the Witch

Onto the world a new mischief shall rise
as the little one holds onto a plan:
unleashing a demise!
Soon her time shall come
and the power of her craft
might never become, by another, undone.

Oh, such dreams of darkness she embraces,
dreams that carry new sights of old places,
with one figure to rule inside them all:
the very witch whose kingdom shall never fall.

The art of the craft she practices every day
yet, alas, 'tis not perfected yet
and her plans might be forced to suffer a delay.
In an attempt to murder a flower,
she simply created another, even more beautiful,
to grow in its place, making her feel sour.

Whilst passing a park with a group of children playing,
she thought it'd be amusing to witness at least one
hit in the head with the ball until their little head starts
decaying.
Yet, once more, the plan backfired:
as her witchcraft made the ball play in their favour,
and because of this, our young witch,
started growing tired.

Unhappy and restless, searching for comfort in the silence of the night,
summoning an ancestor to help her regain her strength and cause the fright.
The ancestor has appeared to offer a solution, but the response did not suit
the witch's plan and hopeful execution!

For the bloodline did not consist of evil, yet of pure delights, she was meant to offer
solutions and of beauty sights.
Never to harm, but only protect: the young witch fell unconscious, for this —
she did not expect.

ELMEDINA HOTA IS AN ARTIST
BASED IN SARAJEVO, BOSNIA
AND HERZEGOVINA.
FOR MORE ABOUT HER
BREATHS OF LIFE VISIT
INSTAGRAM & TWITTER:
@HELLMEDINCIC

THE ROAD FROM COLONUS
BY E.M. FORSTER

I

For no very intelligible reason, Mr. Lucas had hurried ahead of his party. He was perhaps reaching the age at which independence becomes valuable, because it is so soon to be lost. Tired of attention and consideration, he liked breaking away from the younger members, to ride by himself, and to dismount unassisted. Perhaps he also relished that more subtle pleasure of being kept waiting for lunch, and of telling the others on their arrival that it was of no consequence.

So, with childish impatience, he battered the animal's sides with his heels, and made the muleteer bang it with a thick stick and prick it with a sharp one, and jolted down the hill sides through clumps of flowering shrubs and stretches of anemones and asphodel, till he heard the sound of running water, and came in sight of the group of plane trees where they were to have their meal.

Even in England those trees would have been remarkable, so huge were they, so interlaced, so magnificently clothed in quivering green. And here in Greece they were unique, the one cool spot in that hard brilliant landscape, already scorched by the heat of an April sun. In their midst was hidden a tiny Khan or country inn, a frail mud building with a broad wooden balcony in which sat an old woman spinning, while a small brown pig, eating orange peel, stood beside her. On the wet earth below squatted two children, playing some primaeval game with their fingers; and their mother, none too clean either, was messing with some rice inside. As Mrs. Forman would have said, it was all very Greek, and the fastidious Mr. Lucas felt thankful that they were bringing their own food with them, and should eat it in the open air.

Still, he was glad to be there—the muleteer had helped him off—and glad that Mrs. Forman was not there to forestall his opinions—glad even that he should not see Ethel for quite half an hour. Ethel was his youngest daughter, still unmarried. She was unselfish and affectionate, and it was generally understood that she was to devote her life to her father, and be the comfort of his old age. Mrs. Forman always referred to her as Antigone, and Mr. Lucas tried to settle down to the role of Oedipus, which seemed the only one that public opinion allowed him.

He had this in common with Oedipus, that he was growing old. Even to himself it had become obvious. He had lost interest in other people's affairs, and seldom attended when they spoke to him. He was fond of talking himself but often forgot what he was going to say, and even when he succeeded, it seldom seemed worth the effort. His phrases and gestures had become stiff and set, his anecdotes, once so successful, fell flat, his silence was as meaningless as his speech. Yet he had led a healthy, active life, had worked steadily, made money, educated his children. There was nothing and no one to blame: he was simply growing old.

At the present moment, here he was in Greece, and one of the dreams of his life was realized. Forty years ago he had caught the fever of Hellenism, and all his life he had felt that could he but visit that land, he would not have lived in vain. But Athens had been dusty, Delphi wet, Thermopylae flat, and he had listened with amazement and cynicism to the rapturous exclamations of his companions. Greece was like England: it was a man who was growing old, and it made no difference whether that man looked at the Thames or the Eurotas. It was his last hope of contradicting that logic of experience, and it was failing.

Yet Greece had done something for him, though he did not know it. It had made him discontented, and there are stirrings of life in discontent. He knew that he was not the victim of continual ill-luck. Something great was wrong, and he was pitted against no mediocre or accidental enemy. For the last month a strange desire had possessed him to die fighting.

"Greece is the land for young people," he said to himself as he stood under the plane trees, "but I will enter into it, I will possess it. Leaves shall be green again, water shall be sweet, the sky shall be blue. They were so forty years ago, and I will win them back. I do mind being old, and I will pretend no longer."

He took two steps forward, and immediately cold waters were gurgling over his ankle.

"Where does the water come from?" he asked himself. "I do not even know that." He remembered that all the hill sides were dry; yet here the road was suddenly covered with flowing streams.

He stopped still in amazement, saying: "Water out of a tree—out of a hollow tree? I never saw nor thought of that before."

For the enormous plane that leant towards the Khan was hollow—it had been burnt out for charcoal—and from its living trunk there gushed an impetuous spring, coating the bark! with fern and moss, and flowing over the mule track to create fertile meadows beyond. The simple country folk had paid to beauty and mystery such tribute as they could, for in the rind of the tree a shrine was cut, holding a lamp and a little picture of the Virgin, inheritor of the Naiad's and Dryad's joint abode.

"I never saw anything so marvellous before," said Mr. Lucas. "I could even step inside the trunk and see where the water comes from."

For a moment he hesitated to violate the shrine. Then he remembered with a smile his own thought—"the place shall be mine; I will enter it and possess it"—and leapt almost aggressively on to a stone within.

The water pressed up steadily and noiselessly from the hollow roots and hidden crevices of the plane, forming a wonderful amber pool ere it spilt over the lip of bark on to the earth outside. Mr. Lucas tasted it and it was sweet, and when he looked up the black funnel of the trunk he saw sky which was blue, and some leaves which were green; and he remembered, without smiling, another of his thoughts.

Others had been before him—indeed he had a curious sense of companionship. Little votive offerings to the presiding Power were fastened on to the bark—tiny arms and legs and eyes in tin, grotesque models of the brain or the heart—all tokens of some recovery of strength or wisdom or love. There was no such thing as the solitude of nature for the sorrows and joys of humanity had pressed even into the bosom of a tree. He spread out his arms and steadied himself against the soft charred wood, and then slowly leant back, till his body was resting on the trunk behind. His eyes closed, and he had the strange feeling of one who is moving, yet at peace— the feeling of the swimmer, who, after long struggling with chopping seas, finds that after all the tide will sweep him to his goal.

So he lay motionless, conscious only of the stream below his feet, and that all things were a stream, in which he was moving.

He was aroused at last by a shock—the shock of an arrival perhaps, for when he opened his eyes, something unimagined, indefinable, had passed over all things, and made them intelligible and good.

There was meaning in the stoop of the old woman over her work, and in the quick motions of the little pig, and in her diminishing globe of wool. A young man came singing over the streams on a mule, and there was beauty in his pose and sincerity in his greeting. The sun made no accidental patterns upon the spreading roots of the trees, and there was intention in the nodding clumps of asphodel, and in the music of the water. To Mr. Lucas, who, in a brief space of time, had discovered not only Greece, but England and all the world and life, there seemed nothing ludicrous in the desire to hang within the tree another votive offering—a little model of an entire man.

"Why, here's papa, playing at being Merlin."

All unnoticed they had arrived—Ethel, Mrs. Forman, Mr. Graham, and the English-speaking dragoman. Mr. Lucas peered out at them suspiciously. They had suddenly become unfamiliar, and all that they did seemed strained and coarse.

"Allow me to give you a hand," said Mr. Graham, a young man who was always polite to his elders.

Mr. Lucas felt annoyed. "Thank you, I can manage perfectly well by myself," he replied. His foot slipped as he stepped out of the tree, and went into the spring.

"Oh papa, my papa!" said Ethel, "what are you doing? Thank goodness I have got a change for you on the mule."

She tended him carefully, giving him clean socks and dry boots, and then sat him down on the rug beside the lunch basket, while she went with the others to explore the grove.

They came back in ecstasies, in which Mr. Lucas tried to join. But he found them intolerable. Their enthusiasm was superficial, commonplace, and spasmodic. They had no perception of the coherent beauty was flowering around them. He tried at least to explain his feelings, and what he said was:

"I am altogether pleased with the appearance of this place. It impresses me very favourably. The trees are fine, remarkably fine for Greece, and there is something very poetic in the spring of clear running water. The people too seem kindly and civil. It is decidedly an attractive place."

Mrs. Forman upbraided him for his tepid praise.

"Oh, it is a place in a thousand!" she cried "I could live and die here! I really would stop if I had not to be back at Athens! It reminds me of the Colonus of Sophocles."

"Well, I must stop," said Ethel. "I positively must."

"Yes, do! You and your father! Antigone and Oedipus. Of course you must stop at Colonus!"

Mr. Lucas was almost breathless with excitement. When he stood within the tree, he had believed that his happiness would be independent of locality. But these few minutes' conversation had undeceived him. He no longer trusted himself to journey through the world, for old thoughts, old wearinesses might be waiting to rejoin him as soon as he left the shade of the planes, and the music of the virgin water. To sleep in the Khan with the gracious, kind-eyed country people, to watch the bats flit about within the globe of shade, and see the moon turn the golden patterns into silver— one such night would place him beyond relapse, and confirm him for ever in the kingdom he had regained. But all his lips could say was: "I should be willing to put in a night here."

"You mean a week, papa! It would be sacrilege to put in less."

"A week then, a week," said his lips, irritated at being corrected, while his heart was leaping with joy. All through lunch he spoke to them no more, but watched the place he should know so well, and the people who would so soon be his companions and friends. The inmates of the Khan only consisted of an old woman, a middle-aged woman, a young man and two children, and to none of them had he spoken, yet he loved them as he loved everything that moved or breathed or existed beneath the benedictory shade of the planes.

"*En route!*" said the shrill voice of Mrs. Forman. "Ethel! Mr. Graham! The best of things must end."

"To-night," thought Mr. Lucas, "they will light the little lamp by the shrine. And when we all sit together on the balcony, perhaps they will tell me which offerings they put up."

"I beg your pardon, Mr. Lucas," said Graham, "but they want to fold up the rug you are sitting on."

Mr. Lucas got up, saying to himself: "Ethel shall go to bed first, and then I will try to tell them about my offering too—for it is a thing I must do. I think they will understand if I am left with them alone."

Ethel touched him on the cheek. "Papa! I've called you three times. All the mules are here."

"Mules? What mules?"

"Our mules. We're all waiting. Oh, Mr. Graham, do help my father on."

"I don't know what you're talking about, Ethel."

"My dearest papa, we must start. You know we have to get to Olympia to-night."

Mr. Lucas in pompous, confident tones replied: "I always did wish, Ethel, that you had a better head for plans. You know perfectly well that we are putting in a week here. It is your own suggestion."

Ethel was startled into impoliteness. "What a perfectly ridiculous idea. You must have known I was joking. Of course I meant I wished we could."

"Ah! if we could only do what we wished!" sighed Mrs. Forman, already seated on her mule.

"Surely," Ethel continued in calmer tones, "you didn't think I meant it."

"Most certainly I did. I have made all my plans on the supposition that we are stopping here, and it will be extremely inconvenient, indeed, impossible for me to start."

He delivered this remark with an air of great conviction, and Mrs. Forman and Mr. Graham had to turn away to hide their smiles.

"I am sorry I spoke so carelessly; it was wrong of me. But, you know, we can't break up our party, and even one night here would make us miss the boat at Patras."

Mrs. Forman, in an aside, called Mr. Graham's attention to the excellent way in which Ethel managed her father.

"I don't mind about the Patras boat. You said that we should stop here, and we are stopping."

It seemed as if the inhabitants of the Khan had divined in some mysterious way that the altercation touched them. The old woman stopped her spinning, while the young man and the two children stood behind Mr. Lucas, as if supporting him.

Neither arguments nor entreaties moved him. He said little, but he was absolutely determined, because for the first time he saw his daily life aright. What need had he to return to England? Who would miss him? His friends were dead or cold. Ethel loved him in a way, but, as was right, she had other interests. His other children he seldom saw. He had only one other relative, his sister Julia, whom he both feared and hated. It was no effort to struggle. He would be a fool as well as a coward if he stirred from the place which brought him happiness and peace.

At last Ethel, to humour him, and not disinclined to air her modern Greek, went into the Khan with the astonished dragoman to look at the rooms. The woman inside received them with loud welcomes, and the young man, when no one was looking, began to lead Mr. Lucas' mule to the stable.

"Drop it, you brigand!" shouted Graham, who always declared that foreigners could understand English if they chose. He was right, for the man obeyed, and they all stood waiting for Ethel's return.

She emerged at last, with close-gathered skirts, followed by the dragoman bearing the little pig, which he had bought at a bargain.

"My dear papa, I will do all I can for you, but stop in that Khan—no."

"Are there—fleas?" asked Mrs. Forman.

Ethel intimated that "fleas" was not the word.

"Well, I am afraid that settles it," said Mrs. Forman, "I know how particular Mr. Lucas is."

"It does not settle it," said Mr. Lucas. "Ethel, you go on. I do not want you. I don't know why I ever consulted you. I shall stop here alone."

"That is absolute nonsense," said Ethel, losing her temper. "How can you be left alone at your age? How would you get your meals or your bath? All your letters are waiting for you at Patras. You'll miss the boat. That means missing the London operas, and upsetting all your engagements for the month. And as if you could travel by yourself!"

"They might knife you," was Mr. Graham's contribution.

The Greeks said nothing; but whenever Mr. Lucas looked their way, they beckoned him towards the Khan. The children would even have drawn him by the coat, and the old woman on the balcony stopped her almost completed spinning, and fixed him with mysterious appealing eyes. As he fought, the issue assumed gigantic proportions, and he believed that he was not merely stopping because he had regained youth or seen beauty or found happiness, but because in, that place and with those people a supreme event was awaiting him which would transfigure the face of the world. The moment was so tremendous that he abandoned words and arguments as useless, and rested on the strength of his mighty unrevealed allies: silent men, murmuring water, and whispering trees. For the whole place called with one voice, articulate to him, and his garrulous opponents became every minute more meaningless and absurd. Soon they would be tired and go chattering away into the sun, leaving him to the cool grove and the moonlight and the destiny he foresaw.

Mrs. Forman and the dragoman had indeed already started, amid the piercing screams of the little pig, and the struggle might have gone on indefinitely if Ethel had not called in Mr. Graham.

"Can you help me?" she whispered. "He is absolutely unmanageable."

"I'm no good at arguing—but if I could help you in any other way——" and he looked down complacently at his well-made figure.

Ethel hesitated. Then she said: "Help me in any way you can. After all, it is for his good that we do it."

"Then have his mule led up behind him."

So when Mr. Lucas thought he had gained the day, he suddenly felt himself lifted off the ground, and sat sideways on the saddle, and at the same time the mule started off at a trot. He said nothing, for he had nothing to say, and even his face showed little emotion as he felt the shade pass and heard the sound of the water cease. Mr. Graham was running at his side, hat in hand, apologizing.

"I know I had no business to do it, and I do beg your pardon awfully. But I do hope that some day you too will feel that I was—damn!"

A stone had caught him in the middle of the back. It was thrown by the little boy, who was pursuing them along the mule track. He was followed by his sister, also throwing stones.

Ethel screamed to the dragoman, who was some way ahead with Mrs. Forman, but before he could rejoin them, another adversary appeared. It was the young Greek, who had cut them off in front, and now dashed down at Mr. Lucas' bridle. Fortunately Graham was an expert boxer, and it did not take him a moment to beat down the youth's feeble defence, and to send him sprawling with a bleeding mouth into the asphodel. By this time the dragoman had arrived, the children, alarmed at the fate of their brother, had desisted, and the rescue party, if such it is to be considered, retired in disorder to the trees.

"Little devils!" said Graham, laughing; with triumph. "That's the modern Greek all over. Your father meant money if he stopped, and they consider we were taking it out of their pocket."

"Oh, they are terrible—simple savages! I don't know how I shall ever thank you. You've saved my father."

"I only hope you didn't think me brutal."

"No," replied Ethel with a little sigh. "I admire strength."

Meanwhile the cavalcade reformed, and Mr. Lucas, who, as Mrs. Forman said, bore his disappointment wonderfully well, was put comfortably on to his mule. They hurried up the opposite hillside, fearful of another attack, and it was not until they had left the eventful place far behind that Ethel found an opportunity to speak to her father and ask his pardon for the way she had treated him.

"You seemed so different, dear father, and you quite frightened me. Now I feel that you are your old self again."

He did not answer, and she concluded that he was not unnaturally offended at her behaviour.

By one of those curious tricks of mountain scenery, the place they had left an hour before suddenly reappeared far below them. The Khan was hidden under the green dome, but in the open there still stood three figures, and through the pure air rose up a faint cry of defiance or farewell.

Mr. Lucas stopped irresolutely, and let the reins fall from his hand.

"Come, father dear," said Ethel gently.

He obeyed, and in another moment a spur of the hill hid the dangerous scene for ever.

II

It was breakfast time, but the gas was alight, owing to the fog. Mr. Lucas was in the middle of an account of a bad night he had spent, Ethel, who was to be married in a few weeks, had her arms on the table, listening.

"First the door bell rang, then you came back from the theatre. Then the dog started, and after the dog the cat. And at three in the morning a young hooligan passed by singing. Oh yes: then there was the water gurgling in the pipe above my head."

"I think that was only the bath water running away," said Ethel, looking rather worn.

"Well, there's nothing I dislike more than running water. It's perfectly impossible to sleep in the house. I shall give it up. I shall give notice next quarter. I shall tell the landlord plainly, 'The reason I am giving up the house is this: it is perfectly impossible to sleep in it.' If he says—says—well, what has he got to say?"

"Some more toast, father?"

"Thank you, my dear." He took it, and there was an interval of peace.

But he soon recommenced. "I'm not going to submit to the practising next door as tamely as they think. I wrote and told them so—didn't I?"

"Yes," said Ethel, who had taken care that the letter should not reach. "I have seen the governess, and she has promised to arrange it differently. And Aunt Julia hates noise. It will sure to be all right."

Her aunt, being the only unattached member of the family, was coming to keep house for her father when she left him. The reference was not a happy one, and Mr. Lucas commenced a series of half articulate sighs, which was only stopped by the arrival of the post.

"Oh, what a parcel!" cried Ethel. "For me! What can it be! Greek stamps. This is most exciting!"

It proved to be some asphodel bulbs, sent by Mrs. Forman from Athens for planting in the conservatory.

"Doesn't it bring it all back! You remember the asphodels, father. And all wrapped up in Greek newspapers. I wonder if I can read them still. I used to be able to, you know."

She rattled on, hoping to conceal the laughter of the children next door—a favourite source of querulousness at breakfast time.

"Listen to me! 'A rural disaster.' Oh, I've hit on something sad. But never mind. 'Last Tuesday at Plataniste, in the province of messenia, a shocking tragedy occurred. A large tree'—aren't I getting on well?—'blew down in the night and'—wait a minute—oh, dear! 'crushed to death the five occupants of the little Khan there, who had apparently been sitting in the balcony. The bodies of Maria Rhomaides, the aged proprietress, and of her daughter, aged forty-six, were easily recognizable, whereas that of her grandson'—oh, the rest is really too horrid; I wish I had never tried it, and what's more I feel to have heard the name Plataniste before. We didn't stop there, did we, in the spring?"

"We had lunch," said Mr. Lucas, with a faint expression of trouble on his vacant face. "Perhaps it was where the dragoman bought the pig."

"Of course," said Ethel in a nervous voice. "Where the dragoman bought the little pig. How terrible!"

"Very terrible!" said her father, whose attention was wandering to the noisy children next door. Ethel suddenly started to her feet with genuine interest.

"Good gracious!" she exclaimed. "This is an old paper. It happened not lately but in April—the night of Tuesday the eighteenth—and we—we must have been there in the afternoon."

"So we were," said Mr. Lucas. She put her hand to her heart, scarcely able to speak.

"Father, dear father, I must say it: you wanted to stop there. All those people, those poor half savage people, tried, to keep you, and they're dead. The whole place, it says, is in ruins, and even the stream has changed its course. Father, dear, if it had not been for me, and if Arthur had not helped me, you must have been killed."

Mr. Lucas waved his hand irritably. "It is not a bit of good speaking to the governess, I shall write to the landlord and say, 'The reason I am giving up the house is this: the dog barks, the children next door are intolerable, and I cannot stand the noise of running water.'"

Ethel did not check his babbling. She was aghast at the narrowness of the escape, and for a long time kept silence. At last she said: "Such a marvellous deliverance does make one believe in Providence."

Mr. Lucas, who was still composing his letter to the landlord, did not reply.

END.

THE SPIDER

BY ELMEDINA HOTA

It's a foggy November evening. Rays of sunshine have blessed the city the past couple of days, but the mornings and the evenings still feel incredibly cold. The sound of a church bell can be heard in the distance. The dreariness of the night is nothing compared to Aurora's terrible thoughts; the worried expression on her face can be spotted from a mile away. Her right eye is swollen and red, but her left eye - brown in color - is clear. Her lips are coated with dark lipstick. She likes to feel pretty, and even with a swollen eye, she's still trying. Her hair is light brown and layered with bangs. She's fairly slim and appears to be of average height. She looks at the piece of paper Dr. Mandel gave her this afternoon.

75C, Linden Alley, Illnox.

The gate is black, and she can see the path leading to the front door. It's surrounded by bushes. The house is small and looks very cozy, despite its dark exterior. The facade is black. It has an enormous, shiny black door and two outdoor post lights. The roof looks like something out of a dark fairy tale: witchy, with its long, sharp middle reaching toward the sky. To Aurora, this entire picture seems a bit unreal. She sighs and rings the bell.

"Let's get this over with."

A lady opens the door and greets her with a smile. She appears to be in her mid-forties. Her silky hair is falling over her shoulders down to her chest. Her inviting, brown eyes are manifesting warmth and comfort.

"Aurora, I presume?"

"Yes."

"I'm Madeline Regen. Come on in."

Aurora enters and takes off her shoes and coat. Madeline takes the coat and hangs it on the rack.

"This way," she says and proceeds down the hallway to the last room on the right.

Aurora is anxious to hear what Madeline has to say. She starts to feel like she's stepping right into her doom as she follows Dr. Regen to the last room on the right. Luckily, the doctor is comforting, and the disturbing feeling leaves as quickly as it came.

"Sit, please. I usually don't take patients after hours, but I am very much interested in your story. I want you to start from the beginning. Spare no detail. The more you tell me, the better understanding of your situation I'll have. Make yourself comfortable, and if there's anything you need, anything at all, please let me know and I'll get it for you."

"Thank you, Dr. Regen. Before I start, I'd just like to say how much I appreciate you seeing me on such short notice. Thank you, really."

"You're welcome."

"Could I get a glass of water, please?"

"Of course. Just a moment."

Madeline steps out of the room and Aurora can hear her footsteps getting farther away, stopping for a couple of moments, and then she can hear her coming back.

"Here."

"Thank you." Aurora smiles, takes a sip, and puts the glass of water on the table. "I guess it all started two nights ago. ..."

THE WARM, COZY BED IS OFFERING A GOOD NIGHT'S SLEEP. AURORA HAS turned in and is just about to wander off into dreamland. She's forced to open her eyes after her ridiculously tiny bladder screams at her, "Get up, it's bathroom o'clock!"

"Ugh, I was this close. ..."

She gets up, realizing there's no point in trying to fight it. As she rubs her eyes, she notices something on the ceiling, just above her bed. She jumps out of the bed into her fuzzy slippers, thinking it might be a small grasshopper. This thought alone terrifies her. She hates insects. She turns the light on and sees it clearly: it has a long, black body and thick legs. It's not a grasshopper - it's a spider. Usually, she'd put it on a piece of paper and throw it out. But this one looks different. It terrifies her. She's unable to move for a couple of moments.

"What if it's gone when I come back? What if it ends up in my sheets and it crawls up my nose or mouth while I'm asleep?"

She takes a flyswatter and slowly walks towards her bed. Aurora can feel her heart beating faster as she stands just a little below the spider, where she can finally see its terrifying shape and size up close. Her hand starts shaking out of control. She feels like it's looking right at her. Suddenly, her vision blurs. She's having a hard time breathing. She jumps down and looks at the clock. Three a.m.

"What if I ... no. The newspaper, the flyswatter, those might not be enough. It looks so thick and strong. But what if ... oh, please, God let it still be there when I get back!"

She runs out and comes back with a vacuum.

"All right, let's see if this will work."

She plugs it in, turns it on, and puts it on max. She slowly gets back on the bed and raises the end of the plastic hose towards it, certain it will work. Aurora lowers the vacuum, only to find the spider still there.

"Oh, you've got to be kidding me!"

She notices that the spider's long, thick legs are starting to move.

"Oh, my God, here we go!"

The spider uses the web to quickly come down and land on her sheets. It goes underneath her blanket. Aurora takes a deep breath and takes the vacuum again while slowly pulling the sheets onto the floor.

"There it is, trying to run under the bed!"

Aurora turns the vacuum on again, and this time it goes in. She quickly puts the brush head on the hose and leaves it in the living room.

THE SUN FEELS LIKE A LASER THAT FOUND ITS WAY THROUGH THE CURTAIN directly into Aurora's left eye.

"Uuuuugh!"

She turns to the other side with her eyes closed. She feels a ringing inside her head. She opens her eyes and jumps up, with an overwhelming urge to shake her head.

She immediately remembers the vacuum and the spider and feels around.

"Oh, thank God, there's nothing on my face. … Shit, I gotta get it out!"

Aurora takes the vacuum filter bag outside and opens it. She does it carefully, prepared to run back into the house if the spider crawls toward her. But the bag is now empty, and there's no trace of the spider. A sudden realization that it managed to crawl out and is still in the house hits Aurora like a brick. She feels nauseous.

"How the fuck did you get out?!"

Going back to the house, she is cautious and still holding the book in her hands. No sign of the spider. Not on the walls, nothing behind the shoe stand. She proceeds to the bathroom on the left, and it appears clear, too. She proceeds to the living room and her tiny, cozy kitchen. No spider in sight.

"Maybe it got out of the house on its own?"

As the day goes by, she performs her usual tasks, and just like that, it's nighttime again. She decides to take another look around the house before she goes to bed. Still no spider.

"Must've found its way out."

Five minutes after midnight, the sound of someone driving by her house wakes her up from a deep sleep.

"Ughhh, now I have to pee again!"

She stands up and sees the spider on the wall, this time above the door. She runs back into bed and stares at it in horror.

"How am I supposed to get out of the room?!"

The spider is starting to walk across the ceiling toward her. It's coming close with a ridiculous speed and it's getting bigger - even more so than before. Unable to move, Aurora can feel her heart beating wildly in her chest. She is starting to sweat. She wants to open the window and jump out of it.

"Shit! No, no no!"

The spider creates a web and flies directly toward her, straight into her mouth.

She wakes up in cold sweat. Two a.m.

"Oh, thank God! It was just a dream."

She takes a sip of water from her nightstand and gets up to change.

"Fucking spider."

She changes her sheets, too, and checks the room again. Nothing in sight.

With a sigh of relief, she goes back to bed. She's lying down, trying to calm herself. Finally, her tired eyes close and she feels she's about to doze off again.

You didn't have to vacuum me, you know.

She jumps back up and looks around the room after hearing the ominous whisper.

"Hello?"

Silence.

She feels a slight discomfort in her right eye and goes to the bathroom to check it in the mirror.

"Nothing in here. ... But something's itching."

She gasps as she pulls up her eyelid only to see something black. Her hand falls to her mouth as she stares at her reflection in horror.

"What the fuck was that? Oh, my God!"

She takes a deep breath and does it again. There's nothing to be seen this time.

"Thank God."

She goes back to sleep.

The morning arrives, and with it, an incredible headache, and she can still feel her eye itching. The mirror reveals that there's swelling around it, and it's red all over.

Panicking, Aurora googles the closest eye doctors and calls around to see if anyone can see her straight away. After trying four numbers, she finally finds Dr. Evelyn Emmet, who agrees to see her immediately.

She gets ready, puts on a pair of sunglasses, and calls a cab.

Entering the office, Aurora feels terrified.

"What if the spider crawled up my eye somehow? No, that's silly."

Dr. Evelyn's red, long hair is tied, and her cat eyeglasses put an accent on her green eyes. She welcomes Aurora with a smile and invites her into her office to start the examination. Her calm approach to the examination makes Aurora feel slightly better. Dr. Emmet explains that it looks like an infection, even though it's odd to have that much swelling around the eye. She prescribes drops with cream and recommends a checkup in three days.

"These should calm it down, but if you don't see any results, we'll run some further tests."

Aurora feels embarrassed by her terrible thoughts of the spider crawling inside her head, so she keeps them to herself. She feels as if a huge weight has been lifted off her shoulders as she heads home to put the drops in.

The first try at putting the drops in was unsuccessful. She tries again. This time, she feels her eye getting wet.

Hey, that burns!

Again, the voice in her head causes her to flinch.

"What the fuck was that?!"

It's me. Why are you trying to kill me?

"Who? Who the fuck is it? Where are you?"

You know who it is. I'm just behind your eye.

She jumps up, grabs her eyelashes, and pulls up her eyelid again. She can see the black thing once more. Looks like a leg. A spider's leg.

"What? How is this possible?"

All things are possible. Don't you want me here?

"My eye is almost the size of a marshmallow, why would you think I'd want you in there?"

Because you didn't kill me.

"I gotta go to the doctor's!"

Good luck.

"Shut up! SHUT UP!"

Aurora starts to question her sanity. She wants a full scan.

"I'm getting rid of you!"

She heads to her family doctor, Dr. Cole, and explains her concerns. The feelings of embarrassment are overpowered by her fear, a fear of something terrible happening to her, something trying to claim her. He recommends a CT scan and mentions what he thinks is the best place in the city to offer it.

"Let me give them a call and see if they can fit you in now."

Aurora can feel a cold sweat breaking out as she waits. She has to deal with this today. She has to make the voice go away.

He hangs up.

"Good news! He can see you today, but not straight away, I'm afraid. I'm sending him your details via email so you don't have to bring anything with you, aside from your ID. When you get there, state your name and mention that you were recommended by Dr. Cole. You will, however, have to wait until they can fit you in. Will that work for you?"

"That's great, doctor, thank you so much!"

"You're welcome. This is very unusual, the things you've described. We'll have to see if the issue is physiological or if it's psychological. Either way, we'll get to the bottom of it."

"Thank you."

"Good luck!"

Surrender.

Dr. Mandel is a very polite man. He looks fit and, with his glasses and bald head, almost looks like a hipster. After an exhausting afternoon, Aurora feels like her head is about to explode. The scan is over, and it's time to meet the doctor back in his office. She's about to learn her fate.

"Might be a tumor, even. but at least I'll know."

She walks back into Dr. Mandel's office, each step heavier than the one before. She could tell how much he appreciates Dr. Cole when he was explaining that he wants to read the scan immediately.

"I am looking at this, and I don't see any irregularities. Your problem is not physiological after all. It's psychological."

"But what happened to my eye, then? It's a little hard to believe that it's caused by my thoughts now, is it?"

Surrender.

"That might've been an unhappy coincidence. If your eye doctor couldn't find anything and we couldn't find anything, then it's most likely nothing but an infection, as your doctor has established. I can recommend a psychiatrist for you to talk to if you'd like. They can diagnose you and put you on medication that will help and make the voice go away. You want a number?"

"Thanks, but I'm afraid I don't make that much money. This is my third stop at the doctor's office."

"I see. Let me see if there's anything else I can do."

He takes out his notebook and goes through it, page by page.

Surrender.

"Oh, here! She owes me a favor, and she's a great psychiatrist! I'll call her now and see if she can do it free of charge."

ONCE AGAIN, AURORA IS SITTING IN A CHAIR WAITING TO SEE WHAT'S NEXT. She wanders off into a terrible, dark place in her mind, questioning her sanity as she's trying not to scream at the voice telling her to surrender. Her thoughts are interrupted by the doctor's voice.

"Great news. She agreed to see you tonight, after hours. I convinced her that it was an emergency, and she wants to help. Here's the address. Can you be there at eight?"

"Yes, I'll be there!"

"Great! Her name is Madeline Regen. She's a very sweet lady, you'll like her. She'll be able to diagnose you in a record amount of time. You'll see."

"I really hope so! Thank you again, for everything."

Surrender.

"AND THEN I WENT BACK TO DR. COLE'S. AFTER THAT I WENT HOME, TOOK A shower, ate, and came here."

"Did you hear the voice again?"

"Yes."

"When?"

"Just before I left my house."

"What did it say?"

"It asked me not to go."

"Why?"

Aurora notices that Dr. Regen constantly touches the hair around her left ear and slides her fingers across it.

"It said … it said that no one will ever be able to help me."

"I see. And you didn't hear it after that?"

Aurora stares at her in silence.

"Aurora? Can you hear it now?"

"I'm sorry, doctor. I guess I got used to it, so I only mentioned what it said before I left my house since that was different. I could hear it all the time. It kept repeating one word, but it stopped after I sat in this chair."

"What? What was it saying?"

"It was telling me to surrender. Then it asked me not to come here, but I did, so it just kept repeating the word 'surrender.' "

"Thank you for sharing this with me." Dr. Regen takes off her glasses and stands up. "Please excuse me while I go to the bathroom."

Aurora takes a deep breath and feels somewhat relieved that she can't hear the voice anymore.

Dr. Regen is in the bathroom for quite some time, but this doesn't bother Aurora, as she takes the time to look around the wonderfully decorated office. The chairs are black leather, and the entire place has a gothic feel to it, even down to its burgundy walls and black carpet.

It's been around ten minutes since Dr. Regen finally rejoined her. Aurora turns toward her, still sitting in the chair.

"Are you all right?"

"Yes, thank you. I just had a slight stomach ache and kept hearing some sort of ringing in my ear. But I'm fine now."

"Oh, I'm sorry."

"Thank you. I'll kindly ask you to wait there while I try to find the box with the medication." She starts going through the large cabinet behind Aurora and says, "I'm afraid that what you have is a case of schizophrenia, and I have some medicine left over from a patient who moved away."

"Oh, schizophrenia? Are you certain? I've never had any signs of it before. …"

"You tell me after you try these," Dr. Regen says with a smile. "I truly believe that it is."

She opens the box and, again, Aurora notices her hand going toward her ear – only this time, she slaps it. "That was weird," she thinks.

"Will this affect my work and my activities?"

"It might take some time to get used to the meds, but if you don't use them, it might get worse."

Aurora turns around and looks at the certificates and diplomas that are on the wall behind Madeline's chair.

"Wow, you also specialize in dissociative identity disorder?"

"I do, yes."

She can hear Dr. Regen's footsteps coming closer. She's not going through the cabinet anymore.

"Do you have any patients that suffer from it?"

"I do, but I'm afraid I can't share anything."

She grabs Aurora's hair and pulls her head backwards. The sound of a terrible, demonic voice spreads through the house:

"You were not worthy!" She slit Aurora's throat with a razor.

Aurora tries to stop the blood with her hands and looks at Dr. Regen as she falls out of her chair.

Dr. Regen stands above her with the razor in her hand as the ominous voice expresses its disappointment.

Another one bites the dust.

The End

ELMEDINA HOTA IS AN ARTIST BASED IN SARAJEVO, BOSNIA AND HER-zegovina. After studying fashion design at the High School of Textile, Leather, and Design, she obtained a bachelor's degree in journalism at the Faculty of Political Science, University of Sarajevo.

At the age of twenty-two, she discovered her love for mixed martial arts. Even though she proudly represents MMA Fighter Academy Sarajevo in various BJJ & MMA tournaments, her love for sports did not diminish her passion for photography, photo editing, and writing! She enjoys writing dark fantasy, apocalyptic poems, and stories based on her deepest fears and nightmares.

See her on the Web: https://elmedinahota.weebly.com

TAKE A BREAK!!!

What did one ocean say to the other ocean?

Nothing, it just waved.

Want to hear a construction joke?

Sorry, I'm still working o it.

"Tomorrow is the most important thing in life. Comes into us at midnight very clean. It's perfect when it arrives and it puts itself in our hands. It hopes we've learned something from yesterday."
-John Wayne

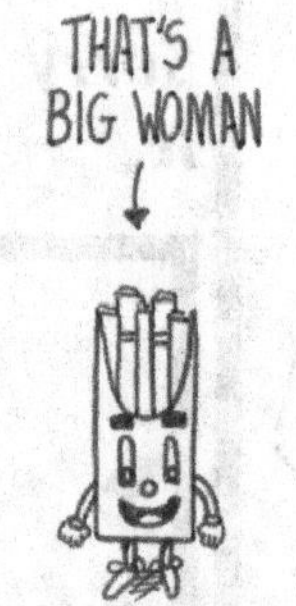

Never Miss a New Release from OffBeatReads...
Receive a FREE copy of an Adventures Issue by Signing Up for Our eMail Brief at OffBeatReads.com

R. RIVETER

AMERICAN ★ HANDMADE

RRIVETER.COM

SUDOKU

	2	3						9
			6			3		5
5					9	1	2	
	3		9			5		
	1				3	7	8	
	5			7		2		
	5			2				
	9	8				6		1
				5	1			

quick

2 out of 3 with someone near.

EXCERPT:

"Did they say anything suspicious?" Jacey asked.

"Everything they say is suspicious," she said wryly. "I remember they were talking about some other dude ... Wade.They said he was gonna have to have a talk with Wade.He did something that pissed the big dude off. And when I drove Crissy home the next morning, she said this Wade guy was a really bad dude, and she wasn't going anywhere near those guys again if she had to be around Wade."

Jacey was silent. At the mention of Wade, she suddenly had memories wash over her, and she felt like throwing up.

The dancer smiled. "That's all I know. That, and you got a blackness surrounding you. Don't come around here again, or you'll be sorry," she said.

"Thank you for your time," Jacey said. Shawnee and Jacey walked through the string lights. Jacey paused, looking back at the dancer.

"That darkness you saw should be a warning to you. I come from a family of real witches, so don't try any of your black magic on me or you'll be the one who's sorry," Jacey said. It was the first time she had admitted it out loud.

FROM: THE DEAD BORN BY MIRANDA MAPLES

A STROLL, A RAID, AND SPIRITS, TOO

BY LUKE D. EVANS

The cemetery is dark. Thin clouds band the half-moon, high above the gnarly branches of old oak and ash trees lording over the markers. Breezes like wraiths whisper in ears and linger among headstones, while fog tarries in hollows and wisps of vapor loiter before entrances to tombs. Death hangs in the air, suffocating the living, terrifying the faint of heart.

This is an old graveyard, of unfettered spirits and stone crypts ravished by the run of time, of patrons long forgotten by the living and bereft with ancient ills, of crumbling tombs of deceased tycoons a century lost and humble patriarchs interred beneath thin stones and simple words.

A thin, dull beam pierces the darkness, and shadows flee behind tombstones and tree trunks and mausoleum walls. To trace the beam to its source is to find a human hand connected to a man walking with a confidence and assurance lost to most humans at night amidst the dead. Spirits hide and fear flees from his boisterous voice. He gesticulates wildly about with his free arm at the form to his rear, tailing him like a lamb.

"Now see," says the foremost form, a large, burly man with thick silvery hair and a thin graying beard. "There is nothing out here to fear. Or do you suppose wild beasts and vindictive spirits roam these yards like cranky nurses in an old hospital? It's all empty here, I tell you."

He turns to face his follower. The young man, blonde strips dangling across his eyes, nods faintly and jumps, startled at the crack of a twig to his blindside.

The large man laughs, a rich hearty sound, a slap in the face of all the vaporous entities hiding in shadows.

"You fear this." He holds out his arms, encompassing the entire cemetery. "All of it! You are a product of society, my boy."

The young man blushes but feels no reassurance.

"Ghosts, you think, while with breath you say 'nonsense'. I know of your kind, Darien, the world is full of them, prevalent in their ideological notions and uncanny tendencies. But come, this occupation, if nothing else, shall cure what ails you. Give it time, and soon you shall be like me, able to peruse these grounds even at the most ignoble of times with nary the bat of an eyelash."

The young man, Darien, reaches out and taps the older man.

Mr. Dastonry leaps into the air, clutching his heart.

"Darien... oh!" He wags a finger in the boy's face and takes a deep breath. "Okay, then, where were we?"

"I have a question," Darien says softly.

"A question? By all means, don't be shy. Fire away."

Darien clears his throat before speaking. "I'm not so sure I'm right for this... position."

"Nonsense! Your old man was one of the best pupils I ever had—he would be proud of you right now. It is in your genes, young man, you can't deny that!" He slaps him on the back briskly.

"Ah, and now memories of your old man are wafting through my brain like aromas sent from above. He was a strong man of firm sensibilities and a stout heart."

Mr. Dastonry turns a critical eye upon Darien and suppresses a cough.

"He never backed down from a challenge, not your old man. Never once. 'Course, backfired in the end, but we all have our faults. May God rest his soul. Did I ever tell you the story of your old man and the well? Some boys, the type no self-respecting mother allows around—you know the type—well, they got ahold of this watch, your old man's, and threatened to throw it down a well. It was hand-dug, mind you, mighty dark and disturbing, not unlike these tombs we're walking past. Your old man, he turned his nose up at them and refused to give in. So they tossed the watch in the well. What does your old man do? He climbs in after it, with the boys watching in amazement. And you know, he got that watch back! Climbed up and down again on those wet stones, and gave it nary a thought. Poor watch never did run again, but to your old man, that wasn't important. It was the *principle* of the matter and not the result, that's what your old man knew."

Darien sighs and nods. His father's questionably adventuresome nature had been both the butt of jokes and the recipient of solemn deference throughout town, both before and after his disappearance. Mostly the jokes, though.

"Now see here, this should cure you, if nothing else." Mr. Dastonry gestures toward a burial chamber, a small building unto itself. "Open the door and enter. Consider it a part of your lesson, my pupil."

The door creaks in reluctantly, to cobwebs and a thick, living darkness. Darien shines his flashlight into the tomb, but it reflects back like high beams on fog. He flicks it back off and glances at Mr. Dastonry.

But Mr. Dastonry has gone off on another one of his tirades, a pseudo-intellectual rant on the shortcomings of civilization, and has not noticed that the flashlight has lost its beam.

"Take me, for instance," Mr. Dastonry says. "I'm a curator for burial grounds."

In between fighting webs like ropes and battling a rising fright, Darien rolls his eyes. Curator? Mr. Dastonry is little more than a bloated groundskeeper, and Darien his fool on a leash.

A scrape sounds to his right, crisp like bone on stone, and the darkness opens up. He fancies he sees an arm move slowly upward from a shelf on the wall of the tomb, and then a head. Behind Mr. Dastonry, still chattering away on welfare and suicide and social security, the stone door slowly swings in an arc to shut them in. Darien's eyes grow large and he shoves Mr. Dastonry out the door before him. It slams shut in their wake.

Mr. Dastonry looks an accusation at Darien, saying in a sharp voice, "Now, Darien, that was really quite uncalled for. I was in the middle of…. Hey, get back here!"

Darien has begun to walk away, but now halts, bends his neck back in exasperation, and turns around. "Have you ever seen one?"

"One what, lad? Speak your mind."

"You know, a ghost. An evil spirit."

"I do *not* know, that is why I asked. Do you suppose I am in the mind of asking that which I already know of my apprentice? I am no childhood school teacher. And as for 'evil' spirits, well! There is no such thing. And I don't simply mean their mere existence. Evil suggests good, and an arbiter of such good and evil, therefore a greater entity or -ties. I, my son, am not prepared for such discussion. We will stick to that which is definite. As such, any being, whether corporeal or not, shall be judged not in entirety but by whatever action is to be judged alone. Is it a just act, or a selfish one? Is it greedy, or generous? Be it kind or cruel? You get the point. A spirit shall not be deemed evil or righteous by mere existence, but instead by its actions. Are they malevolent, or are they benevolent? That is the question. Of course, spirits are balderdash, so you may safely drop the subject entirely."

"Yeah, okay," Darien sighs. "What's next?"

"Eh? Oh, uhhh… good question. Let's see, we've covered markers, stones, tombs, trees… uhhhh, darkness, ghosts, fear." He counts them off on his fingers like a toddler.

He turns to face Darien. "Did you have any questions?"

Darien raises his eyebrows, bites back his words, and says, "No, sir." He manages to not choke on the 'sir,' by some kind fortune.

"Ahhhh," Mr. Dastonry breathes, and wheels around. He squints at an object on the hill before them, shining cheerily on the horizon like a candle in a dark room.

"Well, that looks like the office. See," he says, sweeping his arm around, "we just circled the entire cemetery. Understand?"

Darien nods tautly, no longer trusting himself to speech. The man's patronization irritates him like a bone itch. "It is a nice graveyard," he says at last. He doesn't even know why he bothers. It sounded hollow in his own ears. Any fool could see it wasn't true.

And of course, Mr. Dastonry spins around, no doubt spotting the insincerity.

"My dearest child, how dare you. Do you see any church? A chapel? A cathedral, perhaps, that my old retinas can no longer spot? Then do not speak of graveyards, my simple boy. This here is a *cemetery*. And by god, if I hear 'memorial grounds' come from your mouth, it will be slapped."

Darien freezes, mouth hanging open, stunned. Wait, he didn't catch the insincerity after all? He is concerned about a minor word choice, the use of a supposedly wrong synonym, and a disputed technicality in term?

"And close that trap of yours before one your dastardly spirits rushes in and incorporates." After that, he storms up the hill in abject irritation.

They pass an hour within the cozy confines of the study, Mr. Dastonry's inner sanctum in the office. A fire crackles and lends a warm glow to the living space. Mr. Dastonry sits at a desk, bifocals on, poring over papers. Darien is sprawled across a couch, opposite the fire, his back to the window overlooking the cemetery. Even though only blackness is visible through the panes, Mr. Dastonry insists on leaving the curtains open. Otherwise, he argues, it is a direct shirk of responsibility as curator of the grounds.

Darien bends his neck backward over the cusp of the couch, so that his inverted eyes are trained on the ink outside. The lack of entertainment—of games, of books, of magazines, of music, of *something*—drives him to the verge of boredom; drives him to neck stretches and an open, gaping mouth. Nothing else is to be done but flick lint balls at Mr. Dastonry and stare obliquely at anything and everything. And lint has grown scarce.

Just then, the utter blackness without is interrupted—debased—by a beam of light. Curious, Darien flips around and watches the beam dance, completely enthralled by its random swirling patterns, its source utterly obscured in the pitch.

Not until the beam vanishes like a shooting star does the enchantment break and senses return. Darien leaps from the couch and races to the door.

"Harry, there's a light down in the graveyard. I'm gonna take a look," he shouts, and dashes outside.

Mr. Dastonry peers over the top of his glasses. He opens his mouth to reply, no doubt to correct either the "graveyard" remark or the use of his own first name, or both, but the boy is gone.

With a grunt, he rises and plods to the open door. Darien's thin form can be seen racing down the hill, no more than a smudge on the land. Mr. Dastonry's eyes rove upwards, and he sees an orange haze growing around one of the tombs. He starts to call out after Darien, and stops.

What's the point? It is too late, and the boy too stubborn. Just like his father. And just like his father, his morbid curiosity will be the end of him; meddling in things no person should rightfully meddle in. In fact, he reflects, it was this exact manner that his father disappeared, all those years ago, when Darien was still a little whipper-snapper.

Mr. Dastonry shakes his head in sad acceptance, shuts the door, and trudges back to his desk. Oh well. The lad had such promise. Not nearly like his father, to be sure, but one should not be greedy.

Two shadows penetrate the realm of the undead, undeterred by traditional superstitions, conversing freely. The man in front, of strong build and moderate height, sporting a woolen beret, does most of the talking, while the fellow behind him listens, commenting only when the urge strikes him.

"Light is a funny thing, isn't it?" the man in front says. "All the colors in the spectrum, absorbed by black, reflected by white; harmful rays filtered through our atmosphere, harnessed to cut metal, repair eyesight, treat cancer. It is prevalent everywhere we go, so that we take it for granted. Who among us has been devoid of light, in entirety? And yet finding ourselves without light, a foreboding, a tremor settles on our hearts. Yet all darkness *is*, is the absence of light. And what harm is there in that?"

William suddenly stops and points at a large, grimy headstone, interrupting himself. "What's that one say?"

He glances at his partner behind him, who kneels down and reads the epitaph.

"Darson Lipsinc. 1823 - 1850. Loving Father, Devoted Husband, Terrible Singer. Heaven-sent, may heaven take him back.'" The speaker, a small aging fellow with thinning hair and a dull expression, looks back up like a dog expecting scraps from a meal.

William snorts in amusement. "Good one."

His partner, Lyle, smiles broadly. "Yep." Now the dullness has washed out of his expression, and he appears crafty instead. Perhaps it is the narrowing of his already beady eyes.

"So anyway, light is, in my humblest belief, the sustainer of life. More than food, more than drink, more than air."

His flashlight flickers for a moment, briefly encasing them in the darkness around. William slaps the barrel of the light and the beam returns.

"Without light," he goes on, "the world would cease to exist, life forms would deteriorate, most likely annihilate each other, and all form of society would break down. It is ether, the pillar of the universe, the keeper of time. And so darkness is to deprive one of its life force, the source of its very being."

"But what about the blind?" Lyle asks.

William's face wrinkles up in confusion.

"Well," he says finally, brow still wrinkled, "there is an exception to every rule. It is the proof." He turns a smug smile upon Lyle.

"Furthermore," he continues, "Light does not cease to exist, the blind merely cease to perceive it. I would propose that light continues to sustain them even in their blindness, in ways as yet mysterious to us. But I digress."

He shoves open the door to a crypt and steps within, streaming his beam around the old stones and cobwebs.

"Take us for example," he says while perusing the ancient, neglected mausoleum. "As tomb raiders, we depend on low light. But left with no light, even deprived of our sorry little flashlight, we would be utterly helpless and without further recourse. Do you see? But it goes deeper."

William spins his head around to Lyle. "Close that door, would you? It's getting drafty." Lyle shuts the door.

"It's our life-force. Without it, our spirits would shrivel." He shines the flashlight dead into Lyle's eyes. "I see I'm preaching to the choir."

Lyle blinks, temporarily blinded by the direct beam. He squeezes his eyes shut, returning some semblance of night vision, then eyes the interior walls of the tomb warily. Dank stones and cobwebs like drenched twine glisten in the beam of the flashlight. A wooden casket, half-rotted but still in one piece, lies on a shelf on the right wall and another lies beneath it, but nothing else of interest inhabits the dark burial chamber.

"Nothing here, mate. Let's get outta here," Lyle suggests, but William holds up his hand.

"No, no. Not so fast." He pokes at the stones with a tapping hammer, running over them methodically until one echoes back hollowly. The stone removes with little fanfare to the persuasion of his chisel. Within the wall lies a burlap bag, small enough to lay in the palm of a hand, yet weighty.

"Voila!" William says, grinning broadly. He hands the bag to Lyle and exits the crypt.

Lyle opens the bag and peers inside. "It's… it's gold!" His tone is low but excited. "Ha-*ha!* This is so great!" He races after William.

"This reminds me of some of my theorems on economics," William says, as if in passing. All his grand discussions are said in this manner, as flickers in a crowded mind. "Demand creates greater supply and drives down cost, but if supply is limited while demand remains high, then cost likewise remains high. Now this"--he points at the bag of gold--"is the basis of our economy, the foundation of our currency. This little bit will do nothing to alter the economic landscape, but imagine a scenario where a vast store of gold, say millions and millions of tons, was discovered and suddenly dumped into our economy. What effect would this have? Would it overwhelm the system, plummeting the value of each coin, each bill? Or would it boost the economy exponentially, making every man's monetary possessions slightly more valuable? Or maybe very little would change, that the foundation of the currency is no longer as important as the currency itself, that we as a people are no longer concerned with its basis and only its actuality, and refuse to care that we are dealing in paper and worthless metals and leaving the precious stones to the governments. It is for this reason it was once illegal to own gold bars in this country."

He stops abruptly and waves his beam at a random headstone. "Read that one, would you, Lyle?" He points at a triangular shaped stone, sticking out from the rest like a pimple in a sea of freckles.

"Umm, sure," Lyle mutters, squinting, struggling to read the faded words. "Okay, okay, get this!" he says, waving his arms wildly without removing his gaze from the stone. "Here lies Karlo Mayer, metallurgist, inadvertently killed by the hammer of his apprentice. Well done, good and faithful servant.'"

William inhales, chokes on his own spit, and coughs uncontrollably, in some strange hybrid of humor and tracheal irritation, bent over at the waist. Lyle watches him with a glint in his eye and a smirk on his face.

It takes some moments before William regains his composure. He straightens his back and wipes the tears from his eyes. "*Hummm…*" he breathes. "Well, now that that's over, let's do some more raiding, shall we? This looks like a good one."

He approaches a large mausoleum, an elaborate star ringed by Latin symbols etched in the stone. Vines adorn its face like seaweed on stones at low tide. The door shoves open effortlessly, swinging in on its hinges, and the two thieves immerse themselves in the dark, murky atmosphere.

The light in William's hands reduces to an orange glow, little more than a candle. He smacks the barrel and mutters.

"Batteries don't last worth a darn these days. I should get some rechargeables."

"Or an Android," Lyle mumbles to himself.

Lyle hangs as close as he dares behind William, in constant contact with his clothes but careful to avoid appearing frightened. And yet he is, even after all these years. Of darkness like a living ooze; of creatures of nightmares lurking in the shadows, teeth bared, fur on end; of snakes, and spiders, and centipedes dangling from the ceiling and clinging to the walls; of slime, of grime, of time long past.

Of death and evil—no, *malevolent*—spirits. This tomb nurtures, cultivates the darkness, and it thrives.

William follows his dim beam almost instinctively into a corner to the right. A vase sits on a ledge. Dust hangs from its contours and darkness swells from its opening. William flips it upside-down, emptying it onto the ledge. A black orb caroms off the stones, and Lyle envisions it growing legs and scampering away, like a huge black widow.

It does not. Instead, William bottles up the ebony onyx and cradles it in his palms. For several moments he stands entranced by the stone's swirling, pooling blackness, festering beneath its smooth surface. He covers it and whisks it into his pocket.

He looks to Lyle, whose sunken eyes plead for light. William nods and starts toward the door, when his light gives up the ghost, immersing them entirely in palpable blackness.

As if sensing fear, a nebulous glow rises to their left. A creak, as of rusted hinges long closed, echoes against the stones, followed by a dry cracking, as of twigs crushed beneath heels, or old bones lifting from their coffin.

Behind them, the door snaps shut with a bang and a gust of stale wind.

Lyle breaks into a cold sweat. His lips parch and his heart palpitates.

William looks from the glow to the door and back again to the glow, where a thin, bony hand is now visible.

"Not *this* again," he grumbles.

The air, the darkness, begins surging around them, a vortex of unfettered hatred and rage. The nebula grows, billowing upward and out, an orange haze encompassing the air. Decaying bones rise in its wake, some hovering over their intended locations like UFOs, deprived of ligature. The haphazard skeleton stumbles toward William, its eye sockets gleaming red.

William turns from the approaching skeleton to Lyle, who's clinging to William's shirt like a monkey. He trembles uncontrollably, teeth chattering, eyes bulging.

"Have you tried the door yet?" William asks casually. Lyle wags his head. Sweat pours from his scalp, his eyes riveted by the motley bones inexplicably strolling across the stone floor.

"Don't you think we should?" William says, like a teacher admonishing a student.

The air eddies about them, grabbing words and flinging them against the stones, sending them clashing against each other, marauding the eardrums in fantastic ways.

Lyle hears him and nods enthusiastically, but is otherwise rendered immobile, transfixed by terror.

"Fine," William says, exasperated, and pushes past Lyle to the door. Just before he reaches the handle, the door bursts inward, and moonlight pours into the tomb like water. Darkness retreats, the glow disperses, and bones clatter to the floor.

A thin voice penetrates the tomb, rocking Lyle back to reality. William has come face to face with a boy, a young man. His eyes are wide, but his face skeptical.

"What are you all doing here? This is not public property," the boy states warily.

William's hand hovers over the butt of his club, strapped to his side, but the boy's next words stop him. He is looking past William to Lyle, staring obliquely outward like a man in shock.

"Dad?"

Lyle's hair stands on end. Another ghost? He shall surely die. "Do I know you?" he says doubtfully.

"You look just like…" He shakes his head clear. "It *is* you. I'm Darien. Your *son*? Where the heck have you been?"

Chills dart down Lyle's spine. "Are you a ghost?"

"What? *You're* the one who's supposed to have *died.*"

Lyle stops suddenly, confused. "Died? No, no, I never did that." A grin overtakes his homely face. "I vanished, though, I suppose. But look how you have grown! My young son is a man!"

"Are you really my dad?" Darien eyes Lyle suspiciously. "He used to have a name for me, one only he used, before he… apparated."

Lyle doesn't hesitate at all. "Crapshoot."

Darien's mouth twitches for a moment, then he says softly, "Where have you been? *Dad.*"

A big grin spreads across Lyle's face. "All over. Cemeteries mostly. We—William and I—are tomb raiders. We relieve all these stuffy dead guys of their treasures."

William glares at Lyle, and Darien nods thoughtfully. "So, you comin' home, while you're in town? Or were you planning on just lettin' me go on believing you were dead?"

"Do I have to answer that?" He could see from his son's face that he did. He sighed, then lit up at a thought. "You wanna join us?"

"*What?*" Darien and William say in unison.

Lyle shrugs. "You know, rob tombs. We could use another hand, doncha think?"

"Who says?" William growls. "This is not a racket, just an honest, straight-forward treasure-hunt. Say your hellos and goodbyes and let's get out of here."

"Sure," Darien shrugs. "Can't be any worse than *this* job."

"Wait a minute," Lyle says. "What cemetery is this, William?"

"Heatherside."

"Hmmm…" Lyle turns to face his newfound son. "Did this cemetery ever have another name? Like, I dunno… Wallowford?"

"It's what's on Mr. Dastonry's papers."

"Harry?! He's still curator here, is he? Wow!"

"Curator? Dad, this is not a museum, just dead person storage. He's a groundskeeper, and yes, the old fart's still here. I'm his new apprentice."

Lyle wrinkles up his nose. "I was once, and then I met Will here. Come to think of it, it happened kinda like this. Remember, Will?"

William rolls his eyes, but for once, has nothing to say.

"Let me see your candle," Darien says. "I have a tombstone to show you, it's the funniest thing."

"Candle?"

"Yeah, I saw the orange glow. That had to be a candle, right?"

"Ohh, the *candle*. Yes. Well, the wick got a little low, and..."

"Aw, oh well. It's funny, though, something about a rag and oil. I dunno. You'd laugh."

"Now I want to find it."

A gnarly, bare wood branch stretches out, almost grabbing Darien's shirt. He leans down just in time, swiping dirt from a marker in the ground. The tree manages to snag his hat alone. Lyle lunges for him, stumbles and falls on top of the marker.

"Uhhh, dad?"

"Sorry," Lyle says, brushing himself off as William lurches him to a stand, both with an eye on the tree. It stands innocently erect.

Up on the hill, Lyle notices that the small light in the office window has gone out. All around them, the earth bubbles and broils. Darien doesn't seem to notice. He's pointing at the marker.

"What's this?"

"It's Mom, Dad."

"Mom? Gloria," he says, almost a whisper. "Oh, my Gloria."

William is dragging them both to their feet and shoving them toward the large metal gate. "Let's go. No whistling in the graveyard."

"Actually—" Darien begins.

"—it's not a graveyard, it's a cemetery!" Lyle finishes for him.

They laugh in unison.

"You don't have to worry about Mr. Dastonry. He already walked around the grounds; he won't be doing it again. He's way too fat and old. He probably already fell asleep, if he isn't staying up for me."

"Well, then, you better not keep him waiting," William says dourly.

Dead, rotting bodies have risen out of the soft loam and are now lurching toward them. William urges Lyle toward the gate. "Hurry!" he hisses in his ear.

"Darien, let's go!"

The boy pries himself away from the gravestone and rushes after them.

Safe on the other side of the gate, William turns on him. "So, you're coming with us then?"

Darien nods, and Lyle smiles broadly.

William sighs. "Fine. But I want you to know one thing: if you hadn't opened that door, I would have. Understood? Good. Now let's get out of here."

Darien pats his head. "Hold on, I think I lost my hat." He races back through the gate to the horror of the other men. Walking right up to one of the staggering corpses, he takes his hat from its rotting fingers and pats it on the back. "Thanks, George. I owe you one."

All the dead bodies struggle to turn around, and one by one, sink back into the ground.

At the gate, Darien sets the hat back on his head. "So, we doing this, or what?"

The End

Luke D. Evans has published fiction in TQR, with Muse-It-Up Publishing, and at Pulp Corner, as well as poetry at Dual Coast Magazine, Poetry Quarterly, and The Pedestal. Raised in Maryland, he now lives in Colorado and works in the well water industry. He enjoys scenic mountains, pit beef sandwiches, and a good dream. Find him curating Underside Stories at LukeEvans. substack.com

IN THE MYSTERIOUS ASIA SECTION OF THE PIKE AT THE 1904 WORLD'S FAIR IN ST. LOUIS, A CONTORTIONIST PERFORMS.

SWITCHMAN

BY ISMAIL SOLDAN

"Ow would you feel if you were asked to kill a man?"

Ken looked at his questioner and smiled when he should have gone pale. He had just been about to rise from his chair when Dr. DuPare departed from the usual formula of their sessions.

"Mr. Shimura, I'll need to hear an answer. It's a matter of national security. Do you have that killer instinct or not? Can you take human life?"

Since first stepping foot on MacArthur Base, Ken had wanted nothing more than for the cycle of going from shrink's chair to his radar station to continue forever. It was boring as all hell and the only reason he accepted the job of a 'Switchman'. The sudden change in routine unnerved him almost as much as the question itself.

"If it meant saving others, yes I could."

"How about a million?"

He visibly grimaced.

"I…I hope never to have to make that kind of decision."

"Me neither. But one day Mr. Shimura, you may have to."

Holding the key to his nation's last line of defense had started out stressful, the anxiety diminished with each passing predictable day. 'Codes! Red light, blue light, pull!' was the extent of his duties, even though they put the lives of billions in his hands. DuPare's serious tone made those hands tremble now, jittering with the shock of change. For the first time in his two years on base, something strange was afoot.

"But there's no chance of that happening anytime soon right? I mean, if you knew you'd tell me?"

DuPare leaned back and smiled weakly.

"NTK. Need to know. If the brass thought it was necessary I'd tell you. For now, just answer my questions."

Is she serious?

There was fear in that thought. A dread akin to a drowned man flailing for help and realizing there was none to be had. He was told he'd be a hero when they recruited him. That he would be the one to save or avenge their nation. So why was he scared?

"Codes. Then?"

"Blue light, red light. Pull."

"Good man."

With that he was dismissed. As he rose he heard DuPare purr, "You've been more guarded lately. Try to be as open as you can with me Shimura. Our nation…freedom itself might depend on it."

It was the first time Ken had heard DuPare speak so frankly. The psychiatrist's candid words and stony expression shook his soul. If the world did not end tonight, he thought, he would need a little liquid courage to face it tomorrow.

Stepping back onto the rough carpet lining the cushy civilian outhouses on MacArthur Base brought the comfort of familiarity. His station was about five minutes away, its prize kilometers above the horizon orbiting somewhere around planet earth. Ken was not sure exactly what would happen if he ever had to put in his codes, tap on the red and blue lights and then pull the Doomsday switch. Nor did he ever want to find out.

Is something happening? Lawson would know, he's an officer!

Living on base for a civilian had been like waltzing in a Fred Astair-inspired dream. There were all the trappings of being important and none of the pitfalls. No need to workout around those stern, sweating men and women in their stained gym shirts. No one cared what he did or where he went so long as he worked his shifts on time and met Dr. DuPare three times a week. It was the comfortable civilian job he'd imagined they were offering when he graduated and told him his astrophysics degree might be good for something after all. *An avenger.* It was one thing to imagine it and a whole other thing entirely to actually do it.

Ken stumbled on the way back to his station and glanced at his watch. There was time to stop by the officer's hall and see if Lawson was in. The Lieutenant knew how to allay his fears, make everything seem buttery smooth in that Southern Californian accent Ken had come to trust so much. The last thing he wanted was to sit at his station trembling over every beep and bop. Yes, talking to Lawson would be wise.

Damn…a million? That's the first time she's asked me that.

Somewhere, the fear of impending conflict rose.

Does she know something I don't? A million? That's more than the population of my hometown.

As he drew closer, he heard the thud and thrum of heavy metal trail a lilting falsetto. Lawson was in.

"Catch you at a bad time, eh twanger?"

"Very funny. Didn't think you'd be over here so soon. Got someone to take your place?"

Ken shook his head in answer to Lawson and in wonder at his perceptive nature.

"What's up Kenny?"

The Switchman spoke in a tumble of words, jumping from one sentence to another with all the enthusiasm of Tarzan. Thank God there was no one in the officer's room, for Ken had to have broken at least four regulations in that minutes-long monologue. And all the while Lawson just nodded, even smiled once or twice. Grinned even, while all the anxiety Ken stored away the first day his feet touched the concrete of the base spilled out.

"Look, man, I always told you we were two sides of the same coin. Guys like me, we just buy you the time you need to launch that damn thing. Defense is always easier than offence, which is why guys like you are the ones they always write stories about. You're no different from a Spartan or Roman legionary: you're protecting your home. Sometimes you've got to make war, do the hard thing, so that you can live in peace."

Ken nodded thoughtfully knowing the peace it brought him would not last the night. Maybe only until his shift was over, then he could consult a bottle of aged brandy. Lawson spoke for another three minutes, going all the way back to Julius Caesar and the Gauls to remind Ken that good men had to make tough decisions.

"No guts, no glory," Lawson said with a finality that suggested his pep talk was over. He patted Ken on the shoulder and nodded towards the door.

"Now, don't you have a station to man?"

Ken repeated the words 'no guts no glory' and kept doing so as he lumbered toward the small box of a room and worn office chair that awaited him. The repetition was all that kept him from vomiting when the magic of Lawson's words wore off,

Entering anxiously, he eyed the room, its squeaky-clean surfaces and the massive green screen that loomed above his desk. The 32-inch monitor beeped deep and rhythmically.

Deet. Deet.

Ken clinched his jaws. He eyed the screen like a hawk.

Deet. Deet.

The many lines that filled up the background of the radar disappeared and then flashed again, resurrected by some miracle of technology. Each time his heart thrummed.

Deet. Deet.

Was that a red dot? He wondered if his eyes deceived him but dare not voice the thought. No, he assured himself. An apparition, a direct result of his session with DuPare. A mind trick or a spook, nothing more.

Deet. Deet.

Life would remain normal. There was no need to fear. Ken promised himself, willed himself to imagine waking up as usual, putting one sock on then the other, and following the same mundane routine that led him here five days a week. In the background before work the TV would hum, commercial jingles and talk show gossip would trail him on the lonely road to the office. Cornflakes would fill his stomach during the day, replaced by a turkey sandwich in the afternoon, and something heavy at night. Life would go on just as it always had.

Deeeeeeeeeeeeeeeeeeeeeeeeeeeeeeeeeeeeet.

Tiny flashes of red on the green background. His heart thundered in his chest. The radio buzzed but he could not hear it above the screeching sirens. Each red dot appeared to grow larger as the seconds passed, bleeding into the weblike gridlines pattern of the display.

It had to be a drill! But why did they not tell me? Do they want a simulated response?

He tried to believe it. Paralyzed, he held on to the view of himself brushing his teeth and pouring cereal into a recently cleaned bowl. For moments, only that image mattered. They steadied him even as horns blared somewhere on base.

"Station 01 Switchman! Do you copy! Do you copy God Damnit!!!!"

No, it isn't real.

He did not care if they reprimanded him for failing to act 'realistically' during a drill. They should have let him know, he reasoned. To hell with them and their drills.

"Switchman Shimura do you read me! Answer me right now! This is not a drill!!!!"

Liars. Who cooked this up? Avery? Jones? I'll have to get them back tomorrow.

"Corn flakes, no I think I'll need some honey smacks after this!" he spoke aloud as if to reaffirm the thoughts themselves. As if speaking them made them fact.

More red flashes danced on screen. The station shook. Equipment rumbled to life somewhere below him.

"Kenny! Kenny answer me, please!"

Lawson had never sounded more distressed. Ken was scared. He wanted more than anything to be a baby in his mother's arms.

Why God, why!

"Kenny, are you there?! Answer me!"

"Y…yes Lawson. Is this some sort of prank?"

"Snap out of it damn it! This is not a drill. Get a grip and do your job."

"Are you sure its enemy activity?!"

There was a pause.

"The radars are flashing. That means fire. The coordinates have already been set. What more do you need to know?"

"That this is not a mistake. Heck, we've had flocks of birds cause red flashes and sunspots. Please let's think this through!"

"No time. Be a Spartan. Nut up. If it's a mistake, we'll deal with the consequences later. This is your Thermopylae."

He heard the stories from the Cold War, knew he'd be named and shamed if this were the wrong call. Ken also knew about 'dead drills', exercises designed to rouse a spirit of emergency in Switchmen such as himself. In his two years at MacArthur Base he'd never experienced one but prayed this was the first.

The mantra came back, full powered.

No guts, no glory. No guts, no glory. No guts, no glory.

But he didn't want glory. He wanted to live, not kill.

Why couldn't my boring life continue? How will I live with myself? No, it's a dead drill! Just follow orders.

Muscle memory did the job his own mind could not handle as it warred with itself. Codes were typed in. Two lights came to life on the dashboard in front of him. Blue light, red light.

Are you a killer? Huh, are you a killer?

No, I'm a hero. Aren't I?

He reached his hands to pull. Something within himself hesitated. For Ken, those next milliseconds might as well have been eternity.

END

Ismael is a writer and poet from Seattle, WA. He currently lives in Dayton, OH.

For more, follow Ismail @Lit-Nomad009 on X.

HISTORICAL EMPORIUM
Est. 2003

Buy at... HISTORICAL EMPORIUM

Whose **REPUTATION** is *celebrated* world-wide as the pre-eminent clothing source for the **ADVENTUROUS** and *Fashionable.*

We are...

REVERED by our customers

REVILED by our competitors

RESPECTED by all who know us

NO LOCAL DEALER CAN COMPETE WITH OUR QUALITY, VARIETY AND INCOMPARIBLE CUSTOMER SERVICE!

ACCEPT NO SUBSTITUTE!
If you require **clothing and supplies** as stylish and **stout-hearted** as you, contact us immediately to be outfitted.

800-997-4311

HistoricalEmporium.com

Because humankind fails to learn from past lessons, we find that many circumstances from yesteryear are repeating themselves yet again. The commentaries that follow here and in future issues were originally published by _The Mohave Valley Daily News between 1993 & 2013_--and in many ways they apply to today.
We are grateful to republish these commentaries written by Darryle Purcell in full and unedited. His own brand of humor and style can deliver insight, provoke thought, and even boil blood.

(I wrote this next one for a weekly in 2017. It basically shows that maybe my maturity level peaked many years ago.)

PETA believes silence is golden for retrievers and others

Sept. 20, 2017

WE ALL HAVE SPECIAL INTERESTS THAT WE SUPPORT AT ONE LEVEL OR ANOTHER. One of mine is free speech, so it boils my turnips when one side of an issue demands silence from anyone who disagrees. Of course I have said telephone solicitors that cold-call in the evening, or any other time, with requests to speak to the "woman of the house," or offer resort rewards or seek ridiculous polling information should not only be silenced, they should face the death penalty. But I guess the Supreme Court probably disagrees, and they certainly have that right.

Other folks are embroiled in efforts to protect the 2nd Amendment and ensure legal hunting is not restricted. While there are also people who give their time and energies fighting for the rights of dogs and cats not to be abused. I support a lot of goals that people have, as they are usually launched with the best of intentions.

But some activists are evil, such as Antifa, Nazis, Communists, homeowners' association leaders who measure lawn lengths, and those really nasty folks who want to tax cigar companies out of the country while making it illegal for businesses that hire employees to discriminate against potheads. I think that about covers it.

However, there is one group of caring people who aren't evil, yet they often go over the line. On the surface, PETA (People for the Ethical Treatment of Animals) seems like it is on the right course in defending the "rights" of other species. And I certainly support any efforts to protect Fido and Fluffy from abuse.

But now and then, they go too far – such as wearing pig suits to protest hot dog and hamburger restaurants. They look ridiculous in the suits and that discredits any good the organization does. It's as if I were to wear a pig suit with bunny ears in protest at the next Gloria Steinem appearance. That woman could swear about chauvinists all she wants, pigs or otherwise, while I would be the one with the funny captions pasted all over Facebook.

No, don't get me wrong. I love animals, especially chicken and steak. (*I believe I've been a bit too forthcoming in these columns about being a meat eater.*) And I believe there is a happy medium in the issue of animal welfare, especially since many of those animals also eat meat. I'm sure a few of the vegan PETA people look quite delicious to some of their meat-starved pet hawks, snakes, owls and, probably, some cockapoos. Perhaps the PETA R&D Department could develop a kind of bread that would be a decent alternative to carnivores' prey. If so, sadly they won't be able to name it after their organization, because someone else has already come up with Pita Bread.

I remember several years back when, as the editor of a newspaper, I received a PETA press release on saving innocent cockroaches. The PETA PIO wrote that cockroaches "are really quite fascinating once you get to know them." She stated that cockroaches "smell with their mouths and with the long antennae" and described their cute little versions of "eyes and ears." Sorry, but the concept of having any kind of compassion for allegedly cute cockroaches actually makes pig suits look debonair.

But finally, I've found a PETA issue I might support and, of all things, they are seeking silence. Last week the organization put out a release concerning their efforts to silence New Year's Eve in Seattle. The PETA president wrote a letter asking for a silent New Year's high-tech fireworks show "to offer a stress-free celebration for noise-sensitive animals, children, veterans and the elderly." Apparently, the group's efforts have been successful in Costa Mesa, and I would think that PC California city's explosive entertainment probably comes with subtitles – which now makes me wonder if they also have to put up a large screen to project a woman in a black sweater with moving hands that continue to sign "Boom" in American Sign Language (ASL).

As a Vietnam vet, I've never been a big fan of surprise booms, bangs and popping sounds. Many years ago, I was on my first day of a week of RR in Japan. It was raining. I went to a place that specialized in renting nice suits to guys who just came out of the jungle, so we could at least start out looking spiffy. I left the

building in a blue pinstripe suit and walked across a rainy street. Some youths, who probably pulled the same stunt every time it rained, threw firecrackers behind me. I dived into the gutter only to see the laughing #@^&%*#s running off. Then I went back inside, dried off and rented another suit.

That's a long time ago, but even today there's that shudder that hits when I hear a surprise backfire or firecracker. So fireworks shows are never part of my New Year's Eve plans. And, let's face it; no official fireworks show is as colorful, exciting and adrenaline-laced as a napalm strike.

So I believe I have finally found an issue where both the PETA people and I can agree, silent fireworks. I'm probably alone, again, in my thinking, but it's nice to realize that extreme advocates can find some common ground. And I also think anyone who beats a puppy or kitty should be staked out in a Bullhead City yard for the majority of July.

FRIDAY THE 13TH
A MARNIE REILLY MYSTERIES SHORT STORY
BY SHARI T. MITCHELL

Note to the readers:
This story does not fall within the timeline of the
Marnie Reilly Mysteries series.

Marnie rolled to her side and stared out the window at the sun rising over the paper birches and hemlock spruces on the ridge. Her thoughts took her to a conversation she had with one of her clients yesterday.

"If I tell you I am planning to hurt someone, you are required by law to tell the police, aren't you?"

Jonathan LaRoche steepled his long, chunky fingers on his broad chest as he lay on the couch in Marnie's consulting room. His shoulder-length black hair needed a wash—his clothes were grubby, and he wreaked of perspiration and Axe body spray, and his beard was a matted mess of gray and black whiskers with flecks of food creased into the corners of his unwashed mouth.

Marnie worked hard to maintain her composure, her hand over her nose and mouth to keep from gagging on the odor. "Yes, that's right. If you plan to break the law, I have a duty of care to inform the proper authorities. Is that why you wanted to see me today? Are you planning to harm someone?" Her tone even—her eyes watering from the man's stench.

"I see. Client confidentiality only goes so far, then." He craned his neck to see her reaction.

Moving her hand away from her face, she studied him. "Why would you want to harm someone, Mr. LaRoche?"

"Hypothetically, I would harm someone if they were to say, divulge my innermost thoughts. You know, things that I have discussed with them in confidence." He waved his hand and quickly sat up, hammering his size 16 shoes onto the floor.

Marnie flinched and internally scolded herself for allowing him to startle her. "Mr. LaRoche, we have this conversation once a week. Why don't you tell me what's really on your mind?" She sat forward—eyebrows raised.

He pointed an accusing finger at her. "You don't like me. How can you be my psychologist if you don't like me?"

"Why do you think I don't like you?" She cocked her head, gripping her pen tightly.

"You judge me, Ms. Reilly!" He got to his feet and paced in front of the couch.

Marnie pushed her chair back while he wasn't looking—shortening the distance between her and the door.

"Do I? I don't believe that I judge anyone, Mr. LaRoche. I certainly listen to everything that you tell me and make a professional assessment. Is that what you consider judging?"

Whirling around, he lunged forward, placing his hands on the arms of her chair. His face inches from hers, he snarled, "You! It's you I intend to harm!" Shoving her chair back into the wall with a jolting thunk, he turned his back and sang, "Pop Goes the Weasel." Wheeling back around, he took a step toward her. She leapt to her feet as her consulting room door flew open.

Carl stood in the doorway, jaw and fists clenched. "Your session is over, Mr. LaRoche."

A blue jay squawked by her screened window, jerking her from her thoughts. Glancing down at her smartwatch, a wave of nausea washed over her.

"Argh! It's Friday the 13th!" She rolled to the other side of her bed. Tater sat at the edge, peering into her face. Dickens glanced up from his bed in the corner where he had been licking his foot. His ears perked up when Marnie looked at him.

"You two don't know what Friday the thirteenth means, do you?" Her aquamarine eyes filled with tears as she ruffled a hand through Tater's thick coat and kissed him on top of his head.

The Border Collies, ears up, cocked their heads and mumbled. Dickens stood, stretched out his front legs—rump in the air—then trotted to the side of the bed. Marnie scratched him under the chin, leaned over and wrapped her arms around both of the dogs.

"It means that we stay close to home, keep our fingers crossed and hope for the best." She sat up and swung her legs off the bed. As her feet hit the floor, she saw a shadow move down the hallway outside of her bedroom. Pressing a finger to her lips, she shook her head at Tater, who stared at the figure disappearing around the corner.

RYAN'S DINER BUZZED WITH CAFFEINE-INDUCED ENERGY AS DANNY AND TOM tucked into their breakfasts.

"Your grandmother makes the best scrambled eggs in Creekwood." Tom gulped his coffee while scooping up a forkful of home fries.

"Yes, she does. The bacon is perfect, too." Danny's blue eyes sparkled as he picked up a crispy strip with his fingers and popped it into his mouth.

"It's strange to have a day off. I'm lookin' forward to fishin'—away from Creekwood. I haven't been up north to fish in a long time." Tom pushed away his plate and puffed out his cheeks. "I am stuffed. You ready to go?" He put his hand in his pocket, pulling out a twenty-dollar bill for the tip jar.

"Yeah. Let's hit the road." Danny slid out to the booth and took his wallet out of his back pocket, pulling a twenty out. "C'mon! Let's go before Gram catches us."

Tossing their twenties into the jar on the counter, they made a beeline for the door.

"Where are you going in such a hurry?" Gram appeared in front of them, an order pad in her hand.

The detectives glanced at one another.

"Uh. We're going fishing," Danny said.

Tom nodded in agreement.

"What about Marnie?" She studied them closely.

Both men shrugged.

"She's home—she had stuff to do." Danny fiddled with his phone.

Tom fished his phone from his pocket and glanced down at the screen. Looking up at the ceiling, he sighed. "We're not goin' fishin' today. We're goin' to the ranch."

His partner scrunched up his face. "Why not? We've been waiting all week for this trip."

"It's Friday the thirteenth."

"Yeah. Okay. Are you tellin' me that Madame Séance is superstitious?" Danny pulled a face, laughed, and glanced down at his grandmother with a grin.

Tom pursed his lips, anger flashing in his violet eyes. "Marnie's parents both died on a Friday the thirteenth. We gotta go to the ranch." He dropped his head to his chest, exhaling loudly. Looking up, he shook his head at his partner. "How can you not know that?"

"She never told me! If I had known…"

"Yeah. Well, you know now. Let's go." Tom pulled open the diner door and stalked out.

Danny glanced up at the little bell ringing violently over the door, and then back down at Gram. "I didn't know."

She looked up at her grandson—her blue eyes stormy. "I knew, and I'm not a detective. You need to communicate better, Daniel. Marnie

Reilly is an open book to those interested in readin' her. I hear her ask you about your day all the time. When was the last time you asked her how she's doin'?"

He rolled his eyes. "She'll just say fine."

"No. That's what your late wife always said. Marnie will tell the truth. She always does, whether it's what you want to hear or not. Perhaps that's why you don't ask her." Gram nudged him toward the door. "Go. Make sure she's okay—'cause believe it or not, sometimes she's not."

MARNIE CREPT INTO THE HALLWAY, THE TIMBER FLOORS COOL BENEATH HER bare feet. Tater and Dickens walked in step on either side of her—ears and scruffs up. The old pine floorboards creaked—she held her breath and paused, listening. Tater glanced up at her, waiting for a command. She gently tugged his ear, a signal that everything would be fine. Holding up her hand, she made eye contact with both of the dogs.

"Sit. Stay," she whispered. Both dogs sat motionless, awaiting her next direction.

As Marnie took another step forward, they all heard a shuffling in the guestroom down the hall. The dogs tipped their heads, and Marnie tiptoed slowly toward the door, which was slightly ajar. She pushed the door open to a flurry of black. She screeched, lifted her arms to protect herself, and shouted the command, "Scootchem!"

Tater bounded forward with a high-bitched bark, chasing the shadow away from his mistress. He stopped short when the intruder slammed into the bedroom window with a dull thud. The dog lay down on the floor, resting his head next to a wounded crow. Marnie joined him near the window and kneeled down.

"Ah, geez! The poor thing. You remind me of a pet crow my father used to have." Reaching behind her, she grabbed a pillow, removed the pillowcase, and gently scooped up the bird. Cradling the bird in her arms, she ran her finger lightly over the bird's wings, its head and tail feathers. Tater stood and peered into the cloth bundle at the bird. "He doesn't seem to have broken anything, and his neck doesn't appear to be broken. Let's take him out onto the veranda in case he wakes up. I don't want him to fly into the window again."

Marnie stood, and she and Tater went out into the hallway where Dickens still sat. Waving her hand, she said, "Free!" Dickens stood and walked calmly down the stairs behind his mistress and Tater.

At the bottom of the stairs, Marnie paused and glanced down at her dogs. "How did the crow get into the house?"

"WHY ARE YOU SO PISSED OFF AT ME? I HAD NO IDEA MARNIE'S PARENTS BOTH died on Friday the thirteenth. How should I have known that?" Danny ran a hand through his hair and frowned at his partner.

Tom turned his attention away from the road for a moment to scowl at him. "How can you not know that? You know, she's been goin' through a rough time lately. She's got a new home; a new direction for her practice; and she has a new court-appointed client who is giving her a hard time. When was the last time you asked her how her day was?"

Danny cocked an eyebrow. "Are you and Gram in cahoots? She asked me the same question."

Tom slammed his hand onto his steering wheel. "No! We are not in cahoots. We notice things and actually ask Marnie how she's doin' and she tells us. Are you gonna ask me about the client who's givin' her a hard time?"

"She told me she's got a painful client, but that's all she said."

"Did you push her? She probably would have told you more if you had."

"No. She gets mad when I do."

Danny's phone rang. He answered it. "Hi, Carl." He listened for several minutes, his jaw clenching tighter with every moment that passed. "We're on our way there now. Yeah, he's with me. We'll see you there."

"What's wrong?" Tom turned on the signal light to turn onto the highway.

"You better get your grill lights on and floor it. Carl just filled me in on Marnie's court-appointed client. The guy threatened her yesterday. She made him swear not to tell us, but he got worried. He tried to call her a few minutes ago, and she didn't answer the home phone or her mobile."

Tom turned on the grill lights and pressed his foot down on the gas pedal. The big tires of the truck kicked up rocks, and the backend fishtailed before correcting.

Scowling at his partner, he growled, "Call her again, and keep calling until she answers."

MARNIE'S MOBILE PHONE VIBRATED AND FELL TO THE FLOOR FROM HER BED-side table. Tater and Dickens woofed at the thump from above, but continued following their mistress through the downstairs of their house. Stepping into the library, she flipped on the overhead light, went to her desk, laid the wounded crow on the blotter, and pulled open a large file drawer. Taking a lockbox from the drawer, she punched in a code and it sprang open. The dog's growls alerted her they were not alone. Glancing up, she put her hand to her mouth, stifling a scream. The hulking mass of John LaRoche's malodorous frame stood in the open doorway leading out to the veranda.

Her eyes never leaving the grotesque madman in her doorway, Marnie whispered, "Shush, Tater. Shush, Dickens. Sit. Stay." The Border Collies sat, their intense and intelligent eyes trained on the trespasser.

LaRoche pointed a gun at the dogs. "Remove the mongrels, Ms. Reilly, or I *will* kill them."

She turned to her dogs, making eye contact with Tater, and made a twisting motion with her hand. He tipped his head and put a paw on her knee. Pointing to the door, she gave the command, "Tater. Dickens. Out. Kitchen." Both dogs obeyed and slunk out of the library. Marnie's heart jumped into her throat as the click of their toenails disappeared down the hall. Turning back to the lunatic in her library, she lifted her chin and narrowed her eyes.

"Why are you here, Mr. LaRoche?"

Taking a step into the room, he ran his hand across the back of a leather chair. His mouth formed a grotesque grin—the gun in his hand now pointed at Marnie. "I told you my intentions yesterday."

She kept her eyes on him as she reached out her hand to the lockbox.

"Ah! Ah! Ah! I wouldn't do that. I will shoot you in the heart before you can retrieve your weapon."

Dropping her hand to her side, she glanced down at her desk. One of the crow's eyes opened, and a wing ruffled ever so lightly. Inhaling deeply through her mouth, she lifted her gaze and saw the depth of the man's hatred for her. His soulless black eyes judged her and his mouth moved peculiarly, as if he were reciting a spell. Narrowing her eyes, she studied the man's face—there was something familiar.

"It's you who is judging me, Mr. LaRoche. I can see it in your eyes. Why do *you* hate me? What is it about you that makes you hate someone you don't even know?"

"Oh, I know you, Ms. Reilly. I know you too well. You play with people's minds and then send them to mental hospitals to wither away and die. That's what you were planning to recommend to the court, wasn't it? You were going to tell them to lock me up for an eternity."

Shrugging, she didn't hide a smirk. "That is exactly what I recommended—yesterday, in fact. As soon as you left my office, I wrote a report to the court. I told them you are a sick, twisted, maniacal creature. I told them you direly need soap, a shower, a razor, toothpaste, and a toothbrush. You disgust me, Mr. LaRoche. As a psychologist, I would probably not say that to a client, but you trespassed. You are standing here, in my home, uninvited and unwashed. You are a foul human being! I personally delivered the report to Judge Lawrence last night. And that is that. No matter what you do to me, your sentence is sealed." She laughed at him—her aquamarine eyes wide and mocking. "Now, you should be on your way. Detectives Keller and Gregg will be here soon for breakfast. We have plans."

As he took a step toward her, Marnie weaved to the bookcase behind her desk. Picking up a marble statue of St. Francis of Assisi, she heaved it toward him and sidestepped toward the door. The statue missed and fell to the seat of the leather couch. She crouched as the gun went off and crab-crawled to the door as a loud shriek and the flurry of ruffling feathers attacked LaRoche. Throwing his hands in the air to protect himself, he dropped the gun.

Tater and Dickens appeared at the veranda door, as Marnie scrambled to her feet and raced out of the library—her dogs ran past LaRoche, knocking him down. Sprinting to the kitchen, she smiled when she saw the kitchen door standing open. "Good boy, Tater! Smart boy! Let's go! We need to get to the barn!"

Snatching up her Wellingtons, Marnie hopped awkwardly, pulling on the boots as they ran out the backdoor. Too terrified to look back, she focused on getting to safety—the big red barn would provide that.

CARL PARKINS KICKED A FLAT TIRE ON HIS BLUE CHEVY PICKUP TRUCK. "I have never had a flat tire in my life. Why? Today of all days!" Scowling up the road, he threw up his hands in frustration. "Yes!" He waved down the approaching truck with flashing grill lights.

Tom stopped the truck, and Danny rolled down his window. "Jump in!"

Carl reached into his truck for his briefcase, pulled open the back door of Tom's truck, and climbed inside. "Crap! Am I glad to see you guys. I got a flat tire."

Tom glanced into the rearview mirror. "Did you bring your gun?"

Carl gave a curt nod.

MARNIE AND HER DOGS RACED UP THE STEPS TO THE LOFT. DROPPING THE hatch door, she rolled two bales of hay on top of it. Her stomach lurched when she remembered LaRoche had a gun. He could easily shoot up through the floorboards, harming her dogs and her. Peering through the wall of the barn, she spotted LaRoche running across the pasture. She looked around the hayloft, noting a pitchfork, a tall cabinet, a large chain with a hook, and work gloves.

"What can I do with these?" She raised an eyebrow and walked to the cabinet. The door of the cupboard stood locked with an old padlock. Retrieving the pitchfork, she stuck a tine through the hasp and yanked. The hasp broke off, the door swung open to reveal two shotguns, and a shelf above the guns held boxes of birdshot. She turned to her dogs—both stared up—they were panting, not smiling. "What do you say we have a bit of target practice?" She loaded five shells into a gun, pushed back the sliding door of the loft, and took aim. *Boom!* The ground in front of LaRoche exploded. He veered left but continued running toward them. She took aim again. *Boom!* She hit an old fence post, sending splinters into the air. Peering out, she couldn't see him. He had vanished from sight.

Below them, she heard whistling. It was a familiar tune from childhood—one she had heard last night.

> *Round and round the cobbler's bench*
> *The monkey chased the weasel*
> *The monkey thought it was all in fun*
> *Boom!*

A bullet flew up through the floorboards, and the dogs leapt sideways as another bullet splintered the old boards, scattering loose hay. Marnie muffled a scream and motioned with her hand for her dogs to come to her as the whistling began again. As the dogs ran to her side, she rolled a spent shell casing away from them.

> *Round and round the cobbler's bench*
> *The monkey chased the weasel*
> *The monkey thought it was all in fun*
> *Boom!*

Another round pierced through the floor at the other end of the barn. Marnie tiptoed to the cabinet and took out a full box of shells. She rolled three together to the center of the loft. This time, the lunatic sang:

> *Round and round the cobbler'th bench*
> *The monkey chathed the weathel*
> *The monkey thought it wath all in fun*
> *Pop goeth the weathel!*

A chill ran up her spine, and she swallowed her fear. She stood stock-still, waiting—for what—she wasn't sure.

Grabbing hold of her dog's collars, she pulled them as close to the eaves as she could get them. "Okay, guys. We're going to need some help. It's time for a bit of divine intervention." Marnie closed her eyes and whispered.

Danny turned in his seat. "Okay, Captain Crystals, give us the lowdown."

Carl rolled his eyes, resigning himself to the fact that the nickname wasn't going away. He dug into his satchel for a file and opened it on his lap. "His name is Jonathan LaRoche. He is a 58-year-old Creekwood native. He's six-feet ten-inches tall, weighs two hundred-eighty pounds, and he threatened Marnie with bodily harm yesterday—which is why I can tell you everything I have about the ogre. Judge Lawrence referred him to us—well, one of her clerks did. Ah, a Miss Annabelle LaRock."

Tom glanced up into the mirror. "Did you say Jonathan LaRoche?"

Carl looked down at the file and nodded. "Yeah. It says here that the police charged him with harassment and assault. He shoved a woman in the QuickMart when she reached for the last bottle of Canada Dry ginger ale. His excuse was that he wasn't feeling well and needed the soda. Uh… The woman sustained a minor injury—a contusion to her left shoulder. The lady pressed charges. The court ordered LaRoche to see a court-appointed psychologist for anger management. It looks like Judge Lawrence's clerk sent the asshole our way. Maybe she thought he would land on my desk."

Clicking his tongue, Tom thought. "Hey, is there any history on the guy? Employment? Time served? Anything?"

"Yep. He was a kindergarten teacher here in Creekwood. Hmm… Probably back when you and Marnie were kids. Do you remember him?" He looked up, meeting Tom's eyes.

"Yeah. I remember him. I'm surprised Marnie didn't."

Danny turned to his partner. "Why's that?"

"Back then he was Mr. LaRock, and he was our kindergarten teacher, and he was horrible. He picked on Marnie because she had a lisp and a slight stutter. He used to make her sing some stupid song over and over again, trying to get her to stop lisping. LaRock was cruel, and he got fired for his behavior. Marnie's parents took exception to a teacher bullying their daughter." Tom glanced into the mirror, meeting Carl's eyes.

"What was the song?" Carl asked.

"Pop Goes the Weasel."

Putting his head into his hands, Carl groaned. Meeting the detective's eyes again, he replied, "He said that to her yesterday when he shoved her chair across the room."

MARNIE, EYES CLOSED, CALLED OUT TO HER PARENTS FOR HELP. "I'M BREAKING my rule. Sorry to bother you, but I really need your help today. Do you remember Mr. LaRock? He's trying to kill me. Do you think you could give me a hand?"

A slight breeze rose in the hayloft, whirling chaff and dust into the air. Tater and Dickens whimpered, tilted their heads, and smiled at the figures in the center of the room. Tater leaned on his mistress's leg and tapped her knee with his paw. Opening her eyes, Marnie watched as Jonathan LaRoche climbed up a rope and reached through the door at the other end of the loft. Pulling himself into the barn, he pulled his pistol from his pocket, aiming it at her. Glancing at her parents with fear in her eyes, she saw love in theirs as they looked back at her. Colin Reilly raised up his arms to the sky and shouted, "Osiris!"

TOM PULLED UP THE TRUCK OUTSIDE OF MARNIE'S HOME, AND THE MEN rushed into the house, calling her name.

Danny raced through the kitchen to the stairs, running up the steps three at a time.

"Marn!" Tom called out, sprinting into the library.

Carl walked into the living room, glanced around the room, and went to the library to find Tom, who was standing beside the couch holding the statue of the patron saint of animals—a gift he had given her from Tater and Dickens on Mother's Day.

Danny called out from upstairs. "She's in the barn! I saw her move in front of the hayloft door! She's upstairs!" He jumped down the stairs, twisting his ankle at the bottom. "Argh!"

Tom and Carl met him at the kitchen door. Together, they ran across the pasture to the big red barn.

"Marn!" Tom called up, but Marnie waved him off. "We're coming, Marn! We'll be right there!"

Danny limped up the stairs and pushed up on the door. It wouldn't move.

"Come help me," he shouted.

Tom and Carl ran up the steps, and the three of them pushed with all of their might.

"There's a rope around the other side of the barn. We can climb up it." Danny limped to the back of the barn to the far door. His partner and Carl followed.

Tom glanced up and then pointed to a wall of tools. "I'll climb up. You two see if you can get the loft door open with that pry bar over there."

Danny nodded. "Good plan."

"OSIRIS!" COLIN REILLY CALLED AGAIN—A CAW CAME BACK IN REPLY.

Gun still aimed at Marnie's chest, Jonathan LaRoche took another step toward her. As sunlight streamed through the open loft door, a shadow broke through the sunbeams. The crow swooped over Marnie's head, forcing her and her dogs to dive to the floorboards as a bullet flew over her. Osiris flew into the face of the madman, throwing him off balance and out the door of the hayloft with a fear-filled scream, followed by the sickening, dull thud of death.

Marnie got to her feet and turned to her parents. "How can that be, Osiris? How can he still be alive?"

Her mother and father grinned. "He's not, but neither are we," said her mother.

"We have to go now. We'll see you soon," said her father.

Marnie looked at him with horror. "What's that supposed to mean?"

Her mother giggled. "Geez, Colin, don't scare the girl." Turning to her daughter, she smiled. "Don't worry, darling. We'll come to see you. You won't be coming to us for a very long time."

Marnie exhaled loudly. "Well, that's good to know." Her eyes filled with tears, and as she opened her mouth to speak again, her parents were gone.

"Marnie! Are you okay? We can't get through the door!" Danny called up from below.

She rolled the hay bales off the door and lifted it up. "I'm fine. Nothing a bit of divine intervention can't handle." She reached out her hand to Danny and pulled him into a hug when he reached the top step.

He pulled a face. "You're fine. Really? You're fine? We just heard a gunshot, and you're telling me you're fine."

"Okay. No, I'm not fine. I'm a mess." She leaned into him and embraced tightly. Wrapping his arms around her, he hugged her tighter and kissed the top of her head.

Tater and Dickens trotted over to them and rested against Danny's leg. Carl stepped into the loft and looked around. "Where's Tom?"

"Hey, Marn!" Tom called out from the opposite end of the loft, where he was swinging through the door from the rope. Pointing out the window, he said, "You know that you've got a dead guy down there, right?"

The End

Shari T. Mitchell is the author of the Marnie Reilly Mysteries thriller series, which includes Divine Guidance, Torn Veil, and the upcoming release (mid-2023) Fatal Vow.

Raised and educated in Northern New York State, her hometown and surrounds inspired the series' fictional town of Creekwood, New York. Shari loves developing multidimensional characters with whom her readers can relate, but plotting the twists and turns of a murder mystery feeds her analytical and creative mind. She shares her home in North Carolina with her partner in crime, Harper, and their crazy rescue dogs, Dougal, Callee, Midget, and Mags. Shari, a thirty-plus year marketer, loves spending time with her family, cooking, hiking, gardening, reading and writing.

Online Details:
Website: www.sharitmitchell.com
Instagram: @sharitmitchell
Facebook: https://www.facebook.com/ShariTMitchellAuthor
X: @sharitmitchell

Kirk had never seen the distant planet
called Earth, yet his squadron was now ordered
there—to stem the outbreak of a galactic war!

It was well called the Dragon's Throat, thought Kirk. Throat of fire, of burning suns, a cosmic blind-alley into danger!

You made your decision. You threw a ship, a hundred men, your officers, your friends, your own Commander's badge you threw them all down on the gamble. But when the stakes were stars....

CHAPTER 1

He said to himself, "The hell with it, we're committed."

He said aloud, "Radar?"

Joe Garstang, standing on the bridge beside him, answered without turning. "Nothing has been monitored yet. Not *yet*."

Kirk's palms itched. If they were running into an ambush, if Orion heavy cruisers were waiting for them, they'd soon know it. There could be ships all around them. Radar wasn't too dependable, in the howling vortices of force-field energy flung out around this jungle of stars.

Through the broad bridge-windows—the "windows" that were really scanners cunningly translating faster-than-light probe rays into visual images—there beat upon his face the light of a thousand suns.

It was Cluster N-356-44, in the Standard Atlas. It was also hellfire made manifest, to starmen. It was a hive of swarming suns, pale green and violet, white and yellow-gold and smoky red, blazing so fiercely that the eye was robbed of perspective and these stars seemed to crowd and jostle and rub each other. Up against the black backdrop of the firmament they burned, pouring forth the torrents of their life-energy to whirl in terrific cosmic maelstroms. The merchant ships that boldly drove the great darks between ordinary star-worlds would recoil aghast from the navigational perils here. Only a fool—or a cruiser—would go in here.

There was a narrow cleft between cliffs of stars, with the flame-shot glow of an immense nebula roofing it. The only possible way into the heart of the cluster, this Dragon's Throat of starman legend. But others had gone in this way. At least, so said the rumors, rumors that had reached the squadron as far away as the Pleiades. Rumors too factual, too alarming, to be ignored.

Rumors of cruisers from the squadrons of Orion Sector, that had gone into this cluster. Rumors of a secret base, on a hidden world. The ships of Orion Sector had no business here. Neither, for that matter, did the ships of Kirk's own Lyra Sector. This cluster was no-man's land, part of the buffer zones that were supposed to reduce friction between the five great Sectors of the galaxy. Actually, these stellar wildernesses were the scenes of constant, nameless little wars.

The five governors of the five great Sectors were, all of them, ambitious men. Solleremos of Orion, Vorn of Cepheus, Gianea of Leo, Strowe of Perseus, Ferdias of Lyra—they watched each other jealously. Five great barons of the galaxy, paying only a lip-service allegiance to the shadowy Central Council far away on a half-forgotten world called Earth, in reality independent satraps of the stars, hungry for space, hungry for power. Yes, even Ferdias, thought Kirk. Ferdias was the man he served, respected, and even loved in a craggy sort of way. But Ferdias, like the others, played a massive game of chess with men and suns, moving his squadrons here and his undercover operatives there, laboring ceaselessly to hold on to what he had and perhaps enlarge his domain, just a little, a solar system here and a minor cluster there....

And the game went on. Right now, Kirk thought he was probably heading into a trap. But if Orion cruisers *were* in here, he had to know it. A hostile base here, if left to grow, could dominate all the star-lanes from Capella to Arcturus. It was up to him as a squadron-commander, to go in and find out.

Kirk looked at the looming, overtopping cliffs of stars that went up to the glowing nebula above and down to the black pit of absolutely nothing below.

He thought of Lyllin, waiting for him back at Vega. A starman had no business with a wife.

He said again, "Radar?"

"Still nothing," said Garstang. His square face was no less grim than Kirk's. He was captain of this flagship *Starsong*, and what happened to her was important to him. "If there is a base here," he said, "we should have come in with the whole squadron."

Kirk shook his head. He had made his decision and he was not going to start doubting it now, no matter how lonely and exposed he felt.

"That could be exactly what Solleremos wants. With the right kind of ambush, a whole squadron could be clobbered in this mess. Then Lyra would be wide open. No. One ship is enough to risk."

"Yes, sir," said Garstang.

"The hell with you, Joe," said Kirk. "Say what you're thinking."

"I am thinking that the rumor mentioned cruisers, plural, indefinite. We'd better catch them while they're all asleep."

The *Starsong* forged her way onward toward the two red suns at the end of the Dragon's Throat. And Kirk thought that if he had made the wrong decision, if the *Starsong* never came back again, Ferdias would be very angry. But that would not then make any difference to him.

Looking up at the flaring, tumbling waves of the nebula, like the underside of a burning ocean, Kirk said to Garstang:

"Does it seem to you the pace is speeding up? I mean, this jockeying for power between the Sectors has gone on a long time, ever since Earth lost real authority. But it seems different lately, somehow. More incidents, more feeling of something driving ahead toward a definite goal, a plan and a pattern you can't quite see. You know what I mean?"

Garstang nodded "I know."

The computer banks clicked and chattered. Relays kicked, compensating power, compensating course, compensating tides of gravitic force quite capable of breaking a ship apart like a piece of flawed glass. The two red binaries gave them a final glare of malice and were gone. They were clear of the Throat.

A star the color of a peacock's breast lay dead ahead.

"Ready for approach," said Garstang.

"Stand by," said Kirk. "We'll wait until the last possible minute to shift. If they haven't picked us up already, maybe they won't."

Garstang gave his orders. Kirk watched the blaze of peacock-blue grow swiftly. No ambush in the Throat, so now what? Ambush on the world of the blue star? Or nothing? A wild-goose chase, time and money wasted? Or maybe Solleremos had planted those rumors to draw Kirk's attention while a strike was made somewhere else.

Suddenly Kirk felt very old and very tired. He had been in the squadron for twenty years, ever since he was sixteen, and in all these twenty years the great game of stars, the strain, the worry, had never let up.

It must have been nice in a way, Kirk thought, in the old days a couple of centuries ago when Earth still governed in fact, and all the star-squadrons were part of the Galactic Navy, and the great battle was with the galaxy itself and not with one another.

"We're getting close," said Garstang.

Kirk shook himself and got down to business. There followed a few minutes of split-second activity, and then the *Starsong* had shuddered out of overdrive and was plunging toward a bright world almost dangerously close to her. There was still no sign of any enemy, and the communicators remained silent.

An hour later by ship's chrono they had located the one port of entry listed for the planet and they had set the *Starsong* down in the middle of a large piece of natural desert that served well enough for what space traffic ever came here.

It was night on this side of the planet. There was no moon, but on a cluster world a moon is a useless luxury. The sky blazes with a million stars, so that day is replaced not by darkness but by the light of another sort, soft and many-colored, full of strange glimmers and flitting shadows. In this eery star-glow a town was visible about a mile away. Otherwise there was nothing. No ships.... No legions of Orion Sector.

"The ships could be hidden somewhere," Garstang said. "Maybe halfway around the planet, but waiting to jump us as soon as they get word."

Kirk admitted that was possible. He put on his best dress uniform of blue-and-silver, and strapped a portable communicator between his shoulders. It rather spoiled the effect, but there was no help for that. Garstang watched him.

"How many men will you want?" he asked.

"None. I'm going in alone."

Garstang's eyes widened. "I won't come right out and say you're crazy."

"I was here once before," said Kirk. "When old Volland was commander and I was an ensign. These people are poor but proud. They have traditions of long-ago splendor, claim their kings ruled the whole cluster and so on. They dislike strangers, and won't let many in."

"But if Solleremos' men are already here—"

"That's the reason for the porto." Kirk frowned, trying to plan ahead. "Exactly twenty minutes after I enter the town I'll contact you, and I'll continue to do so at twenty-minute intervals. If I'm so much as a minute late, take off and buzz hell out of the place. It'll give me a bargaining point, anyway."

Garstang said dourly, "A lot can happen in twenty minutes. Suppose you're not able to bargain?"

"Then you're on your own."

In the airlock, open now and filled with a dry, stinging wind, Kirk paused, looking toward the distant town, a lonely blot of darkness between the star-blazing sky and the gleaming sand. Here and there in it lights burned, but they were few and somehow not welcoming.

"She's all yours," he said to Garstang. "If anything looks wrong to you, don't wait for me. Take her away."

"Yes, sir," said Garstang.

Kirk smiled. He climbed down into the sand and began to walk.

The town took shape as he approached it. The stone-built houses, mostly round or octagonal, were scattered out with no particular plan. Under the red and gold and diamond-colored stars that burned above them as bright as moons, they looked curiously remote and evil, like old wizards in peaked hats, peering with little winking eyes. The dry wind blew, laden with alien scents. Apart from the wind there was no sound.

Three men met him at the edge of the town. They wore pale cloaks and carried long staffs tipped with horn. They were all of seven feet tall. They wore their hair high on their heads to accentuate this height, and they were slender and graceful as reeds, walking along with a light dancing step as though the wind blew them. But their faces in the star-glow were smooth and secret, their eyes as expressionless as bits of shiny glass.

"What does the man from outside desire?" asked one of them, in the universal speech.

Kirk said, "He desires to speak with those others from outside who enjoy your hospitality."

But they were not going to make it that easy for him. Their faces remained impassive, and the one who had just spoken said coolly, "Our lord has wisdom in all matters. Perhaps he will understand your words. I do not."

They fell in around Kirk and moved with him into the wide sandy space that went between the wandering houses. The nerves tightened up in Kirk's belly, and his back felt cold. He looked at his wrist chrono, carefully. There was no sound but the whispering of sand under their feet. Garstang would be watching with the 'scope, but once he was in among the houses he could no longer be seen.

That was almost at once. The tall men walked on with their light swaying stride, so that he had to move at an undignified trot to keep up. The stone houses with their high roofs closed in behind him. This dark and brooding town ill accorded with old tales of cluster-kings, he thought. Yet the past held many things.

When they were close to the center of the town, the leader stopped beside a round structure from whose open door came light.

"Will the man from outside enter the dwelling of our lord?"

Kirk breathed a little easier as he went through the door. Apparently there was no truth to the rumors that....

A chopping blow took him on the back of the head. He fell forward. He was stunned but not unconscious, and he tried to roll over, thrashing out blindly with his fists and feet. But at once there were men on top of him, heavy solid men grinding his face into the gritty carpet, pounding the wind out of him, holding him down.

In a minute his hands were tied tight behind him and his ankles lashed together. They cut the straps of the porto and pulled it off him. Then, like a sack of meal, he was dragged to the wall and propped upright.

In an absolute fury of rage, he spat blood out of his mouth and looked up dizzily into the light.

There were three or four men here, obviously not natives of this planet, but he did not pay much attention to them. The one he looked at stood apart, directly in front of Kirk, a lean dark iron-faced man with very alert eyes, and the easy, dangerous manner of one who enjoys his work because he is so admirably well fitted for it, as a cat enjoys hunting.

He said to Kirk, "My name is Tauncer."

Kirk nodded. He looked with feral interest at this most famous of Solleremos' agents. "I should be flattered, shouldn't I?"

Tauncer shrugged. "We all do what we can, Commander. Each in his own way."

"Well," said Kirk. "What do you want?"

"The answer to one simple question."

His face came closer to Kirk's, very tense, very keen, searching for any sign of evasion.

He asked his question.

"What is Ferdias planning to do about Earth?"

CHAPTER 2

There was a long moment of complete silence, during which Kirk stared wide-eyed at Tauncer, and Tauncer probed him with a gaze like a scalpel.

On Kirk's part, it was a silence of sheer astonishment. No question could have taken him so unexpectedly. He'd been prepared to be grilled on squadron dispositions, forces in being, bases, all the things that the men of Orion Sector would like to know about Lyra. But this—

It didn't make sense. Earth was not part of the present-day star struggle. That old planet, so far back in the galaxy that Kirk had never been within parsecs of it—it was history, nothing more. It had had its day, its sons long ago had spread out to the stars and their blood ran in the veins of men on many worlds, in Kirk himself. But its great day had long been done, and the Sector governors who played the cosmic chess-game for suns paid it no heed at all.

"I'll repeat," said Tauncer softly. "What's Ferdias planning to do about Earth?"

"I haven't," said Kirk, "the faintest idea what you're talking about."

Tauncer sighed. "Possibly." He straightened up. "Even probably. But I've been sent here to make the inquiry, and I'll need more than your word and an expression of innocence. Brix!"

One of the other men came forward. Tauncer spoke to him in a low voice, and he nodded, and went into the shadows across the room. Kirk's heart pounded in alarm. He tried to get up, but he had been too well bound. He could not see his chrono, but he did not think that more than seven or eight minutes had elapsed since he had entered the town. Plenty of time for mischief. He said to Tauncer,

"I didn't walk into this with my eyes completely shut. My men have instructions."

"I'm sure they have. And don't feel too badly about this, Commander. The details of the trap were based on a minute study of your psychology and past record. It would have been almost impossible for you to avoid falling into it. Can't you hurry that up Brix?"

"All ready." Brix came back carrying a light tripod with a projector mounted on it. And now Kirk's heart sank coldly into the pit of his stomach. He had seen that particular type of projector before. It was called a vera-ray, and it beamed electric impulses in a carefully-controlled range that absolutely stunned and demoralized a man's brain, making him temporarily incapable of lying or resisting questioning.

Kirk had no information about Earth to give away. But there were plenty of other things in his mind, things of military importance to Lyra Sector that Solleremos would be only too glad to get hold of.

How long now? Ten minutes more? Too long. Even five minutes would be too long, with that projector pounding his skull.

He couldn't get up, but he could roll. He rolled, acting on a split-second reflex that caught even Tauncer by surprise. The projector was only four or five feet away. Brix and the other men were on top of him again almost at once but not quite in time. He fetched the tripod a thrashing kick, with both his feet bound together. It fell over. He could not hope that it was broken, not on this soft carpeted floor, but it would take them time to set it up again.

He tried to keep them busy as long as he could, but Tauncer understood perfectly well what he was up to. He pulled his men off and set Brix to adjusting the projector again, and turned to Kirk.

"You may as well spare yourself, Commander. I have my mission, and the military have theirs. There are three cruisers standing off and on, just out of radar range—they got word the moment you landed, and they're already on their way."

He smiled briefly. "The price you pay for fame, Commander. The Fifth is Ferdias' elite squadron, and nobody gets command of it unless he's in Ferdias' special favor."

"Friendship is one thing," said Kirk hotly, "and favor is another. I don't like your choice of words."

He was just talking, words, sounds with no meaning. Inside he was thinking of Garstang and the *Starsong*, and all the lives of all the men in her. He had led them here.

He looked at Tauncer, and he began now to hate him, with a hate as deep and cold as space.

"Ferdias will tear your heart out," he said.

"Perhaps," said Tauncer. "But he may have other things to occupy his mind."

"Earth? He's never been there. None of us have. It's only a name, and a half-forgotten one at that. Why should Earth occupy his mind? Why, Tauncer?"

How long is twenty minutes? How long does it take three cruisers to come from Point X beyond radar range to Target Zero? How long does it take a man to realize he's through at last?

Brix said again, "All ready."

Tauncer nodded.

Brix touched a stud on the projector.

As though that touch had done it, a dull and mighty roaring echoed from the desert—the full-throated cry of a heavy cruiser taking off.

The men looked, startled, toward the door. Desperately, Kirk rolled sideways, out of the force that was already battering at the edges of his mind.

"You out there!" he shouted at the doorway. "The men from outside avenge treachery! Call your lord—"

One of Tauncer's men kicked him alongside the jaw. Kirk shut up, hanging with blind determination to his consciousness. Fore-thought had provided this one chance. He would not get another. He did not dare to miss it.

The cruiser came low over the town. Dust sifted out of the cracks of the stone walls. The men fell to their knees, covering their heads with their arms. The floor rocked under them, beaten by the rolling hammers of concussion.

The ripped sky closed upon itself with a stunning, thundering crash. After a minute or two the noise and the shock wave ebbed away.

Silence.

The men began to get up again. But Kirk did not move.

The cruiser came back. This time it was even lower. Garstang must have tickled her belly on the peaked roofs. Christ, thought Kirk, he's overdoing it. This time the stones were shaking loose. When it was over, a long thin shape came in through the doorway. It was the leader of the tall men who had brought Kirk here.

His face was a mask of fear and rage as he spoke to Tauncer. "You said that if we helped you, you would keep all other outsiders away!"

"We will," said Tauncer. "Listen—"

"Yes, listen," mocked Kirk. "Listen to it coming back. It'll keep coming back, unless I walk out of here—until your town is flattened."

The tall man stood hesitating. Then the *Starsong* roared back over. When it was gone, he picked himself up and with a knife cut the cords around Kirk's wrists and ankles.

"Oh, no," said Tauncer, starting forward. "You can't—"

The tall man turned on him a face livid with frustrated anger. "Shall the children of cluster-kings be destroyed to serve *you*? Shall I call my people in?"

Kirk, scrambling to his feet, saw outside the door the crowd of tall, pale-cloaked men who had gathered. Tauncer saw them too, and stopped.

As Kirk picked up the porto and started for the door, the man Brix cried violently, "Are we just going to stand here?"

Tauncer said levelly, "Why, yes, there are times when you do just that. But I think we'll see the Commander again."

Kirk went out through the door and through the crowd outside it. No one followed him. He got the porto working and talked fast to Garstang, then dropped the porto and sprinted out of the town toward the desert.

The cruiser dropped down ahead of him, as black and big against the stars as a falling world. The lock yawned open, and Garstang was inside it to meet him. He started to ask what had happened, but Kirk pushed him bodily away down the corridor, heading for the bridge.

"Get in there and do your stuff, Joe. We've got three Orion cruisers on our tail, as of the time we landed."

At that moment they heard the voice of the radarman crying out in sudden anguish, "Sir!"

Garstang said in mild reproval, "You ought to give a man more time, Commander. Radar, what's the bearing? All right, stand by—"

Orders crackled over the intercoms. Men moved swiftly at the control-banks. The last thing Kirk heard before the howling roar of take-off drowned everything was Garstang complaining that this sort of thing was hard on a ship. Then there was a dull crash from somewhere outside. The *Starsong* was shaken as though by a great wind. Both Kirk and Garstang had weathered enough fire to know that she had taken no hurt. But the Orion cruisers were in range now, bearing down on them in normal space at planetary speeds. The next shell would likely be a good deal closer. They dared not wait for star-room to go into overdrive.

"Hit it!" yelled Kirk. Garstang threw the relays open. Sirens shrilled and the lights went dim. The *Starsong* shuddered vertiginously.

And then they were in overdrive and racing out toward the twin red suns that guarded the entrance to the Dragon's Throat.

The scanners and ultra-speed radar came into play, replacing normal instruments, making an illusion of sight. And the voice of the radarman said dismally,

"They're still with us, sir. F-Type cruisers, heavy-armed and plenty fast."

For the next quarter of an hour the *Starsong* gained velocity at a suicidal rate, but the Orion cruisers would not be left behind. The radarman called their coordinates in a steady sing-song and Garstang ordered more power and more power, keeping one eye on the stress indicators and the other on the overhanging star-cliffs of the Throat that seemed to be leaping toward the ship.

There was a limit. You could not take the Throat too fast. In that swarm of suns a ship's fabric could be torn apart in some swift tide of gravity, or vaporized in collision. Garstang had already passed the limit. But the Orionids were refusing to be bluffed.

Kirk said nothing. This was Garstang's job, and he let him do it. But he watched the indicators as closely as the captain. Under his feet and all around him he could feel the *Starsong* quiver, wincing and flinching like a live thing now and again as some wild current wrenched at her. His gaze flicked upward to the nebula, like a fiery thundercloud above the Dragon's Throat, and then to the shoaling suns below, with the narrow pass between them. The twin red stars of the binary flashed by and were gone.

Suddenly, in the screen that mirrored space astern, a tiny nova flared and winked away. The *Starsong* trembled, like a running deer that hears the hunter's gun.

"Wide astern," said Garstang. He looked at the cleft of the Throat and shook his head. "But we'll have to slow down for that, and they know it. They'll have time to range us before they come in themselves. They won't," he added grimly, "have to come in."

Kirk nodded. "So we'll fool them. We won't go into the Throat either."

Garstang stood silent for a moment. Then he said, "I was hoping you wouldn't think of that."

"Have you a better idea? Or even a worse one?"

"No." Garstang took a deep breath and spoke into the communicator. "New course, north and zenith, forty degrees. We're running the nebula. On full autopilot. If anyone wants to pray, go ahead."

The *Starsong* shot upward, plunging high into an area so choked with stellar radiance that it made the Dragon's Throat seem like empty space. The manual control-banks were dark and dead. From the calc-room back of the bridge a new sound came, different from the normal occasional outbursts of chattering. This was a steady sound, a sound of authority, the voice of the *Starsong* speaking. She was flying herself now. The men aboard, Captain and Commander, able spaceman and ensign, were her charges, dependent on her wisdom and her radar vision and her strength. There was nothing they could do but wait.

The *Starsong* spiralled higher, her radar system guiding her on a twisting path between the clotted stars. Then Kirk saw a great glowing edge slide onto the screen and grow into a vastness of dust and cosmic drift illumined by the half-smothered stars it webbed.

The Orionid cruisers had altered course and were coming after them. But the *Starsong* was already skimming through glowing arms that reached like misty tentacles searching for other stars to trap and feed upon. Once in the cloud, she would be screened from the cruiser's radar beams by the most effective scrambling device in space, the nebula itself.

Effective. Yes. But potentially as deadly as Orionid warheads. The only difference was that with the nebula you had a chance. Against three cruisers you had none.

Kirk strapped himself into the recoil chair beside Garstang. Nothing moved now within the ship. The frail, breakable organism of breath and heart and bone were encased in protective webs. This was the hour of the ship, the hour of steel and flame and the racing electron, faster than thought.

The *Starsong* spoke to herself in the calc-room, and plunged headlong into the cloud.

CHAPTER 3

The universe was swallowed up in golden light, in racing, streaming tides of luminous dust. Like an undersea ship of old the *Starsong* raced with the gleaming currents and burst through denser, darker deeps where the stars were faint and far away, to leap once more into a glory of wild light where the drowned suns burned like torches in a mist. And the voice in the calc-room rose to an unhuman crying as the computers strained to take in the overwhelming surge of data from defensive radar, analyze it, and send imperative commands to the control-relays.

It had almost a sound of insane music in it, that voice, and the *Starsong* danced to it, whirling and swaying between the fragments of the drift that threatened her with instant destruction if she faltered for a fraction of a second. Kirk, half-dazed, clung to his padded chair and gasped for breath, and felt, and listened.

The same illusion gripped him now that had mastered him before when forced to run a cloud—the feeling that the suns and star-worlds were all gone, that he was enwrapped in the primal fire-mists of creation. Mighty tides seemed to bear the ship forward, everything was a boil and whirl of light, millrace currents seemed to rush them endlessly through infinity, with all space and time cancelled out. He wondered briefly, once, how the Orionids were doing, and then forgot them. The agony, the intoxication, the godlike joy and the terror were far too great to admit any petty worries about anything human.

Then, with almost shocking abruptness, they broke into clear space, and the cloud was behind them. Like men enchanted waking from a dream, Kirk and Garstang shook themselves and stood erect again, and the voice of the *Starsong* was stilled, and human voices spoke once more.

And human problems were still with them. Somewhat farther astern now, but still doggedly following, three tiny flecks of darkness came after them out of the cloud.

Kirk went into the com-room and made contact with his squadron far ahead. He gave crisp orders, and then rejoined Garstang on the bridge.

"Larned's on his way," he said. "Can you keep clear?"

"I can," said Garstang, and ordered full power. He had nothing between him and the Pleiades now but light-years of elbow room, and he took full advantage of it. The Orion cruisers apparently had intercepted Kirk's message, and made a frantic last attempt to overhaul him.

When that proved impossible, and their trial shots fell so far short that it was obvious the range could not be made before the *Starsong* reached the point of convergence with the squadron, they turned tail and ran back for the cluster. When the squadron did arrive, space was empty of everything but themselves and the distant stars.

The hard, excited voice of Larned, Kirk's Vice-Commander, came rapidly as they joined the squadron.

"So there *is* an Orionid base in there! By God, we'll soon—"

"No," Kirk cut in. "There was no base in there. There was a trap, for me—only I still don't know just why they set it."

He went to the com-room and set up a message on the coding machine. Top secret, to Ferdias at Vega, briefly detailing his encounter with Tauncer.

"—am unable to explain interest in Earth, and your plans concerning. Suggest attempt to distract from some other objective? Await instructions. Kirk."

In a remarkably short time the answer came back.

"Report Vega at once with full squadron." And it added, "Unfortunately, no distraction. Ferdias."

Looking at the cryptic tape, Kirk had an uneasy feeling that he had all unknowingly stepped over one of those thresholds into a new phase of existence, where nothing was going to be quite the same as it had been ever again. He had once more that premonition that the pace, the tempo of the great game for suns, was about to step up still faster.

He said nothing of that to Garstang or the others. To them, the unexpected recall to home base meant an unlooked-for leave. And to him, it would mean returning to Lyllin sooner than he had hoped. But even that could not quite banish his uneasiness.

The squadron wheeled in tight formation and set its course toward the great blue-white sun that burned in Lyra, capital of a mighty Sector that was in everything but name an empire of stars.

When they made their world-fall, when the squadron swept down through the bluish glare over Vega Town and landed on the spaceport, Larned came at once from his own ship. The Vice-Commander, a blocky, brusque and competent young man, bristled with questions.

"What the devil is all this about, Kirk? Pulling us in like this—"

"I haven't an idea," Kirk said. "But I'm about to find out. Call Lyllin for me and tell her I'll be along soon."

An air-car with a uniformed driver took him across the great city. It was really two cities. The older city of graceful white towers had been built long ago by the native Vegans, Lyllin's people. But then, more than a century ago, the starships had come to Vega, the first wave of explorers and colonizers from the inner galaxy. They had not been all Earthmen, even though that wave had first started from Earth. By the time they reached here, Earthmen had already mixed and mated with many other human star-folk. It was these newcomers who had built the new part of Vega Town.

It was to the newer city that the air-car took him, to the looming, dominating mass of Government house. A lift took him down from the roof, and he went through the corridors, a tall man with a faintly worried look on his copper-bronzed face. Efficient secretaries shunted him smoothly and quickly into a room few people ever entered.

It seemed a small room, to be the center of government of so many stars. For this was the center—the Sectors each had their elected legislatures but it was the Governors who wielded the power.

"Stop saluting, Kirk," said Ferdias. "You know you're at ease when you step in here."

Ferdias came around the desk. He limped, from the crash of a Class Twenty long ago. But you never remembered his limp, or how small a man he was. You saw only his face, and when you saw it you knew why, at the age of forty, he was one of the five great Governors.

"Now let's have it," he said.

Kirk let him have it, the full story of the trap in the cluster. And Ferdias' face got just a trifle longer.

He said, finally, "You had no business going in alone. But since you got out, I'm glad you did it. For I'm sure now of what I only suspected before. In his eagerness to find out how much I know, Solleremos has told me what I *wanted* to know."

Kirk, frankly puzzled, said, "I just don't get it. What is Ferdias planning to do about Earth? What plans *would* you have about it?"

Ferdias limped back to his chair, and sat down, and then looked up keenly. "Kirk, you're at least half Earth blood. Tell me, how do you feel about Earth?"

Kirk said, "But I've never been there. You know that—I was born in a transport off Arcturus, and have never been farther back in than Procyon."

"I know. But what do you think about Earth?"

Kirk made a gesture. "What's there to think about? It's a third-rate planet, from what I hear, important only because star-flight began there. Its Galactic Council tried to hold all the galaxy together in one government, but of course that proved impossible. Hell, it's hard enough to hold a Sector together, let alone the whole galaxy."

"But Earth isn't any of the Sectors, of course," said Ferdias.

Kirk looked at him keenly. "Of course not. Sector Governors don't touch Earth's small federal district...." He stopped. He said, after a moment, "Or do they? Do they, Ferdias?"

"Solleremos would like to," said Ferdias.

Kirk was astonished. "You mean, he wants to take *Earth* into Orion Sector?"

"He wants to very much indeed," said the other. "Listen, Kirk. Solleremos' pressure on our borders lately has been only cover-up. It's Earth he's after."

"But *why*? That unimportant little star system—"

"Is it so unimportant?" Ferdias' blue eyes, hot and flaring now, fascinated Kirk. "Materially, maybe it is—a worn-out, third-rate world. But psychologically, it's a very important world indeed. Think of the Earth blood mingled in all the galaxy races now—in you and in me, in half the civilized peoples! Think of the feelings they have, perhaps without altogether realizing it, toward that old planet they've never seen! They know it no longer directs things, they know its Council and Navy are a shadowy sham—but still it's Earth, it's the old center of things, the old heart-world. Suppose one of the other Governors gets Earth into his Sector, and speaks from it thereafter?"

Kirk saw it now. He realized, not for the first time, that when it came to galactic intrigue he was a babe in arms.

It *would* give any of the rival Governors a colossal psychological advantage, to make the old center of the galaxy his seat of government. Commands that came from Earth would have a psychological potency hard to withstand.

"But you're not going to let Solleremos get away with it?" he exclaimed.

"No Kirk. *I* don't want Earth. But I'm not going to let Orion Sector grab it, either!"

He went on. "Solleremos knows I'll try to stop him. That's why he had Tauncer, his right-hand man, set that little trap for you. They know I trust you. They hoped I'd have told you how I plan to block them."

Kirk looked at him, and then said, "How *are* you going to stop them?"

Ferdias said, "There's a big celebration coming up on Earth soon. The two-hundredth anniversary of the first space-flight from Earth. It means a lot to them. Their Council invited me to send an official delegation to represent Lyra Sector. So I'm sending you."

Kirk stared. "Me—to Earth? But what can *I* do if—"

Ferdias interrupted. "The Fifth Squadron will go with you. To take part in the commemoration pageant, the fly-over."

Now Kirk began to understand. "Then if Solleremos tries anything, the Fifth will be there waiting for him?"

"Exactly." Ferdias spoke the word like a wolf-snap. "I know Solleremos' intentions. I know about when he plans his grab for Earth. Earth can't stop him, not with their small forces. But the Fifth can!"

Kirk felt a bit stunned. Fighting the hidden border wars of the rival Governors was one thing. But a full-fledged struggle between Sectors, back there at old Earth, was quite another. It could rock the galaxy....

Ferdias went on matter-of-factly, "You'll take off five days from now. You may be there a while, so you'll take full supply auxiliaries and transports."

Kirk looked up. Transports meant the families of all personnel would accompany the squadron—and that meant Lyllin would go with him. He was glad of that.

"But when we get there," he said. "Besides taking part in that celebration, what do we *do*?"

Ferdias said, "Go and look up your ancestral home."

"My—what?"

"Ancestral home. Place where the Kirks came from, on Earth. I had it hunted out, and it's still standing. It's in Orville, a place near the city New York. You go and look it up first thing."

Kirk began to get it. "You'll send me orders there?"

"You'll hear from me. And you'll get warning if Solleremos moves on Earth. But Kirk—one more thing."

"Yes?"

"You're not to talk of this to anyone. *Anyone.*"

Kirk, as the air-car took him homeward across the city, hardly saw the brilliant Vegan capital flashing by beneath. He was badly worried. A deadly, secret galactic struggle was moving toward crisis, and he was not the man to combat conspiracies, he was no good at plots and plans. But— and his jaw set hard—if Solleremos *did* try to grab Earth by force, there was one thing the Fifth was very good at, and that was fighting.

He couldn't tell Lyllin about any of this, not against Ferdias' strict injunction. But at least she would be going with him this time, and that would be good news to her. He strode eagerly into the metalloy cottage that was home to him. Its familiar rooms were cool and silent. He found Lyllin waiting for him on the terrace.

The blue sun was touching the hills, and the sky was flooded with a purple dusk. Lyllin came toward him. She was all Vegan and looked it, her flesh showed pale as new gold, with the darker masses of her hair picking up the same tint and turning it to copper. She was dressed in the fashion of her own people, in a chiton so mistily transparent that her fine slender body seemed to be draped in a bit of the oncoming dusk itself.

He held her, and then told her his news, and was surprised that it did not seem to make her happy. "To Earth?" she murmured. "Just for the space-flight anniversary? It's strange——"

"But this time you'll be with me," he said. "Not on the voyage—you'll ride transport, of course—but on Earth, all the time I'm there."

"How long will that be, Kirk?"

He didn't know, and said so. Lyllin's face shadowed subtly. But she had a way of silence, and it was not until later that night that she spoke of it.

She said, suddenly, "I shall hate it at Earth."

Kirk was shocked. "But why in the world? That's ridiculous. A place you've never seen, and hardly know about——"

"It's your place, your people. Not mine." She was not looking at him. "You'll be going home. But what will they think of me there? What will *you* think of me there, among your own people?"

Kirk turned her around with rough and angry hands. "I'm ashamed of you. If you could even think a thing like that——" He shook her. "Listen to me. Earth is no more to me than it is to you. It's a name, a place where my grandfather five times removed happened to be born. I've as much blood of other worlds in me as Earth blood. And as for you——"

Her eyes had tears in the corners of them, now. Her mouth was soft and uncertain, like a child's. He said, in a different tone, "No matter where we go, you'll be Lyllin. And I'll love you."

She came close in the circle of his arms, and she kissed him with a wild possessiveness. And her lips were bitter with those sudden tears.

But Kirk felt that she was not convinced. She had the Vegan pride, and if they treated her at Earth like a freak, an alien....

In the depth of his soul, he cursed Solleremos and his ambitious schemes. For the worry that was in him had deepened. The danger that the Fifth was going into, the danger that would explode if that unscrupulous grab for the old planet was attempted, was not the only one. He felt now that beside that there was another, subtler danger waiting for Lyllin and himself at Earth.

CHAPTER 4

The squadron was out of overdrive, cruising at normal approach velocity. There was a sun ahead in space. Compared to the blazing giants of deep space, it was not much, merely a small yellow star looking rather lonely in the midst of a great emptiness. Kirk studied it. The Sun. Not just any sun, *the* Sun. How should he feel about it? Like a child seeing its father for the first time, or like a man returning to an ancient hearth that has long ago lost any meaning for him? Kirk searched his heart, and nothing came. It was only another star.

Garstang touched his arm and pointed, to where far off a little green planet swung to meet them.

"Earth."

The squadron rushed toward it, the cruisers and supply-ships and transports, the men and women and children, strangers from the far reaches of the galaxy. And yet not quite strangers either, for the names that had come from this world were still among them, and the traditions, and even some of the blood. Two hundred years ago, their forefathers had left it. And now they were coming back.

A quiet had settled on the bridge. Kirk supposed it was the same with the whole squadron, everybody staring and thinking his or her own thoughts. He wondered what Lyllin was thinking, and wished she were with him instead of back there in one of the transports.

Earth came closer. He could see clouds, and the white splash of a polar cap. Closer still, and there were seas, and the outlines of continents. Colors began to show more clearly, and the land became ridged with mountain chains. Great lakes took form, and dark-green areas of forest, and winding rivers. A nice world. A pretty world. Kirk hated it. Its other name was Trouble.

"Why did Ferdias have to pick *us* for this job?"

Unconsciously he had spoken aloud, or loud enough for Garstang to hear. "It's only for a visit," said Garstang. "Just a celebration. What's wrong with that?" His tone was mild, without mockery.

But Kirk looked at him sharply. He knew that Garstang and Larned and all his other officers and men must have been talking and wondering. Wondering why they'd been pulled out of their needful place for this rather meaningless celebration.

They came down past the shoreline of a blue-green ocean, past a city that sprawled over islands and peninsulas and up inland river valleys, and then beneath them was a big spaceport. The squadron roared in to its appointed landing, bristling on its best behavior, every ship set down with masterly precision, and there was a crowd assembled there to meet it. Flags whipped in the wind. The brassy music of a band blared out, immensely stirring with a solemn throb of drums beneath it.

The men of the Fifth debarked and formed in marching order, every boot polished and every uniform immaculate, a solid line of blue and silver glittering in the soft blaze of this golden sun. Kirk felt the heat of it in his face. His heels struck solidly on the ground, and the wind touched him, balmily, laden with fragrances strange to him. And he thought, "This is Earth." He looked around at it.

He could see only the spaceport, and that was old and worn and poor. The tarmac was cracked and blackened, the ancient buildings weathered. Opposite the squadron were drawn up twelve cruisers with the old insigne of the Galactic Navy on their bows, and with their crews standing at attention in front of them. Those old, small ships—why, they were Class Fourteens, obsolete for years! He supposed they were all Earth had.

Two men walked toward him. One was a middle-aged civilian, the other an arrow-straight, elderly man in black uniform that also bore the old Navy insigne. He stiffly returned Kirk's salute.

"Nice landing, Commander," he said. "I'm First Admiral Laney, and I welcome your squadron."

Incredulously, Kirk realized that the old admiral was keeping up the pretense that the Fifth Squadron was still part of the Navy.

It was so preposterous it was funny! Not for a century had the old Galactic Navy had any real existence. Its staff never sent any orders out to the squadrons of the five Governors, any more than Central Council dared send orders to the Governors themselves. Yet this old Earth officer was trying hard, in front of the crowd, to act as though he really were Kirk's superior officer....

Then, seeing the faintly desperate look in Laney's eyes, Kirk softened. After all, what difference did it make—it was only a pretense and he felt sorry for the old chap trying to play this part.

He saluted again and said, "Fifth Squadron, Kirk commanding, reporting for orders, sir!"

A look of grateful relief crossed Laney's face. He said uncertainly, "At ease, Commander. Let me present Council Chairman John Charteris."

Charteris, a graying, eager, anxious man, shook hands warmly. He began a little speech, into the tele-cameras close by. "We welcome back one of the gallant squadrons of the Galactic Navy to take part in our commemoration of—"

When the speeches and handshaking and bandplaying were over, Kirk gave an order, and his men broke ranks. Larned came up to him.

"Shall we debark our people now?"

The old admiral told Kirk, "Quarters are all ready for them."

Charteris said, "But you and your wife, Commander, must be my guests."

They walked back between the lofty, looming ships. The women and children and babies of the men of the Fifth started coming out of the transports, and efficient Earth officers began smoothly shuttling them into cars to take them to their quarters. From around the fences, a big crowd of Earth folk watched interestedly.

Of a sudden, for the first time his men's families seemed a little outlandish to Kirk. The women and children were of so many different star-peoples, so many different ways of speech and dress. He looked resentfully for amusement in the Earth faces, but could not detect any.

At the transport he excused himself and went in to Lyllin's cabin. He stopped short when he saw her. He had never seen her like this. She wore an Earth-style dress of impeccable lines, was perfect in a smart, sophisticated way. She still didn't look like an Earthwoman, not with that skin and eyes and hair. But she looked stunning, and he said so.

"I'm glad I look civilized enough for your people," Lyllin said sweetly.

"My people?" Kirk drew back stiffly. "So you're still brooding on that? That's fine. I'm not in a tough enough spot here, my wife has to get super-sensitive and make it tougher."

Lyllin's expression changed. "What kind of spot?" He was silent. She looked at him steadily. "It's something dangerous, isn't it?"

"I'd have told you if it were something I could tell you," he said. "You know that. Will you forget it? And forget about these people being *my* people!"

He went out with her, and Lyllin went through the introductions, cool and proud. Kirk told Larned aside, "Two-day leaves for all personnel in regular rotation. Port facilities will take care of refitting and fueling."

Larned grunted. "I've seen better facilities on fifth-rate planets. Plenty old! But we'll make out."

Charteris' car swept them along a broad highway to New York. It had a stiff, strange look to Kirk, its vertical towers huddled together bold and black against the setting sun. He thought it a cramped and crowded place, though Charteris' terrace apartment high above the myriad lights was pleasant.

There was a dinner there that night, and drinks, and more speeches, and much talk about the Commemoration. Sector politics were unobtrusively avoided. Kirk fretted and worried through it all. What was Solleremos doing, where were his squadrons? Ferdias had said he'd get warning if they moved, but would that warning come in time?

In the morning, he found Charteris oddly changed. He looked at Kirk with a queerly doubtful expression.

Kirk said, "Before we make arrangements about the Commemoration, I—"

"Oh, there's no hurry about that," Charteris said hastily. Then suddenly he asked, "Do you know if Orion Sector will send a token squadron too?"

Alarm rang a bell in Kirk's brain instantly. What was behind the question? Had Charteris heard something that he hadn't?

He answered, "Why, no, I don't. But surely you would know—"

Charteris continued to eye him with that dubious expression as he said, "We sent an invitation to Governor Solleremos to take part, of course. But doubtless we'll soon hear from him."

Kirk thought swiftly, he *has* heard something—something that he doesn't want me to know! But what? Was Orion already moving, were Orionid forces coming to Earth on the excuse of the celebration, just as he had?

He'd get no information from Charteris. He'd better contact Ferdias, as quickly as possible. He was only a naval commander, and he felt an enormous desire for definite orders in this crisis. He could only get such orders at the rendezvous Ferdias had told him to go to.

Kirk said casually, "While I'm here on Earth I want to look up my ancestors' old home here, and now would be a good time. It's in a village not too far away, I understand. If we could borrow a ground-car—"

Charteris seemed glad to comply. "Of course. A sentimental pilgrimage, in a way? Very understandable—"

Kirk refused the offer of a driver. But by the time he and Lyllin got out of New York and were rolling northward, he almost regretted that decision. It seemed ridiculous for a man who could pilot a squadron half across the galaxy in full overdrive, but the traffic frightened him. He hadn't done much driving, and certainly none on highways like this big northern boulevard. On this crowded Earth, people apparently still used ground-cars in great numbers for short distances, and it was not until they branched off on a subsidiary highway that Kirk felt easy.

He said then, "I want to explain about this ancestral home business."

Lyllin, looking straight ahead, said, "You don't have to explain. It's perfectly natural that you should want to see where your people came from."

"Will you stop behaving like a woman and listen?" he said angrily. "*My* people, again. What the devil would I care where my seventh great-grandfather lived. I'm doing what Ferdias ordered." He added, "I wasn't supposed to tell you even that, but I couldn't very well go off on this supposed sentimental pilgrimage without you."

Lyllin's expression changed. "Then there'll be someone from Ferdias to meet you there secretly, is that it? And I'm not to know about what?"

"That's it," he said. "Ferdias' orders were not to tell anyone."

He thought that Lyllin looked somehow relieved. "I don't mind. I'm worried, I wish I knew, but it's all right if you can't tell me."

It came to him that she was relieved to learn he didn't really care about his Earth ancestors, that that had only been an excuse.

Kirk felt a sharp relief himself, to be on his way to Orville, to the old house there where Ferdias' agent would be waiting to tell him what to do. In this gathering crisis he couldn't act blindly! It was vital to get directive information as soon as possible.

They turned off the big boulevard onto quiet, tree-lined back roads. These roads were old and rambling, accomodatingly twisting around hills and ponds and even houses. Some of the houses were modern chromaloy villas, but there were antique stone houses also, and once he and Lyllin both exclaimed when they saw a very old house that was built all of wood.

Out here away from the city, everything looked ancient. Stone fences that had the moss of centuries on them, a steepled church mantled thick with ivy, worn fields that had been tilled for ages. In the fields, driverless automatic tractors were lumbering about their work, but there seemed little bustle or activity. Kirk thought that this was an old, worn world....

A brilliant bird flashed across the road and he and Lyllin argued what it was. "A robin, I think," Kirk said doubtfully. "In school, when I was little, we had an old Earth poem about Robin Redbreast. I didn't know then what it was."

"Not nearly so splendid as a flame-bird," Lyllin said. "But the red of it, and the green trees, and the blue sky.... It's a pretty world, in its way."

They rolled finally down a little hill and over a bridged stream into the town of Orville. It was only a village, with shops around a big open square. There was a corroded statue of a soldier at the center of the park, and benches on which old men sat in the sun.

Kirk asked directions of a merchant standing in front of his shop, a chubby man who stared open-mouthed at the two visitors. And Kirk suddenly realized how strange indeed they must look in this sleepy little Earth village—he in his blue-and-silver starman's uniform, his face dark from foreign suns, and Lyllin whose beauty was a breath of the alien.

He was glad to drive on out of the village, on the designated road. It was an even more rambling road, looping casually along the side of a shallow valley whose neat farms and fields and woods lay silent in the blaze of the soft golden sun. They met no other ground-cars, though an occasional air-car hummed across the blue sky. Kirk kept counting houses, and when he had counted five he turned in at a lane, and stopped.

The house was of field-stone, an ancient, brown dumpy structure that had a faintly forlorn, deserted look. Under the big, stiff, dark-green trees in its front yard—were they the trees called "pines?"—the grass was high and ragged. The lane went on past the house, past an orchard of gnarled trees heavy with green fruit, to a big old barn. There was no one in sight, and no sign that anyone was here.

"Are you sure it's the place?" asked Lyllin.

He nodded, moving toward the porch. "It's the place. Ferdias had his agent here buy it, weeks ago, so we'd have this quiet place for contacts. There should be someone here."

There was a bell-push at the door, but no one answered it. Kirk tried the door. It swung open, and they went in.

They went into a room such as they had never seen before. The walls were of painted wood, instead of plastic. The furniture was wooden too, and of archaic design. The room, the house, were very silent.

"Look at this," said Lyllin, in tones of surprise.

She was touching a chair, and the chair rocked back and forth on its bottom. "I thought it was a child's toy but it's not made for a child."

He shook his head. "Beyond me. And it's beyond me too why Ferdias' man isn't here!"

He called, but there was no answer. He went through all the rooms, and there was no one.

Kirk felt a mounting alarm. Had something gone wrong with Ferdias' careful plans? Where was Ferdias' agent, where was the man who should have met him in this secret rendezvous with the information and orders he must have?

Suppose that man didn't come—who then could give him warning of Solleremos' strike, if Orion *did* strike?

CHAPTER 5

Kirk stood, his dismay and anxiety increasing by the minute. What was he going to do?

He said, finally, "We'll have to wait. Ferdias' man is bound to be along soon."

"You mean—perhaps stay here all night?" said Lyllin. "But food, and beds—"

"We'd better look around," he said unhappily.

They found fairly new blankets on the beds. And in the old kitchen cupboards was food in the self-heating plastipacks.

"We can make out," he said. "But it's a hell of a thing."

While Lyllin prepared their supper, he went out and restlessly walked around the place. The weedy yard ran into brushy fields and nearby woods. The old barn was empty, and the outbuildings were shabby and forlorn.

He did not think much of Earth, if this was a sample. He went back inside, and helped Lyllin solve the puzzle of an ancient sink. Even the reddening sunset light pouring through the windows could not make the old wooden walls and worn cupboards look less dingy.

He said so, and Lyllin smiled. "It's not so bad. We'll eat out on that back porch—it's less musty there."

The porch was not screened, and friendly insects dropped in upon them as they ate. The whole western sky was a flare of red, great bastions of crimson cloud building ever higher. Under the sunset, beyond the fields, the ragged woods brooded darkly.

A small animal came soundlessly out of the high grass and stared at them with greenish eyes.

"What is it, Kirk—a wild creature?"

He looked. "It's a cat, that's what it is. An Earthman in the *Stardream* had one for a pet, kept it at Base. He called it Tom." He tossed a bit of food onto the step. "Here, Tom."

The cat stalked carefully forward, eyed them coldly, then bent to the food. After a moment it turned its back on them and departed.

Darkness fell. Kirk began to feel a little desperation. Ferdias' man hadn't come. What if he didn't come at all? How long could they wait in this forgotten backwater, not knowing what was going on out there in deep space?

Lyllin said, "Isn't it possible your man is waiting in Orville, that village—and doesn't know you're here?"

"It could be, I suppose." Kirk grasped at the straw. "I'll go down to the village. If he's there, he'll see me. Mind waiting—just in case someone does come here?"

She said she didn't mind. But he took the compact shocker from his coat-pocket and left it for her before he went out.

Kirk drove rapidly down the lonely, dark road to the village. But the little town looked dark and lonely too, when he got there. The shops were almost all closed. He saw only a few people. It was very quiet. In the shadows of the square, the old iron soldier stood stiffly.

The lights of a tavern caught Kirk's eye, and he went toward it. It seemed about the only place where his man might be, and he needed a drink anyway. He shouldered in, and instantly a small buzz of talk fell silent. Kirk went to the bar, and the men at the farther end of it followed him with their eyes. The tavern-keeper, a bustling, skinny man, hurried up and tried to act as though a deep-space naval Commander was no unusual visitor at all.

"Yes, sir, what'll it be?"

Kirk's eyes searched the rack of unfamiliar bottles. He shook his head. "You pick it. Something strong and short."

"Yes, sir, some fine old whisky right here." Whisky—well, he'd heard of that. He drank it, and didn't like it. He let his eyes rest on the other man. Could one of them be Ferdias' agent?

He didn't think so. Most of these men looked like farmers or mechanics, hearty-looking, sunburned men, the younger ones tall and gangling. One was a very old man with a straggling beard who shamelessly stared at Kirk with bright, beady eyes. They weren't unfriendly, but they were aloof. Kirk had an idea he'd get little out of this insular bunch. He might as well go— none of these could be Ferdias' man.

But as he set his glass down, the bearded old man limped forward, peering bright-eyed and inquisitive at him.

"You're the fellow who was asking directions to the old Kirk place today," he said, almost accusingly.

Kirk nodded. "That's right."

The old Earthman was obviously waiting for an explanation. It occurred to Kirk that he'd better give one, if he didn't want this whole countryside wondering audibly why a starman had come here.

He said, "Kirk's my name. My great-great something grandfather, a long time ago, came from here. I'm just looking up the old place, that's all."

He turned to go then, feeling that he was wasting time here. But one of the middle-aged Earthmen came forward to him with hand outstretched.

"Why, if your folks came from here, that makes you sort of an Orville boy, doesn't it? What do you know about that! Vinson's my name, Captain."

"Commander," Kirk corrected, as he shook hands. "Glad to know you. I guess I'll be on my way."

"Say, now, not without me buying you a drink," boomed Vinson. "Not every day one of our own boys comes back from way out there."

There was a chorus of agreement, and more outstretched hands, and hearty introductions. Kirk stared at them in wonder. What in the world— Then he got it.

All over space, the pride of Earthmen was proverbial, and their clannishness. He'd met it and he didn't like it. He was therefore all the more astonished now, that they should suddenly accept him as one of their own. Seven generations, and the whole width of the galaxy between him and this place, yet they claimed him as "one of our own boys"!

He wanted to get out now, he'd found no trace of Ferdias' agent here and time was passing, but it wasn't easy to get out. More men kept coming into the tavern, as word got around, to shake hands with and buy a drink for the "Orville boy" from far-off space. Vinson, a jovial master of ceremonies, rattled on with introductions Kirk only half-heard—"Jim Barnes, whose farm's up beyond your folks' old place", "here's old Pete Marly, he can remember when there were still Kirks living there," on and on until in desperation, Kirk thanked them and shouldered toward the door.

"Have to go, my wife's waiting," he said, and a friendly chorus of voices bade him good-night, "I'll ride with you far as my own house," said Vinson.

Kirk was sweating as he drove out of the village. A hell of a way to conduct a secret job, with the whole village bawling his name! And it had got him nowhere—

Vinson's house was the second on the same road. As he got out of the car, he said, "Sure does beat all, your coming back from so far. Shows it's a small world."

"It's a small galaxy," Kirk said, and Vinson nodded. "Sure is. Well, I'll be seeing you. Drop over. Good-night."

As Kirk drove on, he was faintly startled by an upgush of yellow light that silhouetted the bending trees ahead. A great segment of silver was rising in the sky. Then he realized—it was that moon that they'd passed on their way in.

The moon of Earth, the "Moon" of the old Earth poems people still read. Not too impressive, but pretty. But how the threads of all you'd read and heard kept subtly running back to this old planet! He supposed some of these flowers whose fragrance he could smell on the warm night air were "roses". Funny, how much you knew about Earth that you didn't realize you knew.

The old road gleamed beneath the rising moon. He glanced up at the star-pricked sky. Had the Kirk who was his seventh grandfather, all those years ago, looked at the starry sky as he walked this same road? He must have. He'd looked too long, and finally he'd gone out to that sky and not come back.

The house was dark when he turned in at the lane, but he saw Lyllin's dim figure sitting on the front porch.

"No. No one came," she said, as he sat down beside her.

"And no sign of any agent of Ferdias in the village," Kirk said. "A fine thing. We'll have to wait."

They sat a while in the soft warm darkness. Kirk's thoughts were more and more gloomy. They couldn't wait here forever, yet he had to make contact as Ferdias had ordered—

Strange, glowing little sparks of light drifted across his vision, and now he became aware that the whole dark yard and woods were swarming with such floating sparks. They winked on and off, in a fashion he had never seen, dancing and whirling under the dark trees.

"What are they?" asked Lyllin, fascinated.

"Fireflies?" Kirk said doubtfully. "I remember that word, from somewhere...."

Then he suddenly started and exclaimed, "Hell, what—"

A small sinuous body had suddenly plopped into his lap. Two green eyes looked insolently up at him. It was the cat.

"It's very tame," said Lyllin. "It must have been somebody's pet."

"Probably belonged to the last people who lived here," Kirk said. "It's tame, all right."

He stroked its furry back. The cat half-closed its eyes and emitted a rusty purring sound. "Like that, eh, Tom?"

Tom settled down cozily, in answer. Lyllin reached to stroke its head.

With startling swiftness, the cat recoiled from her and leaped off Kirk's lap. It stared green-eyed back at them, then started across the lawn.

Kirk turned, laughing. "Crazy little critter—" He stopped suddenly. "Lyllin, what's the matter?"

She was crying and he had rarely seen her cry. "Did it scratch you?"

"No. But it feared me, and hated me," she said. "Because it knew I'm alien."

Kirk said, "Oh, rot. The wretched beast is just afraid of strangers."

"It wasn't afraid of you. It sensed that I'm different—"

He put his arm around her, mentally cursing Tom. Then, as he wrathfully looked after the cat, Kirk stiffened.

Tom had started across the lawn toward the dark brush nearby. But the cat had stopped. And, as Kirk looked, Tom suddenly emitted a hiss and recoiled. It went away from the dark clumps, in long swift leaps.

Kirk's thoughts raced. The cat had recoiled from that brush, exactly as it had recoiled from Lyllin. For the same reason? Because someone alien, not of Earth, was in those shadows? He thought he could hear a slight sound, and his muscles suddenly strung tight. Ferdias' agent wouldn't approach so secretly. Non-Earthmen skulking in those shadows meant only one thing.

He said, "Come on in the house and forget it, Lyllin. I could stand another drink—"

But instantly, when inside the house, Kirk made a lunge toward the nearest bedroom and grabbed for the blankets there. He tossed one of the blankets to Lyllin with frantic speed.

"Wrap it around your head—*quick*!"

She was intelligent. But she was not used to obeying orders instantly and without question "Kirk, what—"

He grabbed the blanket out of her hands and started wrapping it many times around her head, speaking in a whisper as he did so.

"Out there. Someone. If they want to be quiet about it, they're sure to use a sonic knockout-beam. *Hurry*—"

He pulled her to the floor. The blanket swathed her head. He wrapped the other one around his own head, fold after fold. They lay, tense, waiting.

Nothing happened.

He thought how foolish they would look, lying on the floor with their heads swathed, if nothing at all did happen.

He still did not move. He waited.

A series of small sounds began in the back of the house, just vaguely audible through the blanket-folds. A chattering of windows, creaking and rattling of beams, clink of dishes.

The sounds came slowly through the house toward them. *Chatter, rattle*—leisurely advancing. He knew then he'd guessed right. The sonic beam itself was pitched too low to hear. But it was sweeping the house.

It hit them. Lyllin stirred suddenly with a small sound, and Kirk gripped her arm, holding her down. He knew what she was feeling. He felt it himself, the sudden shocking dizziness, the keening inside his head. Even through the swathings of thick blanket, the beam made itself felt. Without protection they'd already be unconscious.

The shock passed. The beam was sweeping on to the front of the house. Kirk remained on the floor, his hand still holding Lyllin's arm. He'd used sonics himself. He had a pretty good idea of how this one would be used.

He was right. The small, half-audible sounds of the house and its shuddering contents came walking back toward them.

Chatter—clink. Rattle—clink—

It hit him again, and he set his teeth and endured it. And again it passed them, and once more the kitchen dishes started talking.

Kirk suddenly thought of the unsuspecting Earth folk in the nearby farms, sleeping peacefully in their old houses, without ever a dream that in their quiet countryside, alien folk from the stars were pitted in a secret struggle that had this whole ancient planet as its prize.

The sounds shut off abruptly. Kirk unwrapped his head, and twitched at Lyllin till she did the same. He made a warning motion to her, to keep down, and he himself crawled forward to the old living-room. He had the little shocker in his hand now.

In a corner of the living-room, behind a grotesque old table, he waited. There was no sound at all.

Then there was one. Footsteps, on the porch outside—coming fast and confidently to the door.

A man came into the room. He wore a dark space-jacket and slacks, he carried a shocker, and he walked like a dancing panther.

Kirk knew him.

His name was Tauncer.

CHAPTER 6

Behind Tauncer came an older man, as gray and solid and rough at the edges as an old brick. He could have been an Earthman, and probably was. He was loaded down with a porto, and some other piece of equipment in a carrying case slung over his shoulders.

Taking no chances at all, but allowing himself to feel a deep and vicious pleasure, Kirk fired from behind the table.

Even so, warned by some faint sound or perhaps only by the instinct of the hunter, Tauncer swung toward him in the instant before the burst of energy hit. He did not quite have time to fire. The impetus of the turn made him hurtle halfway across the room to hit the floor headlong.

The brick-like man was slower. He had only managed to open his mouth and lift his hand halfway toward his armpit when Kirk's second blast dropped him quietly where he stood.

Kirk got up. He found that he was shaking. He looked down at Tauncer, thinking how easily a man could die, flexing his fingers in a hungry way. Lyllin came into the open doorway, and he said angrily,

"You were to stay back there."

Her eyes did not leave his face. She murmured, "Yes. I did wrong." Then, looking at the sprawled bodies, "Are they dead?"

"We're not out on the Sector frontier," Kirk growled. "I wish we were. But here on these old planets they take violence seriously. No, I just used stunning bursts on them."

He rummaged the house until he found wire, and bound the hands of the two men very securely behind them. Then he searched them. He did not find any documents, which was no surprise. He removed a shocker from the brick-like man, and took it and the porto and the heavy carrying case far out of reach.

The carrying case contained a vera-ray projector with its tripod collapsed. Possibly the same one Tauncer had tried to use on him in the cluster world. Tauncer seemed extremely fond of the vera-ray. Probably, in his business, he never traveled without one.

He gave Lyllin the shocker that Tauncer had dropped. "Watch them. Back in a moment."

He went out and rapidly, carefully, searched the grounds of the old farmhouse. He found the sonic device squatting heavily behind a bush. He stood by it for some moments, perfectly still, listening, but there was no sound except the faint stirring of the breeze. There did not seem to be anyone else around. Tauncer and the Earthman must have come alone. Kirk frowned. He picked up the sonic device and stood for a second longer, uneasy but baffled. There was no sign of an air-car. They must have landed far back in the woods to avoid betraying themselves by the noise of the motors. But he could not search the whole woods, not tonight.

He went back to the house.

"They're coming around," said Lyllin. She was sitting in a chair in front of the two bound men, watching them. She rocked back and forth in a rhythmic motion, making the old floorboards squeak. "Look," she said, in a voice just a little too high, "I found out what this queer chair is for. It's rather pleasant."

"I don't find it so," said Tauncer suddenly. "The creaking irritates me." He opened his eyes, and Kirk had the feeling that he had been keeping them closed for some time, shamming, while he took stock of the situation.

"Well," he said to Kirk. "I'm an acknowledged expert with the sono-beam. Would you mind telling me how you did it?"

Kirk said, "We had warning—a friend of mine named Tom." He motioned Lyllin to get up. "Go on in the other room, dear. I don't think you'd enjoy this."

She looked at him as though he was someone she had just met and was not sure she liked.

"Try to understand," he said. "I don't do this sort of thing every day. It's hardly ever necessary."

"Of course," she said. She went into the next room, and he shut the door behind her. Then he sat down in the rocking chair, with the shocker held ready in his hand.

Kirk looked at Tauncer. "I'm a peaceful man," he said, "visiting my ancestral home. What did you want with me?"

Tauncer smiled. There was something about him that made Kirk more and more uneasy—a lack of concern, a deep-based confidence that didn't fit a man in his position.

Tauncer said gently, "You are the Commander of the Fifth Squadron, Lyra Sector, awaiting orders from your Governor. You are wasting your time."

Kirk's nerves tightened painfully, but he kept his face impassive. "Go on," he said. "I'm listening."

"Ferdias' agent was supposed to meet you here secretly with certain—information." Tauncer spoke with deliberate clarity, as one who explains some problem to a child. "He is not coming. We've known who he is, for some time. And I got to him, before he ever left New York." He nodded to the vera-ray projector across the room. "I used that extremely useful invention on him, and of course he told me all about this place and how he was supposed to meet you here. So I came instead."

Kirk looked at the vera-ray himself, but Tauncer shook his head. "It wouldn't do you any good. The particular piece of information you need—namely, when and where to move—is not known to me, and your contact man had not received it yet either. When it does come through, one of our men will get it—probably already have."

Tauncer's eyes looked up brightly at Kirk, the eyes of the adroit and wily man measuring the honest clod for another defeat.

"You might just as well free me, Kirk. It was a good try, but your cause is hopeless now."

"Not as long as I'm on my feet," said Kirk, getting up. He was a very angry man. "Not as long as the Fifth will follow me. If I don't get orders, I'll make my own."

"No," said a familiar voice behind him. "The Fifth isn't going anywhere, Commander."

Kirk whirled around.

Joe Garstang was standing in the front door. He had a shocker in his hand, pointing with rocklike steadiness at Kirk's breast.

"Drop your weapon," said Garstang.

A red haze swept over Kirk's vision. Through it he saw Garstang, wavering and distorted. Blood hammered in his temples. "You," he said, so choked with rage at this enormity that he could hardly form the words. "My own captain. My friend. Traitor. Working for him—"

Distant and strange in the red mist, Garstang's face became twisted as though with pain.

"I'm sorry," he said, and fired.

Kirk fell onto the floor. Garstang must have pressed the stud back to a light charge, because Kirk was still conscious and only partly paralyzed. His own weapon dropped out of his nerveless fingers.

Garstang came and kicked it away. Kirk flopped around like a gaffed fish, trying to get his reflexes working again. He heard the inner door open, and then Lyllin screamed, partly in fear but mostly in fury, a purely animal sound. She went for Garstang, ignoring his shocker, with a single-minded intent to kill. Her own hands were empty. She was content with them.

Garstang dropped his weapon in his pocket and caught her, holding her hands away from his face and eyes.

"Please," he said. "Please, Lyllin. He's not dead, he's not even hurt." He turned to Kirk. "You should have dropped your shocker. I told you." There was a fresh onslaught, and a red line sprang out on Garstang's cheek. It began to drip slowly, small bright drops against the leathery brown. "Kirk, for God's sake call her off," he said.

Kirk managed to sit up. He mumbled, shook his head two or three times, and finally the words were intelligible. "I'm all right. Come here, Lyllin. Help me up."

She relaxed then, dropping her hands. Garstang let her go. She hissed at him in furious Vegan and then ran to Kirk. "I should have used that weapon," she said. "I should have killed him. I forgot it. I'm sorry." She began to struggle, trying to lift him.

Garstang went immediately into the next room. Through the open door Kirk saw him look around and then pocket the shocker that Lyllin had laid down and forgotten. Lyllin didn't notice, and he said nothing. What was the use?

"Push that chair over here," Kirk said. "Now don't worry, this'll wear off. I'll be all right in just a few minutes. Yes. That's it."

He sat in the rocker, rubbing his numb right arm with his left, trying to stamp his foot, but he couldn't move it yet. He glared up at Garstang, who had come and was standing near Tauncer, looking from him to Kirk with a faint frown.

Tauncer had not spoken, and he did not speak now. He sat where he was and waited, and watched them.

"Well," said Kirk, "what are you waiting for, Joe? Go ahead and untie him."

"No," said Garstang, shaking his head slowly. "No, I'm not going to untie him."

"Why not?" demanded Kirk bitterly. "Or have you decided to double-cross him, too?"

"I don't think you understand," said Garstang. "I'm not working with Tauncer. I'm not working for Solleremos at all."

Kirk stared, for a moment surprised out of his rage. "But then who—"

"My loyalty," said Garstang, "is to Earth."

"Oh, hell, that doesn't make sense," said Kirk. "You're no more Earthman than I am—"

"I am, Kirk. You never knew it, but I'm all Earthman. And I've been in Earth Intelligence for fourteen years."

Garstang went on slowly. "Earth may be old and partly helpless, but she is not so blind as to let five powerful hungry Governors go unwatched. We've seen this grab coming for a long time. The only thing we didn't know, and couldn't find out, was which one of the five would try it first. But now I think we know."

"What do you think you know?" said Kirk.

Garstang looked at him steadily. "Ferdias was the only Governor who sent a squadron to Earth, for the Commemoration. Why?"

Kirk cried, "To protect Earth from Solleremos! It's Orion who's going to try the grab!"

"I thought you'd say that, Kirk. Maybe you believe it. But ask yourself—if that's so, why didn't Ferdias warn us openly? Why did he have you sneak off to this undercover rendezvous?"

Garstang shook his head. "No, Kirk. I think you're an honest man. And I think you've been had. I think you've been had all the way."

CHAPTER 7

Kirk began to laugh. He laughed until tears of rage and desperation stood in his eyes.

"Christ," he said, "If Earth agents are all as bright as you are, Joe, God help her."

He pointed to Tauncer. "Allow me to introduce you. This is Tauncer, Solleremos' right-hand man."

Garstang nodded. "I know."

"I've just fought him off, and now I have to fight you. A fine thing. A damn fine thing. Listen, Joe. The Fifth was sent here by Ferdias to protect Earth. Solleremos will attack—"

"When?" asked Garstang.

"I don't know. Ferdias' agent was supposed to meet me here and give me final orders. Tauncer has taken care of that. Why do you suppose he did that? Why do you suppose he came here and attacked me? He—"

Garstang turned to Tauncer. "Yes," he said. "Why did you?"

Tauncer said quietly, "You were perfectly right, Garstang. Ferdias *has* been planning to grab Earth. We knew that, in Orion. We had to know when and how Ferdias would do it—and it was my mission to find out. I was trying, there in the cluster. I tried here, but the Commander was too much on guard."

"You're lying," said Kirk between his teeth. "Not two minutes ago you were telling me I couldn't stop Solleremos from taking over Earth. Lyllin, you heard it—"

Lyllin whispered, "I am sorry—but you sent me away from the room. Remember?"

Tauncer turned to the Earthman. "Harper will tell you I'm not lying. You heard every word, didn't you, Harper?"

The Earthman wrinkled his seamy cheeks and said in a tone of ringing honesty, "I sure did."

Kirk was not yet able to stand up and kill him, or Tauncer, so he shut his jaws tight and tried to think. I mustn't be drawn into a verbal slanging match, he thought. That's what Tauncer wants. The more I yell and swear the worse I look. What must I do? Something. Something....

"—so we're going to act suddenly to disarm the Fifth Squadron," Garstang was saying. "Charteris has been suspicious from the first, and what I told him there last night made him more so. And—"

"Disarm the squadron?" cried Kirk. "Are you insane?" He had a sudden nightmare vision of the Orion ships sweeping in, of the cruisers and transports of the Fifth disappearing in a storm of smoke and fire, the men falling like dead leaves.

"We can't take any chances," Garstang said, moving toward the phone. "The Earth Navy—"

"Ha!"

"The Earth Navy," repeated Garstang, "is on full alert right now."

"Solleremos will eat it up," said Kirk savagely. "Don't be a fool, Garstang. I don't care how loyal you are to Earth, you've got to admit her navy can't face Orion Squadrons for five minutes."

Garstang hesitated. His face was grim and sad, and Kirk felt sorry for him in spite of his anger. Garstang said, "We'll have to do what we can. We'll fight enemies if they come, but we'll make sure first we don't get stabbed in the back."

He picked up the phone. A gleam of satisfaction crossed Tauncer's face. Kirk saw it, and suddenly the inspiration came to him.

He exclaimed, "I've been an idiot! Listen, Joe—put that phone down. I can prove what I said in three minutes. If I don't—then go ahead and call."

Garstang looked at him, frowning.

Tauncer said, with the first edge of tension his voice had yet shown, "Go ahead, Garstang, don't let him make a fool of you."

Kirk said, "Shut up." He rose and hobbled over to the vera-ray projector. "Help me set this up, Joe. Tauncer used it on Ferdias' agent, and he was going to use it on me. Now let's see what it'll get out of *him*."

Garstang came over. "A vera-ray? Why didn't you mention it before?"

"I was too damn mad to think straight," said Kirk.

They set it up, and Tauncer watched them, not speaking, yet still the look of apprehension in his eyes was tempered with some underlying confidence. He seemed to be thinking, very hard.

Garstang got the projector going. Harper, the seamy Earthman, winced away from Tauncer as far as he could get. Behind the projector Kirk could not feel anything, but Tauncer's face was briefly agonized, and then it went slack and his eyes lost their keen brilliance, becoming vague and unfocused.

"Tauncer," said Garstang. "Can you hear me?"

"Yes."

"Is Solleremos planning to take Earth into his Sector?"

Some dim vestige of a censor barrier seemed still to survive in Tauncer's mind, because there was a long delay and Garstang asked the question again, more sharply. But when the answer came it was clear enough.

"Yes."

Kirk looked at Garstang, and Garstang's cheeks reddened. Lyllin said triumphantly, "You see?"

"All right," said Garstang, and turned again to Tauncer.

"How will he do it?"

"Direct attack. The Earth naval forces are negligible. Lyra Squadron will be caught on the ground, disorganized by absence of command."

"Absence of command," said Kirk slowly. A sudden alarm came into his face. "You were going to keep me from returning to the squadron."

"Yes."

"But not here at this farm. Too many people knew where I was. Charteris, folk in the town—"

"Oh, no," said Tauncer, "not here. Fast scout. The ship that brought me to Earth ahead of your squadron. It's been waiting out beyond radar range. It will take us all off."

Now, thought Kirk, I know why he's been so confident. He's been planning for time. "You sent word to the scout-ship?"

"Yes," said Tauncer. "On the porto, right after I beamed your house. I was sure you'd be unconscious."

Over Kirk's shoulder, Garstang said sharply, "When will it land?"

Tauncer made a vague movement as though trying to get his arm around where he could see his chrono. Garstang said, "It's exactly two minutes after eleven, Earth time."

Tauncer's lips moved. "Before midnight," he said. "Soon."

He seemed, dazed as he was, to be smiling.

Garstang said to Kirk, "You've got to get out of here, and fast!" He started to turn hurriedly away, as though to hustle him and Lyllin out of the house at once, but Kirk said, "No, wait, let me think."

He spoke to Tauncer. "You don't know exactly where Solleremos' squadrons are, or exactly when they'll strike."

"No."

"But there must be a signal, some word they're waiting for."

"Yes," said Tauncer. "When the scout takes us off, that will be the signal. Means we've got Commander. Means Lyra Squadron confused."

Garstang tugged at Kirk. "Come on."

"But," said Kirk to Tauncer, "suppose the scout doesn't find anybody here."

"All the same. They'll know I've failed, and plan may be known. So order will be to strike like lightning before defensive measures taken."

Kirk shut off the projector. He bent over Tauncer. "Get up," he said. "Joe! Give me a hand." They got Tauncer wobbling to his feet. "Put him in the ground car and take him back to Charteris. Try and convince Charteris to let the Fifth go on battle-alert. Every minute may count—if we're caught on the ground, we're sunk."

"Kirk—"

"Don't argue. If anything happens to me, Larned is to take over and cooperate fully with Admiral Laney. You—"

"What do you mean, if anything happens, you're coming too."

"No."

They wrestled Tauncer down the front steps.

"But the scout—"

"That's just it. You heard what he said. The scout must *not* take off again."

"So what are you going to do?" asked Garstang. "Stand and hold it with your bare hands? We can't possibly get any help from New York in time."

"Yeah," said Kirk. "So I'm going to try to get help right here."

"From these people?"

"Haven't you heard?" said Kirk. "I'm a local boy."

"So if you get it? A bunch of farmers. Even if they'll listen to you, which they probably won't—"

They shoved Tauncer into the car. "Better tie his feet too," said Kirk. "Lyllin! Lyllin, you're going with Joe."

"No," she said from the porch. "I am not."

"But you can't stay here!"

"If you are going to get yourself killed here, I stay!"

She was determined to make a fight about it, and Kirk had no time right then. "All right," he said. "I guess you'll be safe enough with the Vinsons." He slammed the door after Garstang. "Get going."

Garstang swore but he roared the ground car out in a cloud of dust and gravel. Kirk ran back into the house. Most of the feeling had come back in his side, and he could move pretty fast. The Earthman, Harper, was squirming around the floor trying to get free. Kirk gave him one ruthless blast with the sono-beam that would put him to sleep for a day or so. He could be dealt with later, when more important things were out of the way. Then he got on the phone and called Vinson.

A sleepy voice answered. "I was just going to bed. What do you want?"

"When you have an emergency around here," said Kirk, "what do you do to get help in a hurry?"

Vinson's voice waked up. "Why, I phone around fast. The boys turn out quick for fire, flood or whatever. Hey, you got a fire, Commander?"

"Worse," said Kirk. "Do your people have guns of some kind?"

"Sure, nearly every farm has a hunting-shocker. But—"

"Tell 'em to come armed, and come fast. Your place. My wife and I are coming now."

"Say Commander, is this a joke or what?"

"It's the unfunniest joke ever to hit Earth," Kirk said grimly. "Call them!"

He slammed the phone down, grabbed Lyllin by the hand, and lit out, full tilt down the path and into the moonlit road.

By the time they reached Vinson's house, all the lights were on and Vinson himself was standing in the road, waiting for them.

"I hope you know what you're doing," he said to Kirk worriedly. "The boys don't like getting hauled out for nothing. What's up?"

Kirk told him, rapidly, between gasps, as he helped Lyllin up on the porch. Mrs. Vinson, a pleasant-looking dark-haired woman in a pink robe, cried out from the doorway and took Lyllin's hand to welcome her in.

"What on earth is going on?" she demanded. "Why, you poor thing, he's run the legs off you! Come in, sit down—" Then she caught sight of Vinson's face. "What is it?" she asked quietly. "Tell me, so I'll know what to do."

"There's going to be a fight," said Vinson, in a wondering, half-incredulous tone. "There's a war going to start, and the first fight is going to be right here, in Orville."

"In the woods," said Kirk hastily, pointing. "You'll be quite safe here. And if we can take them by surprise, there won't even be a skirmish."

"He says that the fate of Earth depends on us," said Vinson, still in that wondering tone. "Well. I'm damned. What do you know!"

A car roared up outside. Another followed it, and then others at irregular intervals. Pretty soon Vinson's yard and porch were crowded with men carrying hunting-shockers. They looked at Vinson, and at Kirk, curious, doubtful, not exactly hostile but in no mood to be hurried into anything they didn't understand. Kirk glanced up at the sky and groaned. Then he spoke, as rapidly and forcefully as he could.

"So that's the picture," he finished. "If that Orion scout takes off again after it lands, your Earth may be a different place tomorrow. We can stop it—if you will."

He wailed. There was no reaction at all for a moment, the leathery faces looking silently at him. Then one man said,

"If people come bothering us, we'll bother them back—plenty. But we don't need any stranger telling us what to do."

Kirk's heart sank. The cursed Earth mulishness was going to defeat him, after all.

Vinson said loudly, "What do you mean, stranger! This is one of the old Orville Kirks. *He's* no stranger. It's strangers that he wants us to help slap down."

They thought that over for a moment, and again Kirk looked up at the sky. It must be very close now. In minutes, maybe, it would drop down, and there would be nothing at all to stop it from going away again and giving the signal. And these stolid farmers....

The one who had spoken peered bleakly at Kirk, and said, "Well. Like I said, we don't want strangers interfering with us. Do we, boys?"

The men nodded assent, and stalked toward their cars. Kirk turned away, defeated and furious. He'd have to try by himself—

Motors roared to life, and the cars started to go by him. A big red truck paused beside him, and Vinson reached down from it to haul him aboard.

"What are you standin' there for?" he cried to Kirk. "You said it might come any minute!"

Kirk, a little dazedly, scrambled up into the truck beside him. "You mean they're going back with me—"

"What did you think? Like Fred said, no blasted strangers from away outside are going to come sneaking in here!"

The truck roared away down the moonlit road, following the speeding cars back the way Kirk had come, waking hurrying echoes, raising a great cloud of dust to redden the moon.

Kirk thought, "I'll never understand these damned Earthmen—never!"

CHAPTER 8

At three minutes and fourteen seconds before midnight a small, fast spacecraft with the insigne of the striding warrior on her bows dropped down out of the sky and landed in the brush-grown meadow at the edge of the Kirk woods. There was nothing anywhere in sight around it but the dark quiet mass of the trees, the patches of bramble and pale white blossoms of the Queen Anne's Lace. Across the meadow was the Kirk house, with a single lamp burning in it.

A hatch opened and a party of men came out, climbing down a collapsible ladder. There were fifteen of them, armed. They stood still, looking around and listening. Then they began to move toward the house, scrambling and stumbling among the briars and the tufts of bunch-grass, fanned out like skirmishers.

Kirk, lying behind a hazel bush in the fringe of the woods, waved one hand slowly in an outward arc, and there were several small rustlings in the brush to his left. He waited, feeling tense and prickly all over, sweating heavily, though the night was cooler now. He counted, slowly and carefully, moving his lips. Held tight in the crook of his arm was the heavy sono-beam device, snatched up from the house as they came past it. Vinson was beside him, and among the trees nearby were eight more men, waiting for Kirk's signal. Kirk could not see Vinson's face in the dark, but he could hear his breathing, quick and excited. He leaned his head close to the Earthman's, and whispered,

"Remember, keep down out of the way until you see me go in."

He raised up cautiously.

"All right. Now."

He began to creep rapidly toward the slash of light from the scout-ship's open hatch. The others came behind him. He was not used to this sort of stalking, and he made more noise than the other nine put together. He hoped no one would hear it.

From the direction of the house there came a sudden crackling of shocker-beams. Kirk flung himself forward, over the last few feet. Secrecy was a lost hope now, and all that mattered was getting the sono-beam projector into the open hatchway. The bloody thing weighed a ton when you carried it, but its heft was only relative. Against armor-plate and the strong double-hull of a space-ship it would be no more effective than a bullroarer.

There was a guard of two in the hatchway. They sprang to the lip of the opening, staring toward the house, their shockers lifted. Kirk yelled, "Get 'em!" Vinson and a man on the other side of him fired almost together. The guards came tumbling forward onto the ground. Kirk dodged between them and set the sono-projector on the edge of the hatch floor. He had to reach high to do it. The others, following his orders, were hugging the curve of the hull on either side of the ladder. Kirk slammed the stud full charge and wide open.

"They're coming back this way!" yelled Vinson. He was looking toward the house. Kirk craned his neck.

The shocker-flashes flickered like heat-lightning in the night. They moved back toward the ship—probably the fifteen men, or what was left of them, were retreating from the Orville men whom Kirk had stationed in the house and yard.

He said desperately, "Stop them, damn it, can't you stop them?" The sono-beam projector was sliding out of his hands, walking itself with its own vibration across the smooth-worn metal. He had to turn to hold it.

Inside the ship there was bedlam going on, a sound of things breaking and men's voices raised in inarticulate cries. A tall gray-haired man with a captain's stars on his shoulder-tabs came at a staggering run into the passage and dropped, and lay still. His hands quivered with the jarring of the floor.

Kirk shut off the projector and threw it away. He went up the ladder, and at the top he paused a second to look at what was happening in the meadow. The Orville men who had gone in behind the invaders had risen out of the brush. Their shockers flared in a line of ragged light amid the brambles and the white flowers. Then there was darkness and a sudden peace.

"Come on!" Kirk shouted, his voice carrying far across the meadow. Then he ran down the passage, with Vinson and the other eight pounding at his heels. The gray-haired captain did not move as they went by.

And it was almost easy. Seven, eight, nine, of the crew lay sprawled in the main passage or in doorways opening from it, unconscious. The communications man was still making vague pawing motions at his dials, but the motions were only reflex and the equipment was jarred to fragments of splintered glass and plastic. In the small, compact bridge, best protected by intervening bulkheads, the two junior officers and three crewmen were still conscious but too dazed to offer resistance.

"Well," said Vinson, breathing hard, his eyes shining. "We did all right."

"We did fine," said Kirk, grinning. The other eight grinned, too, nodding their heads at each other and at him. They had fought together and won together, and now they were all comrades, men of Orville, men of Earth. It was a good feeling, Kirk discovered. A very good feeling.

Some of the men came in from the meadow. The fifteen from the scout were all taken. The Orville men had suffered some casualties in the way of burns and shock, but no fatalities.

"Good," said Kirk. He looked at the Orionids. "Where can we put 'em for safekeeping?"

Vinson said, "The local jail is pretty small, but I guess we could pack them in."

"It won't be for long," said Kirk. "The high brass will take them off your hands in a hurry."

"We'll see to it," said Vinson. "I guess you'll want to call New York. And don't worry about the women, I'll stop by the house and let them know we're okay."

"Thanks," said Kirk. He went out across the meadow to the house, and put in his call to Charteris.

After that things happened with desperate speed. A fleet of air-cars descended on Orville and the Kirk house. Charteris was with them. He inspected the Orion scout, conferred briefly with his aides, and then spoke to Kirk.

"I suppose I should apologize, Commander," he said, rather stiffly, "but I'm not going to. In our position we have no choice but to suspect any force too strong for us to deal with easily."

"I don't care about anything," said Kirk, "except to get my squadron off the ground before Orion strikes."

Charteris nodded. "Your squadron is being fitted for action now. I suggest we return to New York at once to confer with Admiral Laney and decide strategy."

The next few hours were hectic ones. Orders, preparations, requisitions, arguments. And Kirk found himself up against a totally unexpected stumbling-block—the stiff-necked, stubborn pride of Earth.

"We recognize perfectly," Admiral Laney said frostily, "our position as a fifth-rate naval power, but we have never yet run from battle and we don't intend to start doing it now."

"But against Orion Sector's two crack squadrons—"

"We're grateful for the presence of the Fifth Lyra," said Laney, "but our own ships will bear the brunt of the attack."

"Sir," said Kirk, and he meant it, "I would be proud to fight under you. But facts are facts. I think you understand that the Fifth Lyra has a certain pride too. But we're not going to bear the brunt of any attack where we know in advance we're outnumbered two to one. In short, if you meet Solleremos head on, you meet him alone."

"Now here," he went on, turning to the huge depth-chart of the Solar System, "was my thought. We know from the vera-ray examination of the captain of that Orion scout, that the scout's take-off was literally to be the signal for the attack. They didn't dare risk a radio message, even in code, that might be intercepted. So the course of take-off, on the exact coordinates of the hidden fleet, was to serve as a message. They could spot this by ultra-wave scanner, using relays at previously-arranged points in deep space. So, we have the coordinates—"

He wrote them down on the chart.

"Carried to point of convergence, that would put the Orion fleet about there—far off this chart, of course, but roughly south-east of the star Saiph. They will presumably attack along this line—" He drew one, bold and red, a dagger pointed at Earth's heart.

"Roughly nadir-point zero six, from our viewpoint," said Laney. "Well?"

"Here," said Kirk, "you seem to have a natural sort of chevaux-de-frise, to borrow an ancient term."

He pointed to a blurred and speckled area lying between Mars and Jupiter.

"The Asteroid Belt," said Laney. "Yes. We know our way around in it, but anyone else would find it hard going." His eyes brightened. "Plenty of places for ambush. Yes, I see what you're driving at. If we could entangle their superior forces in the drift—"

"Exactly. Bait them in there, harry them all you can. Now, then. They'll be expecting to catch the Fifth Lyra on the ground. As far as they know, Tauncer succeeded and all is well. So perhaps they won't be too watchful. We'll be up here hiding above the Sun, screened by it from their radar. When you have them hooked—"

He made a downward slashing motion with his hand.

"That suits me," said Laney. He shook hands with Kirk solemnly. Then he turned to Charteris and the others who were gathered with anxious face? in the conference room. "I think we may as well get started."

Charteris sighed. He picked up the intercom and spoke into it briefly.

Northward, the fields around Orville were brightening with a new day. In the meadow behind the Kirk house the briars and the Queen Anne's Lace were beaten down by the passage of men and trucks. They were all gone now except for one truck with massive electronic equipment, pulled back to a safe distance from the Orion scout. The necessary changes had been made in the ship's control system. Now the crew of the truck waited for a signal from the house.

It came.

The truck crew went to work, activating the remote-control relays, setting up a locked-in series of coordinates. Then the firing key was pressed.

With every semblance of life, the Orion scout took off on its destined course—a Judas goat, empty and silent, with no living thing inside its hull.

Standing on the steps of the Vinson's house, Lyllin watched it rise and vanish in the blue air. She had had one short call from Kirk. *Wait there. I'll come back.* Now the small dying thunder of the scout-ship's flight seemed like the receding footsteps of everything she had ever loved, passing over the distant hills.

She turned slowly and went back into the house.

CHAPTER 9

The sky screamed light, beneath them. The Sun, its atoms ceaselessly riven and then reborn, shrieked raving energy, magnetism, electricity, light, radiant heat, a rage across the heavens, a cosmic storm flinging up wild plumes and spindrift of violet calcium, of yellow sodium, of blue and red and purple.

Over it, as over a limitless fiery ocean, hung the shoal of silver ships. Tossed and twitched by storms of radiation, wrenched by the mighty claws of the titan magnetic field, scorched by the blaze of the star, they fought to hold position. Their formation wavered, sagged, re-formed and wavered again, and still they held together.

On the bridge of the *Starsong*, clutching a stanchion as the deck heeled and shuddered under him, Kirk stood with Garstang watching the screens.

"Not a sign!" said Garstang in his ear. "And we can't sit up here forever!"

The rim of the Asteroid Belt showed on one screen, a jagged wheeling of rock fragments, dust and pebbles and little naked worlds, black on their shadow-sides flashing like heliographs where they caught the light. Beyond them was space, very deep, very dark, very empty, looking toward Orion and his pendant sword.

In that deep emptiness out there, five ships moved slowly. Earth ships, behaving like a normal patrol. The remainder of Earth's fleet was hidden among the asteroids. Even the searching rays that fed the screen could not see them.

Suddenly Garstang caught Kirk's shoulder. "There!" he said. He leaned forward and pointed his blunt forefinger at the screen.

Out of the depths toward the star Saiph came a swarm of tiny flecks that might have been nothing more than bits of cosmic drift, except that they moved together and very fast. They swept in toward the Solar System with a gathering rush, growing, picking up the sunlight on their polished sides. Two full squadrons of Solleremos' fleet, on planetary approach.

The five Earth ships out there wheeled in perfect formation and went on out to meet them.

Kirk's mouth was dry. Runnels of sweat crept down his temples, down his body. The palms of his hands were clammy.

"Screen's gone again," he said, and swore.

The screens blazed useless white, even the powerful rays that served them wrenched and cut by an outburst of solar electricity. Then they cleared again.

The Earth ships had not gone far out. Suddenly they wheeled again, abandoning formation now. Spurts of light came from their launching tubes in quick rotation, each ship firing as she bore on the target. Then they cracked on speed and ran for the Belt.

One of the Orionid cruisers burst into a great flame and was gone.

Garstang shouted, and as though at a signal the screen went out again.

Kirk ran his uniform sleeve over his face, and kept still. There were so few of the Earth ships, and so many of the others, something more than double the strength of his own squadron. Far below, Earth lay naked, stripped, utterly without defense. Kirk thought of Lyllin, and the Vinson house with the dusty road in front of it. He thought of the woods and the meadow where they had fought in the night, and curiously enough he thought of the cat. Insolent little beast....

He waited for the screen to clear, and watched.

A number of Orion ships detached themselves from the main fleet and raced after the Earth ships. They were much faster. The long aim of Solleremos was reaching swiftly now, and one of the Earth cruisers winked out with a brave, brief burst of flame. The other four reached the Belt.

The Orionids plunged in after them.

"Now," whispered Garstang. "Now, now——"

The eight Orionid cruisers, apparently detailed to mop up this patrol, sped down a deceptively open "lead" through the asteroid drift. The scanner beams swung to a better angle to follow them, and now the screen showed a closer view of that stony wilderness. The Earth ships had vanished. The lead pinched out in a cul-de-sac of wildly gyrating rocks. The Orion cruisers did a fast-about, practically on each others' heels, but before they were finished the four Earth ships and half a dozen others appeared from nowhere, all around them.

"Hit them," muttered Garstang. "Oh, hell, get onto it and *hit* them!"

They hit them. There was a quick holocaust of light-bursts and the Orionid cruisers in there were gone.

"That hurt them," said Garstang. "They're hooked——"

He turned and looked at Kirk. Kirk lifted his hand, his body bent slightly forward, his eyes intent upon the screen.

Out there in the Asteroid Belt, the trap was sprung. And now the Orionids knew they had the whole Earth fleet, such as it was, to deal with—a force too small to stop them, but too formidable to leave on their flank and rear. The squadrons altered course, curving in a long bow-shaped line toward the Earth ships that hovered, in apparent doubt, above the fringes of the drift.

Kirk brought his hand down in a slashing gesture. "*Now!*"

The Fifth Lyra swooped out of the sun.

Now.

Now is the moment, the one right time, there will not be another. Either you make it or you don't. Outnumbered, outmanned, and outgunned the element of surprise is all you've got.

The Sun falls behind, the edge of the Belt shifts and tilts and swings as you cut the plane of the ecliptic. Out of the furnace into the fire, at full drive.

The long line of the Orion ships is very beautiful, strung against the glittering emptiness of space.

The *Starsong* groans and quivers like a living thing. You can hear the beating of her heart, the pounding throb of power pushed to the limit, and beyond. Garstang, in the captain's place, has a face of iron, dark and still. Sweat shines on the edges of it. The men are quiet.

The Commander is afraid.

Ships, lives, men, a planet. Who would say *Now!* and not be afraid?

The Orion fleet springs at the viewports. The ships grow large, the intervals between them widen out. The *Starsong* flies at the point of a wedge shaped like an axe-blade. Behind her, on either side, the squadron follows in close formation.

In a tight, flat voice, the Commander says, "Prepare to engage."

The Fifth Lyra, the falling wedge, the axe-blade, hits the line of cruisers from above and cuts it in two.

Instantly the close-held wings fan out, driving the severed sections apart, opening the gap so wide it can never be closed again. Shells burst, little blinding suns, little fountains of hellfire, racking the ships, burning them, destroying them. But the wings sweep on. Part of the Orionid line is rolled up and driven into the drift of the Belt, where the Earth ships strike and strike again, and the proud cruisers with the polished sides become wreck and flotsam to join the cosmic debris in its endless journey around the Sun. The other section is driven outward into space, back toward Orion.

And the *Starsong* hunts down the *Betelgeuse*, flagship of Solleremos' fleet.

Kirk says, If we can get her, I think the rest will all go home. Fire One—

Fire Two.

The *Betelgeuse* answers, and space is drowned in a flaming cloud. The *Starsong* staggers and men are thrown down on the reeling iron deck. A red light flares on the telltale board. Somewhere deep in the ship's vitals the bulkhead doors slam shut, sealing off. The *Starsong* has a hole in her and some men have died, but she's still alive, still strong to move and strike.

Fire Three.

The *Betelgeuse* dives clear and her own tubes spout hellfire, a double flowering of death and destruction. The *Starsong* wrenches away, desperate, shaken, and once more the ports are filled with fire and a red light glimmers on the board.

Fire Four.

The *Betelgeuse* quivers strangely. With a dreamlike slowness two pieces of her appear out of the brilliance and the flame, bow and stern at odds with each other, going different ways. Then there is a white blinding flash, and she is gone.

And the Orion fleet, leaderless, surprised, mauled and clawed and wounded, is pulling out. One by one, in pairs, in little groups, they turn tail and streak for open space, and are gone.

The Fifth Lyra and the ships of Earth follow them, but not far. Space is empty, and in the ships there is a great silence, while the men breathe softly and look at nothing and feel that they are still alive. There is no light now but the light of the Sun and the distant stars. The Belt wheels on its way, and bits of riven metal that once were ships fall slowly toward it.

After a time, on the bridge of the *Starsong*, Garstang turned to Kirk. His face was sweating and wild, and his eyes had a dazed look. He said, "What now?"

"We wait and see what," said Kirk. "Maybe nothing."

"Nothing?"

"Solleremos has missed his spring. I've an idea he may prefer to make like it all never happened, if we don't give any official news of this fight. I think Charteris will see it that way."

Charteris did. The battle couldn't be kept secret really, but Earth's authorities pretended that it had never happened. There was no profit in starting a full-fledged war, and there wouldn't be one if Solleremos had learned his lesson.

He had learned it, it seemed. From Orion there was a long silence. Then came a routine congratulation on the Commemoration. The Governor of Orion Sector, it appeared, was happy for Earth.

"The so-and-so must be raging, but he won't try *that* again," said Kirk.

To him, and to the Squadron, had come another message, from Ferdias. Well done. That was all. But from Ferdias, it was plenty.

And the Commemoration blazed, on Earth. The lights, the bands, the speeches, and then the fly-over—the battered mighty giants of the Fifth roaring across the sky with the even more battered Earth cruisers leading the way.

From its museum they had brought the first of all the space-ships, and everyone held their breath and kept fingers crossed while it lurched, coughed and wobbled up into the sky, and labored bravely around the planet, and by some miracle came down safe again.

And the great day was over.

Garstang, looking strange now in the black uniform of Earth, spoke earnestly to Kirk the day before the Fifth was to leave.

"You know you're pretty much a hero here now, Kirk. You'll be retiring from service in not too many years. Why don't you come back to Earth to live?"

"Why does everyone say, come *back* to Earth," Kirk complained. "Just because I had ancestors here I'm no Earthman!"

He added, "And whatever you do, don't mention that bright idea to Lyllin! I'm going up to Orville now to get her."

Garstang only smiled at him, a queer sort of smile.

Kirk drove up through the quiet roads, the green countryside. The golden sun was soft upon his face. The breeze held a faint, smoky tang of oncoming fall. Earth's fall—he'd heard about that.

Peaceful, beautiful—but it was no world for him! Come "back" to Earth, indeed! Why, he'd lived on many worlds and none of them had ever got that kind of sentimental hold on him. Though he could understand why people felt that way about this old place—

Hell, he must be getting sentimental himself! He put a curb on such thoughts and drove on. And when he drove into Orville, there were frantic handwavings from every street-corner, his name was shouted by the kids along the sidewalks.

Vinson came running out of his house to meet him when he pulled up.

"Your wife's over at your house," Vinson explained. He shook hands. He was vastly excited and proud. "You know what—the village is going to put up a plaque. With all our names on it. Just saying, 'They fought the Battle of Orville'. Nothing else, account of diplomacy."

Kirk said, "It deserves the plaque, that fight. If you chaps hadn't turned out that night—"

"Hear you're leaving tomorrow," Vinson went on. "Thought I'd keep your old place going better, while you're gone, by working the fields. I'll keep an eye on your house, too."

Kirk said, "What makes you think I'm coming back?"

Vinson said, puzzledly, "Why, you are, aren't you? I mean—you're an Orville boy—this is your real home—"

Kirk suppressed the impatient words he'd been about to utter. No use upsetting a nice guy. He said, "Oh, sure, I'll be back—"

He drove on to the old house. Lyllin sat on the porch. He saw, to his surprise, that on her lap there cozily reclined a large black cat.

Lyllin smiled. "I think I've been accepted. By the people here—and by Tom."

Tom yawned and looked with insolent green eyes at Kirk. "His sides are bulging," Kirk said. "You've been bribing the beggar with food."

She laughed. "I don't know how he'll like space-travel. But we'll be bringing him back some day."

"Will we?" said Kirk.

She looked up at him. "Joe Garstang was talking to me. You *will* be retiring from active service in a few years. And I like it here now, Kirk. I really do."

He said, loudly, "Why in the world must everyone assume that I *want* to come back to this place? Will you tell me that?"

"Don't you?"

He started to answer, then didn't. He looked out from the porch of the old house, at the sunset light sweeping the green valley, at the old trees beyond the fields, at everything that had somehow got a queer grip on him without his knowing it.

He said, "Well, I don't know. Maybe."

Lyllin smiled.

That night the Fifth went skyward in a great thundering that rolled louder and louder across the cities and the countryside. Great black bulks flying up fast across the glittering sky, roaring, bellowing, shouting a gigantic farewell down to the watching millions as they rushed out toward the stars.

END

Orchard Corset

OrchardCorset.com

Ph. 1-866-456-7411

★★★★★ 04/23/19

Customer service and sizing experts

Customer service and sizing experts are very helpful and responsive. Feeling great about my order!

koma876omen

★★★★★ 04/25/19

Very comfortable

Fits like a glove and is super comfortable. Highly recommend for daily use.

Dayna L.

★★★★★ 04/24/19

Gorgeous!

I knew I had to get this one when I saw the teaser picture for it. It's even more gorgeous in person. Fits well even though I have...
Read More

Amy H.

-Sizing Experts Available 7 Days a Week
-Only Steel-Boned Corsets, Never Plastic
-Interest Free Pay Over Time Option!
-Rewards program
-Men's Corsets too

THE RED-HAIRED GIRL
A WIFE'S STORY

By Sabine Baring-Gould

First Published in *The Windsor Magazine* in 1903

In 1876 we took a house in one of the best streets and parts of B——. I do not give the name of the street or the number of the house, because the circumstances that occurred in that place were such as to make people nervous, and shy—unreasonably so—of taking those lodgings, after reading our experiences therein.

We were a small family—my husband, a grown-up daughter, and myself; and we had two maids—a cook, and the other was house- and parlourmaid in one. We had not been a fortnight in the house before my daughter said to me one morning: "Mamma, I do not like Jane"—that was our house-parlourmaid.

"Why so?" I asked. "She seems respectable, and she does her work systematically. I have no fault to find with her, none whatever."

"She may do her work," said Bessie, my daughter, "but I dislike inquisitiveness."

"Inquisitiveness!" I exclaimed. "What do you mean? Has she been looking into your drawers?"

"No, mamma, but she watches me. It is hot weather now, and when I am in my room, occasionally, I leave my door open whilst writing a letter, or doing any little bit of needlework, and then I am almost certain to hear her outside. If I turn sharply round, I see her slipping out of sight. It is most annoying. I really was unaware that I was such an interesting personage as to make it worth anyone's while to spy out my proceedings."

"Nonsense, my dear. You are sure it is Jane?"

"Well—I suppose so." There was a slight hesitation in her voice. "If not Jane, who can it be?"

"Are you sure it is not cook?"

"Oh, no, it is not cook; she is busy in the kitchen. I have heard her there, when I have gone outside my room upon the landing, after having caught that girl watching me."

"If you have caught her," said I, "I suppose you spoke to her about the impropriety of her conduct."

"Well, caught is the wrong word. I have not actually *caught* her at it. Only to-day I distinctly heard her at my door, and I saw her back as she turned to run away, when I went towards her."

"But you followed her, of course?"

"Yes, but I did not find her on the landing when I got outside."

"Where was she, then?"

"I don't know."

"But did you not go and see?"

"She slipped away with astonishing celerity," said Bessie.

"I can take no steps in the matter. If she does it again, speak to her and remonstrate."

"But I never have a chance. She is gone in a moment."

"She cannot get away so quickly as all that."

"Somehow she does."

"And you are sure it is Jane?" again I asked; and again she replied: "If not Jane, who else can it be? There is no one else in the house."

So this unpleasant matter ended, for the time. The next intimation of something of the sort proceeded from another quarter—in fact, from Jane herself. She came to me some days later and said, with some embarrassment in her tone—

"If you please, ma'am, if I do not give satisfaction, I would rather leave the situation."

"Leave!" I exclaimed. "Why, I have not given you the slightest cause. I have not found fault with you for anything as yet, have I, Jane? On the contrary, I have been much pleased with the thoroughness of your work. And you are always tidy and obliging."

"It isn't that, ma'am; but I don't like being watched whatever I do."

"Watched!" I repeated. "What do you mean? You surely do not suppose that I am running after you when you are engaged on your occupations. I assure you I have other and more important things to do."

"No, ma'am, I don't suppose you do."

"Then who watches you?"

"I think it must be Miss Bessie."

"Miss Bessie!" I could say no more, I was so astounded.

"Yes, ma'am. When I am sweeping out a room, and my back is turned, I hear her at the door; and when I turn myself about, I just catch a glimpse of her running away. I see her skirts——"

"Miss Bessie is above doing anything of the sort."

"If it is not Miss Bessie, who is it, ma'am?"

There was a tone of indecision in her voice.

"My good Jane," said I, "set your mind at rest. Miss Bessie could not act as you suppose. Have you seen her on these occasions and assured yourself that it is she?"

"No, ma'am, I've not, so to speak, seen her face; but I know it ain't cook, and I'm sure it ain't you, ma'am; so who else can it be?"

I considered for some moments, and the maid stood before me in dubious mood.

"You say you saw her skirts. Did you recognise the gown? What did she wear?"

"It was a light cotton print—more like a maid's morning dress."

"Well, set your mind at ease; Miss Bessie has not got such a frock as you describe."

"I don't think she has," said Jane; "but there was someone at the door, watching me, who ran away when I turned myself about."

"Did she run upstairs or down?"

"I don't know. I did go out on the landing, but there was no one there. I'm sure it wasn't cook, for I heard her clattering the dishes down in the kitchen at the time."

"Well, Jane, there is some mystery in this. I will not accept your notice; we will let matters stand over till we can look into this complaint of yours and discover the rights of it."

"Thank you, ma'am. I'm very comfortable here, but it is unpleasant to suppose that one is not trusted, and is spied on wherever one goes and whatever one is about."

A week later, after dinner one evening, when Bessie and I had quitted the table and left my husband to his smoke, Bessie said to me, when we were in the drawing-room together: "Mamma, it is not Jane."

"What is not Jane?" I asked.

"It is not Jane who watches me."

"Who can it be, then?"

"I don't know."

"And how is it that you are confident that you are not being observed by Jane?"

"Because I have seen her—that is to say, her head."

"When? where?"

"Whilst dressing for dinner, I was before the glass doing my hair, when I saw in the mirror someone behind me. I had only the two candles lighted on the table, and the room was otherwise dark. I thought I heard someone stirring—just the sort of stealthy step I have come to recognise as having troubled me so often. I did not turn, but looked steadily before me into the glass, and I could see reflected therein someone—a woman with red hair. Then I moved from my place quickly. I heard steps of some person hurrying away, but I saw no one then."

"The door was open?"

"No, it was shut."

"But where did she go?"

"I do not know, mamma. I looked everywhere in the room and could find no one. I have been quite upset. I cannot tell what to think of this. I feel utterly unhinged."

"I noticed at table that you did not appear well, but I said nothing about it. Your father gets so alarmed, and fidgets and fusses, if he thinks that there is anything the matter with you. But this is a most extraordinary story."

"It is an extraordinary fact," said Bessie.

"You have searched your room thoroughly?"

"I have looked into every corner."

"And there is no one there?"

"No one. Would you mind, mamma, sleeping with me to-night? I am so frightened. Do you think it can be a ghost?"

"Ghost? Fiddlesticks!"

I made some excuse to my husband and spent the night in Bessie's room. There was no disturbance that night of any sort, and although my daughter was excited and unable to sleep till long after midnight, she did fall into refreshing slumber at last, and in the morning said to me: "Mamma, I think I must have fancied that I saw something in the glass. I dare say my nerves were over-wrought."

I was greatly relieved to hear this, and I arrived at much the same conclusion as did Bessie, but was again bewildered, and my mind unsettled by Jane, who came to me just before lunch, when I was alone, and said—

"Please, ma'am, it's only fair to say, but it's not Miss Bessie."

"What is not Miss Bessie? I mean, who is not Miss Bessie?"

"Her as is spying on me."

"I told you it could not be she. Who is it?"

"Please, ma'am, I don't know. It's a red-haired girl."

"But, Jane, be serious. There is no red-haired girl in the house."

"I know there ain't, ma'am. But for all that, she spies on me."

"Be reasonable, Jane," I said, disguising the shock her words produced on me. "If there be no red-haired girl in the house, how can you have one watching you?"

"I don't know; but one does."

"How do you know that she is red-haired?"

"Because I have seen her."

"When?"

"This morning."

"Indeed?"

"Yes, ma'am. I was going upstairs, when I heard steps coming softly after me—the backstairs, ma'am; they're rather dark and steep, and there's no carpet on them, as on the front stairs, and I was sure I heard someone following me; so I twisted about, thinking it might be cook, but it wasn't. I saw a young woman in a print dress, and the light as came from the window at the side fell on her head, and it was carrots—reg'lar carrots."

"Did you see her face?"

"No, ma'am; she put her arm up and turned and ran downstairs, and I went after her, but I never found her."

"You followed her—how far?"

"To the kitchen. Cook was there. And I said to cook, says I: 'Did you see a girl come this way?' And she said, short-like: 'No.'"

"And cook saw nothing at all?"

"Nothing. She didn't seem best pleased at my axing. I suppose I frightened her, as I'd been telling her about how I was followed and spied on."

I mused a moment only, and then said solemnly—

"Jane, what you want is a *pill*. You are suffering from hallucinations. I know a case very much like yours; and take my word for it that, in your condition of liver or digestion, a pill is a sovereign remedy. Set your mind at rest; this is a mere delusion, caused by pressure on the optic nerve. I will give you a pill to-night when you go to bed, another to-morrow, a third on the day after, and that will settle the red-haired girl. You will see no more of her."

"You think so, ma'am?"

"I am sure of it."

On consideration, I thought it as well to mention the matter to the cook, a strange, reserved woman, not given to talking, who did her work admirably, but whom, for some inexplicable reason, I did not like. If I had considered a little further as to how to broach the subject, I should perhaps have proved more successful; but by not doing so I rushed the question and obtained no satisfaction.

I had gone down to the kitchen to order dinner, and the difficult question had arisen how to dispose of the scraps from yesterday's joint.

"Rissoles, ma'am?"

"No," said I, "not rissoles. Your master objects to them."

"Then perhaps croquettes?"

"They are only rissoles in disguise."

"Perhaps cottage pie?"

"No; that is inorganic rissole, a sort of protoplasm out of which rissoles are developed."

"Then, ma'am, I might make a hash."

"Not an ordinary, barefaced, rudimentary hash?"

"No, ma'am, with French mushrooms, or truffles, or tomatoes."

"Well—yes—perhaps. By the way, talking of tomatoes, who is that red-haired girl who has been about the house?"

"Can't say, ma'am."

I noticed at once that the eyes of the cook contracted, her lips tightened, and her face assumed a half-defiant, half-terrified look.

"You have not many friends in this place, have you, cook?"

"No, ma'am, none."

"Then who can she be?"

"Can't say, ma'am."

"You can throw no light on the matter? It is very unsatisfactory having a person about the house—and she has been seen upstairs—of whom one knows nothing."

"No doubt, ma'am."

"And you cannot enlighten me?"

"She is no friend of mine."

"Nor is she of Jane's. Jane spoke to me about her. Has she remarked concerning this girl to you?"

"Can't say, ma'am, as I notice all Jane says. She talks a good deal."

"You see, there must be someone who is a stranger and who has access to this house. It is most awkward."

"Very so, ma'am."

I could get nothing more from the cook. I might as well have talked to a log; and, indeed, her face assumed a wooden look as I continued to speak to her on the matter. So I sighed, and said—

"Very well, hash with tomato," and went upstairs.

A few days later the house-parlourmaid said to me, "Please, ma'am, may I have another pill?"

"Pill!" I exclaimed. "Why?"

"Because I have seen her again. She was behind the curtains, and I caught her putting out her red head to look at me."

"Did you see her face?"

"No; she up with her arm over it and scuttled away."

"This is strange. I do not think I have more than two podophyllin pills left in the box, but to those you are welcome. Only I should recommend a different treatment. Instead of taking them yourself, the moment you see, or fancy that you see, the red-haired girl, go at her with the box and threaten to administer the pills to her. That will rout her, if anything will."

"But she will not stop for the pills."

"The threat of having them forced on her every time she shows herself will disconcert her. Conceive, I am supposing, that on each occasion Miss Bessie, or I, were to meet you on the stairs, in a room, on the landing, in the hall, we were to rush on you and force, let us say, castor-oil globules between your lips. You would give notice at once."

"Yes; so I should, ma'am."

"Well, try this upon the red-haired girl. It will prove infallible."

"Thank you, ma'am; what you say seems reasonable."

Whether Bessie saw more of the puzzling apparition, I cannot say. She spoke no further on the matter to me; but that may have been so as to cause me no further uneasiness. I was unable to resolve the question to my own satisfaction—whether what had been seen was a real person, who obtained access to the house in some unaccountable manner, or whether it was, what I have called it, an apparition.

As far as I could ascertain, nothing had been taken away. The movements of the red-haired girl were not those of one who sought to pilfer. They seemed to me rather those of one not in her right mind; and on this supposition I made inquiries in the neighbourhood as to the existence in our street, in any of the adjoining houses, of a person wanting in her wits, who was suffered to run about at will. But I could obtain no information that at all threw light on a point to me so perplexing.

Hitherto I had not mentioned the topic to my husband. I knew so well that I should obtain no help from him, that I made no effort to seek it. He would "Pish!" and "Pshaw!" and make some slighting reference to women's intellects, and not further trouble himself about the matter.

But one day, to my great astonishment, he referred to it himself.

"Julia," said he, "do you observe how I have cut myself in shaving?"

"Yes, dear," I replied. "You have cotton-wool sticking to your jaw, as if you were growing a white whisker on one side."

"It bled a great deal," said he.

"I am sorry to hear it."

"And I mopped up the blood with the new toilet-cover."

"Never!" I exclaimed. "You haven't been so foolish as to do that?"

"Yes. And that is just like you. You are much more concerned about your toilet-cover being stained than about my poor cheek which is gashed."

"You were very clumsy to do it," was all I could say. Married people are not always careful to preserve the amenities in private life. It is a pity, but it is so.

"It was due to no clumsiness on my part," said he; "though I do allow my nerves have been so shaken, broken, by married life, that I cannot always command my hand, as was the case when I was a bachelor. But this time it was due to that new, stupid, red-haired servant you have introduced into the house without consulting me or my pocket."

"Red-haired servant!" I echoed.

"Yes, that red-haired girl I have seen about. She thrusts herself into my study in a most offensive and objectionable way. But the climax of all was this morning, when I was shaving. I stood in my shirt before the glass, and had lathered my face, and was engaged on my right jaw, when that red-haired girl rushed between me and the mirror with both her elbows up, screening her face with her arms, and her head bowed. I started back, and in so doing cut myself."

"Where did she come from?"

"How can I tell? I did not expect to see anyone."

"Then where did she go?"

"I do not know; I was too concerned about my bleeding jaw to look about me. That girl must be dismissed."

"I wish she could be dismissed," I said.

"What do you mean?"

I did not answer my husband, for I really did not know what answer to make.

I was now the only person in the house who had not seen the red-haired girl, except possibly the cook, from whom I could gather nothing, but whom I suspected of knowing more concerning this mysterious apparition than she chose to admit. That what had been seen by Bessie and Jane was a supernatural visitant, I now felt convinced, seeing that it had appeared to that least imaginative and most commonplace of all individuals, my husband. By no mental process could he have been got to imagine anything. He certainly did see this red-haired girl, and that no living, corporeal maid had been in his dressing-room at the time I was perfectly certain.

I was soon, however, myself to be included in the number of those before whose eyes she appeared. It was in this wise.

Cook had gone out to do some marketing. I was in the breakfast-room, when, wanting a funnel to fill a little phial of brandy I always keep on the washstand in case of emergencies, I went to the head of the kitchen stairs, to descend and fetch what I required. Then I was aware of a great clattering of the fire-irons below, and a banging about of the boiler and grate. I went down the steps very hastily and entered the kitchen.

There I saw a figure of a short, set girl in a shabby cotton gown, not over clean, and slipshod, stooping before the stove, and striking the fender with the iron poker. She had fiery red hair, very untidy.

I uttered an exclamation.

Instantly she dropped the poker, and covering her face with her arms, uttering a strange, low cry, she dashed round the kitchen table, making nearly the complete circuit, and then swept past me, and I heard her clattering up the kitchen stairs.

I was too much taken aback to follow. I stood as one petrified. I felt dazed and unable to trust either my eyes or my ears.

Something like a minute must have elapsed before I had sufficiently recovered to turn and leave the kitchen. Then I ascended slowly and, I confess, nervously. I was fearful lest I should find the red-haired girl cowering against the wall, and that I should have to pass her.

But nothing was to be seen. I reached the hall, and saw that no door was open from it except that of the breakfast-room. I entered and thoroughly examined every recess, corner, and conceivable hiding-place, but could find no one there. Then I ascended the staircase, with my hand on the balustrade, and searched all the rooms on the first floor, without the least success. Above were the servants' apartments, and I now resolved on mounting to them. Here the staircase was uncarpeted. As I was ascending, I heard Jane at work in her room. I then heard her come out hastily upon the landing. At the same moment, with a rush past me, uttering the same moan, went the red-haired girl. I am sure I felt her skirts sweep my dress. I did not notice her till she was close upon me, but I did distinctly see her as she passed. I turned, and saw no more.

I at once mounted to the landing where was Jane.

"What is it?" I asked.

"Please, ma'am, I've seen the red-haired girl again, and I did as you recommended. I went at her rattling the pill-box, and she turned and ran downstairs. Did you see her, ma'am, as you came up?"

"How inexplicable!" I said. I would not admit to Jane that I had seen the apparition.

The situation remained unaltered for a week. The mystery was unsolved. No fresh light had been thrown on it. I did not again see or hear anything out of the way; nor did my husband, I presume, for he made no further remarks relative to the extra servant who had caused him so much annoyance. I presume he supposed that I had summarily dismissed her. This I conjectured from a smugness assumed by his face, such as it always acquired when he had carried a point against me—which was not often.

However, one evening, abruptly, we had a new sensation. My husband, Bessie, and I were at dinner, and we were partaking of the soup, Jane standing by, waiting to change our plates and to remove the tureen, when we dropped our spoons, alarmed by fearful screams issuing from the kitchen. By the way, characteristically, my husband finished his soup before he laid down the spoon and said—

"Good gracious! What is that?"

Bessie, Jane, and I were by this time at the door, and we rushed together to the kitchen stairs, and one after the other ran down them. I was the first to enter, and I saw cook wrapped in flames, and a paraffin lamp on the floor broken, and the blazing oil flowing over it.

I had sufficient presence of mind to catch up the cocoanut matting which was not impregnated with the oil, and to throw it round cook, wrap her tightly in it, and force her down on the floor where not overflowed by the oil. I held her thus, and Bessie succoured me. Jane was too frightened to do other than scream. The cries of the burnt woman were terrible. Presently my husband appeared.

"Dear me! Bless me! Good gracious!" he said.

"You go away and fetch a doctor," I called to him; "you can be of no possible service here—you only get in our way."

"But the dinner?"

"Bother the dinner! Run for a surgeon."

In a little while we had removed the poor woman to her room, she shrieking the whole way upstairs; and, when there, we laid her on the bed, and kept her folded in the cocoanut matting till a medical man arrived, in spite of her struggles to be free. My husband, on this occasion, acted with commendable promptness; but whether because he was impatient for the completion of his meal, or whether his sluggish nature was for once touched with human sympathy, it is not for me to say.

All I know is that, so soon as the surgeon was there, I dismissed Jane with "There, go and get your master the rest of his dinner, and leave us with cook."

The poor creature was frightfully burnt. She was attended to devotedly by Bessie and myself, till a nurse was obtained from the hospital. For hours she was as one mad with terror as much as with pain.

Next day she was quieter and sent for me. I hastened to her, and she begged the nurse to leave the room. I took a chair and seated myself by her bedside, and expressed my profound commiseration, and told her that I should like to know how the accident had taken place.

"Ma'am, it was the red-haired girl did it."

"The red-haired girl!"

"Yes, ma'am. I took a lamp to look how the fish was getting on, and all at once I saw her rush straight at me, and I—I backed, thinking she would knock me down, and the lamp fell over and smashed, and my clothes caught, and——"

"Oh, cook! you should not have taken the lamp."

"It's done. And she would never leave me alone till she had burnt or scalded me. You needn't be afraid—she don't haunt the house. It is *me* she has haunted, because of what I did to her."

"Then you know her?"

"She was in service with me, as kitchenmaid, at my last place, near Cambridge. I took a sort of hate against her, she was such a slattern and so inquisitive. She peeped into my letters, and turned out my box and drawers, she was ever prying; and when I spoke to her, she was that saucy! I reg'lar hated her. And one day she was kneeling by the stove, and I was there, too, and I suppose the devil possessed me, for I upset the boiler as was on the hot-plate right upon her, just as she looked up, and it poured over her face and bosom, and arms, and scalded her that dreadful, she died. And since then she has haunted me. But she'll do so no more. She won't trouble you further. She has done for me, as she has always minded to do, since I scalded her to death."

The unhappy woman did not recover.

"Dear me! no hope?" said my husband, when informed that the surgeon despaired of her. "And good cooks are so scarce. By the way, that red-haired girl?"

"Gone—gone for ever," I said.

THE END

Choking smoke
where sad jazz plays
Endless drinks drown this bloke
in an endless haze

"Just leave that bottle.
Yes I'm alright—
and don't worry, I'll pay,
I'm not tight."

Sober can't fight lonely
while she lies in that bed
such a pitiful state
my heart breaks with dread

"One more bottle.
I'll be alright
Just let Helen sing
for my mother tonight."

SODUKO ANSWERS

4	7	2	3	1	5	8	6	9
8	1	9	2	6	7	3	4	5
5	3	6	4	8	9	1	2	7
7	8	3	6	9	2	5	1	4
9	2	1	5	4	3	7	8	6
6	4	5	1	7	8	2	9	3
1	5	7	9	2	4	6	3	8
2	9	8	7	3	6	4	5	1
3	6	4	8	5	1	9	7	2

Thanks for reading!
Issue 10 Coming this Winter!

www.ingramcontent.com/pod-product-compliance
Lightning Source LLC
Chambersburg PA
CBHW010554170726
48285CB00011B/2898